Dragon Bones

Also by Lisa McMann

» » « «

THE UNWANTEDS SERIES

The Unwanteds

Island of Silence

Island of Fire

Island of Legends

Island of Shipwrecks

Island of Graves

Island of Dragons

» » « «

THE UNWANTEDS QUESTS SERIES

Dragon Captives

Dragon Bones

Dragon Ghosts

» » « «

FOR OLDER READERS:

Don't Close Your Eyes

Visions

Cryer's Cross

Dead to You

LISA McMANN

THE UNWANTEDS QUESTS

Dragon Bones

Aladdin

NEW YORK   LONDON   TORONTO   SYDNEY   NEW DELHI

ALADDIN

An imprint of Simon & Schuster Children's Publishing Division

1230 Avenue of the Americas, New York, New York 10020

First Aladdin paperback edition February 2019

Text copyright © 2018 by Lisa McMann

Cover illustration copyright © 2018 by Owen Richardson

Also available in an Aladdin hardcover edition.

ALADDIN and related logo are registered trademarks of Simon & Schuster, Inc.

For information about special discounts for bulk purchases, please contact
Simon & Schuster Special Sales at 1-866-506-1949 or business@simonandschuster.com.

The Simon & Schuster Speakers Bureau can bring authors to your live event.
For more information or to book an event, contact the Simon & Schuster Speakers Bureau at 1-866-248-3049
or visit our website at www.simonspeakers.com.

Book designed by Karin Paprocki

The text of this book was set in Truesdell.

Manufactured in the United States of America 0119 OFF

2 4 6 8 10 9 7 5 3 1

The Library of Congress has cataloged the hardcover edition as follows:

Names: McMann, Lisa, author. Title: Dragon bones / by Lisa McMann.

Description: First Aladdin hardcover edition. | New York : Aladdin, 2018. | Series: The Unwanteds quests ; book 2 |
Summary: Trapped underground in the catacombs and made to transport the bones of ancient dragon rulers to the
extracting room, where others extract the magical properties dormant in the bones, twin Thisbe must learn how to
control her own fiery magic and use it to escape.

Identifiers: LCCN 2017013555 (print) | LCCN 2017049490 (eBook) |
ISBN 9781481456845 (hardcover) | ISBN 9781481456869 (eBook)

Subjects: | CYAC: Adventure and adventurers—Fiction. | Magic—Fiction. | Brothers and sisters—Fiction. |
Twins—Fiction. | Dragons—Fiction. | Island—Fiction. | Fantasy.

Classification: LCC PZ7.M478757 (eBook) | LCC PZ7.M478757 Dp 2018 (print) | DDC [Fic]—dc23
LC record available at https://lccn.loc.gov/2017013555

ISBN 9781481456852 (pbk)

For Tricia, with love and thanks

Contents

Dragon
Bones

Breaking the News

There was a rare thunderstorm over Artimé when Simber returned, carrying Thatcher and an unconscious Fifer Stowe on his back. All was quiet in the mansion, for it was not quite dawn, and the dark skies kept most of the mages in their beds with the covers pulled up around them, listening to the rumbling in their dreams.

A three-headed tiki statue stood guard in Simber's place to the left of the door, and Jim the winged tortoise, with his brightly colored mosaic shell, floated lazily in the air on the right, his white feather wings flapping just enough to keep him rising and falling without hitting the ceiling or the pedestal

LISA McMANN

below him. They hadn't sensed Simber coming until he burst through the door.

"Get Alex and Henry!" Thatcher shouted. "Bring them to the hospital ward right away!" His voice was harsh and gravelly, for he'd barely slept in the days it had taken them to return home from the land of the dragons. With Fifer limp in his arms, he slid off Simber's back and stumbled to his knees, his legs numb and body aching from the journey. He got up and hobbled toward the hospital ward as the two statues figured out what was happening. Simber followed Thatcher.

Jim flew upstairs with the tiki statue behind him, mysteriously able to glide up the steps on his flat, legless bottom. At the balcony Jim headed for the family hallway to locate Henry Haluki, Artimé's chief healer and Thatcher's partner in all things, while the tiki statue slid to the farthest hallway on the left. Many of Artimé's mages couldn't see that magical hallway—they saw a mirror on the wall instead—but the tiki statue had no problem finding it. He charged toward Alex's apartment and pounded his top head against the door.

In the hospital ward, Thatcher gently lay Fifer on a bed and looked around, feeling helpless and a bit guilty that he knew so little about the medicines Henry had so lovingly created. He went to get a cup of water and a sponge to soak and press against the young twin's parched lips, in hopes that drops of water would seep inside her mouth and trickle down her throat without choking her.

While Thatcher lifted Fifer's head and administered the sponge, he swept his troubled gaze over the girl. Her clothing was full of rips and stained dark with blood after Simber, the enormous winged-cheetah statue, had unintentionally smashed through the glass barriers in Dragonsmarche, sending shards like a thousand daggers into Fifer's body. An instant later Fifer's twin, Thisbe, had been snatched up by the Revinir—someone Thatcher and Simber had recognized as the former Queen Eagala from Warbler Island, who should've been dead—and taken underground to her lair among the catacombs.

They'd had to leave Thisbe behind. In order to save Fifer's life, they'd flown nonstop for days, all the way to Warbler, where they'd learned of even more heartrending news: Sky had been swept underwater into the mouth of the plunging volcanic Island of Fire and was gone.

Thatcher heard a commotion on the stairs and looked up, feeling his heart in his throat. He and Simber had a lot of explaining to do, and there was no easy way to go about it. Delivering this news to Alex was the hardest thing Thatcher had ever faced, including everything he'd just been through.

"Thank goodness," Thatcher murmured when he saw Henry racing toward him, one arm slid inside the sleeve of his healer's coat, the rest of it flying behind. The two quickly embraced; then Henry slipped his other arm into the jacket and reached for his medical supplies. "Tell me everything," he demanded.

Before Thatcher or Simber could begin to tell him, Alex arrived inside the ward. At the sight of his sister on the bed he paled, and his mouth slacked in shock. "What happened? Is she okay? How did this come about?" He looked around frantically. "Where's Thisbe? Carina said—Carina told me— You were all supposed to be coming right behind them!"

Simber looked to Thatcher to fill in everyone as Henry began assessing Fifer's condition, then working on her wounds, cleaning them and applying the magical plant-based concoctions he'd developed over the years. Thatcher spoke hastily about what had transpired after Carina and Seth had left the castle Grimere with the five young dragons. Things had not gone as planned.

Alex listened, stunned. He could hardly take in the information about Thisbe or how the Revinir had snatched her up and disappeared. Or who the old woman really was. "Queen Eagala is the Revinir?" he whispered. "How can that be? She's been dead for over ten years!"

"We don't know," said Simber. "But I'm cerrrtain it was herrr."

"We have to go after Thisbe," Alex said, growing frantic. "She must be absolutely sick with fear! But Fifer—is she . . . ?"

"We'll go after Thisbe," said Thatcher, trying to calm Alex down. "Shortly we'll start to organize and figure out a plan for that. But . . ." He gave Simber a pleading look.

"Rrright," said Simber in a grave voice. "Alex, therrre's . . . something else."

Alex looked at Simber. His hand shook, and he reached for a bedpost. "Something else?" he said weakly. "What more could there possibly be?"

Simber's body sagged, and he closed his eyes as if he couldn't

LISA McMANN

bear to see Alex hurt even more. After an agonizing moment, he opened them and looked squarely at the mage. "It's Sky," he said quietly. "She was worrrking on the Island of Firrre, and it plunged below the waterrr without warrrrning. She was swept in." He paused for a moment as he watched Alex, dazed, sink heavily to the bed next to Fifer's. And then Simber growled, "She's gone."

When Everything Shatters

Henry turned sharply away from treating Fifer to look at Simber. "*What?* Good gods! You can't be serious."

"Sky?" Alex stared in disbelief. "No," he said, faltering. Then: "No!"

Thatcher, his expression wretched, went over to Alex and sat beside him. "I'm so sorry. I'm afraid it's all true." He put a gentle hand around the head mage's shoulders.

Simber bowed his head. "I'm sorrry. I can't begin to imagine yourrr pain. The shock of all of this must be overrrwhelming."

LISA McMANN

Alex was numb inside, and his skin turned cold and aching. He'd heard the words and understood their meaning, but he couldn't absorb the wrenching truth of everything he'd experienced in the past few moments: Fifer lying bloody and unconscious, Thisbe kidnapped by Queen Eagala, and now his beloved Sky, gone? The scope of the news was beyond his ability to comprehend. He was completely struck down. He couldn't catch his breath. He couldn't see—everything wavered in front of him. He felt like his soul had left him and risen above his body to escape the words. Like he was a spectator looking down on this horrible scene. He doubled over, the world spinning, and put his hand over his face. This couldn't be real. It had to be a nightmare. "Tell me what happened," he cried. "Tell me everything." Then he slid off the edge of the bed to the floor and crumpled there, sobbing.

"Go get Aarrron rrright away," Simber ordered Thatcher. "And Crrrow. Hurrry!"

Thatcher nodded and dashed out of the hospital ward without a word. Simber watched Alex shuddering on the floor, then closed his eyes and sighed heavily. He knelt next to the mage to let him know he was there and quickly filled him in. He could do nothing else for him right now. It was the worst moment in Simber's memory.

After a time Alex quieted. He lifted his head and looked through red-rimmed eyes at Simber. When their eyes connected, more tears started pouring down the head mage's cheeks, and he moaned in pure agony, feeling physically sick, the losses hitting him in waves until he wished he could slip into unconsciousness to escape it.

He began to cry harder. And when he could finally catch his breath and speak a few words, he turned to Henry. "Is Fifer . . . ? Is she . . . ?" He couldn't finish.

"She's hurt very badly, but she's going to live," said Henry, determined and working steadily. His face didn't betray the range of emotions he felt. He had one job, and that was to see Fifer through. He couldn't bear the thought of Alex losing all three of them, especially after having lost so much in his life already. "She's waking up now, Alex. I need your help—can you come and stand by the head of her bed? Let her know you're here?"

The grief surged again. Alex didn't know if he could get up, much less walk over to Fifer's side. But he reached his right arm around Simber's neck and pulled himself up off the floor. The stone cheetah helped him walk. Alex quickly tried to dry his tears on his shirt so Fifer wouldn't be scared. "What do I tell her?" he said to Simber, in agony. "Does she know about . . . this? About Thisbe or any of it?"

Simber's expression was filled with sorrow. He shook his head. "I don't think so," he said. "She's been unconscious. Just tell herrr that you'rrre herrre. Tell herrr that you'rrre with herrr and she's safe. Just like you'd have done forrr any of us back in the old days."

Alex stared at Simber, a look of bewilderment on his face. His role as chief comforter in times like these had all but disappeared since the final battle. And he'd focused his care inward since that time, so much so that it felt strange to remember he wasn't the only one who needed a guiding hand in this moment. With a start he realized that no matter how much he was hurting, he *was* the guiding hand . . . like he used to be. Like after Mr. Today, the original head mage, had died and all the magic in Artimé had disappeared. How would Fifer feel once she heard the news? And Crow? And Aaron? "It hurts," he whispered, and choked back a sob. "Worse than any pain I've ever known."

"I know," said Simber, standing by him. There was nothing else to say that could possibly help. He could only stand by.

Alex's mind awhirl, he reached Fifer's side and stood near her head. He gripped the bedpost as a new wave of pain went through him and stifled a moan, then tried to smile as his sister's eyes fluttered. "Hey there, Fife," he said softly. "It's me, Alex. You're home. You're safe."

Fifer opened her eyes and focused on her brother's face. She was confused. Her lids closed for a moment, then squeezed shut, then blinked open again. Her eyes filled with tears. A jumble of horrifying memories bounced around in her head. "I'm so sorry, Alex," she choked out. She began to cry inconsolably.

Alex lost it again and cried with her. He smoothed her hair from her face and kissed her cheek, his tears raining down on her. "It doesn't matter," he said. "It doesn't matter. I'm just so glad you're okay. You're . . . alive." As he said the words, he couldn't stop the next wave of pain that came with the thoughts about Thisbe and Sky, and everything inside him shattered once more. He was in turns frozen, overwhelmed, and on the verge of blacking out from the pain stabbing through him. Yet here was Fifer. Alive. He clung to her life like a raft in the sea.

LISA McMANN

A tiny piece of his shattered heart found another tiny piece, and they melded back together. Fifer was here. Awake. Alive. He hadn't lost them all.

In that moment he loved her ferociously, more than he'd loved any other human being or creature in his life, and he swore in his heart to protect her from anything like this ever happening again. "Never again," he whispered.

Alex had lost one sister, but Fifer had lost her twin. Alex had known that feeling once and the physical pain that went with it. She would need him to be strong for her now.

In the midst of Alex's grief, something inside him, a remnant of his old self, fluttered awake after a long sleep. He planted his feet and then took Fifer's hand in his. He looked her in the eye with a lifetime's worth of compassion and, as gently as he could, told Fifer what had happened to Thisbe.

She didn't have the strength to comprehend or react and soon slipped into unconsciousness, the words twisting around her mind like a nightmare.

Alex's survival mode switched onto autopilot, and he began running things as usual, pushing the pain and distracting thoughts back so he could govern properly. He ordered Thatcher to dispatch Spike Furious, the intuitive magical whale, to go in search of Sky. Then he stoically delivered all the terrible news to Aaron and Crow.

Their reactions were about what Alex had expected, and the pain remained raw. But Alex soldiered on, with support from Simber and Thatcher.

"How is my mother handling this?" Crow asked. He ripped his hand through his long dark hair, feeling completely frantic to be a full day's journey across the sea from her with not only the news of the girls, but of his sister, Sky. "And Scarlet? Is she okay?"

"Copper and Scarlet are together on Warbler," said Thatcher. "They have each other for comfort until you can get there. Simber will take you once you're ready."

Aaron appeared stunned at the news and handled it with little outward reaction at first. He reverted back to turning off his emotions, which was reminiscent of how he'd grown up in Quill. Moving abruptly away from the others, he went to stand near Fifer, who was asleep, and tried to make sense of it all.

After a while he reached for Fifer's hand and held it. He

LISA McMANN

studied it, watching how her long thin fingers curled naturally in his. He felt like he was drowning and kept trying to surface long enough to let some of his emotions out, but he could barely breathe. And his mind kept going back to his youth, to when he'd said good-bye to Alex for what he'd thought was the last time, at the Purge. It sparked something still raw in him, and his grief was bitter.

"They've been forced to grow up like we did, Al," he said, looking over his shoulder to where Alex sat. "All in one day. Separated and everything." Then he shook his head, and the tears began. "This is *their* Purge." He was quiet for a moment, thinking back to when the governors of Quill had taken Alex away while he stood there watching and thinking his life would be the better of the two. How wrong he'd been. "But which of them is me," he added softly, turning to Alex, "and which is you?"

Alex looked away, curling into his pain. He couldn't answer.

Word spread through Artimé. Soon Samheed and Lani hurried into the hospital, followed by Seth and Carina and Sean. Seth ran to Fifer's side, his pale face turning gray from the sight of Fifer's many wounds. The news of Thisbe's capture made the panic well up in Seth anew. How could this have happened? Why hadn't they stayed? Maybe they could have saved her. Guilt flooded him—he'd survived unscathed. He vowed to stay by Fifer's side until he knew she was truly going to be okay.

A steady stream of friends from Artimé and nearby Karkinos, the giant crab island, came into the hospital ward once they'd heard the news. They were all shocked and brought to tears for the victims and their loved ones, expressing their grief and sorrow to Alex and Aaron and Crow. But, as it always happened in Artimé, there was little time to mourn. The exact whereabouts and well-being of Thisbe and Sky were unknown, and Alex wouldn't rest until he had answers. Things had to be done.

With Fifer stabilized and being cared for, and Seth staying by her side, Crow slipped away to pack his things, though he wouldn't leave until he was certain Fifer was okay—he'd helped take care of the twins for most of their lives, and he wouldn't abandon Fifer now.

Alex also forced himself away from the crowds at her bedside. He beckoned to Aaron, Lani, Samheed, and some of the others and led them out of the hospital ward. "Let's meet in

LISA McMANN

my office in five minutes," he told them as he headed up the stairs. "We've got work to do."

Moments later Simber, Aaron, Samheed and Lani, Thatcher, Carina and Sean, and Florence, the ebony-colored stone warrior statue who taught Artimé's people how to fight with magic, assembled in Alex's office to discuss what to do next. Alex came in through the magical entrance from his private quarters, eyes still red rimmed but his face splashed clean. He greeted everyone with a look of determination that covered the pain he felt.

"We can't waste any time," he announced, and dropped heavily into his chair. "We've got to go right away. We need to find Thisbe and bring her home. And Sky—Spike and our other aquatic friends are already out there searching, doing more than we ever could. I just hope they find . . . something." He leaned forward and pressed the heel of his hand to his forehead, feeling sick and helpless, knowing there was little hope for Sky to have survived. He pressed back the pain and took a sharp breath—he couldn't deal with that right now.

"But first, Thisbe," Alex went on, looking up. "It's been days since she was captured—she must have lost all hope by now. I can't stand thinking about it. Who should go? And how soon can we leave?" He looked up at the ones who'd gathered around him: "Which of you will come with me?"

Lani's lips parted in surprise. "What—you mean *you're* going?"

"I . . . Yes." Alex gave her a challenging stare. "Do you have a problem with that?"

"Me? Are you kidding? Not at all! It's just that . . . Well, what I mean is that you haven't been doing . . . because of your disability . . ." She sighed and gave up trying to explain. "Oh, never mind! I'm going too."

"Somehow I knew you'd say that." Alex looked around the room. "Who else is with us?"

Samheed opened his mouth to speak, but Florence interrupted. "We're all with you, Alex. Obviously. But let's back up a little. Rushing into this rescue without preparing properly isn't going to do us any good, and it could get us killed—and Thisbe, too."

"Yes. Thank you, Florrrence." Simber nodded in hearty agreement. He looked at Carina and Thatcher. "I think these two can tell you how they werrre caught flat-footed and immediately capturrred in the forrrest in Grrrimerrre. Don't you think a rrrefrrresherrr courrrse could have helped you?"

Carina looked mortified. "Definitely."

Thatcher nodded emphatically. "I still don't feel comfortable. It's been too long since we've trained."

Florence nodded. "Most of you haven't taken a Magical Warrior Training class in many years. You're rusty. I don't care how good you were back then—your aim will be off. We need to lay out a plan to train and prepare ourselves."

"Well, of course we do," said Alex impatiently, "but we also need to get moving as soon as possible."

Florence put her hands in the air. "Just slow down and listen to me for a moment, Alex. I can't imagine how desperate you must feel. But please give me a little time to gather information from those who've been to the land of the dragons, and we'll figure out what kind of fighting to focus on and how to do this the right way—so you don't *all* end up in the dungeon."

Alex looked like he was about to object again, but Aaron gave him a warning look. "Okay," said Alex. "But let's at least talk through the rescue plan."

"Of course," Florence said. She gave him a strained smile,

then turned to look at Simber. "First, a question to someone who's actually been to this foreign world. Do you think Eagala—the so-called Revinir—is going to hurt Thisbe?"

"Frrrom the inforrrmation we have, I don't think she will," said Simber. "Therrre seems to be some monetarrry value given to black-eyed people therrre—though they arrre used as slaves, so it's a bit confusing. But the Rrrevinirrr prrrobably intends to use Thisbe as a serrrvant of some sorrrt. She could have taken Fiferrr too, but instead she left herrr forrr dead, so perrrhaps she saw herrr as useless. That makes me feel strrrongly that Thisbe is alive and being put to worrrk in some way."

"That's all very comforting that you think she's alive," argued Alex, "and perhaps she really is. But she's got to be terrified. She could lose hope if we don't get there to rescue her quickly."

"She'll be okay," Lani said quietly but firmly. "Sam and I turned out okay after something like this happened to us, remember? And after all, she's your sister—I'm sure she has plenty of drive in her to see her through this. Florence is right. Let's plan this properly the first time so we don't add any other disasters on top of this one." She turned back to Florence and motioned for her to continue.

"Okay," said Florence. "Thank you. Now, maybe Simber, Thatcher, and Carina can help me figure out who is going to be best suited for this rescue mission. First off, how are we going to get there?"

"Flight is the only way to get past the waterrrfall," said Simber. He frowned, as if puzzling over something that didn't seem quite right, but the conversation continued.

"Should our rescue team go with just Simber as our ride?" asked Samheed. "That would have to be a pretty small group."

"I can take thrrree, prrresuming we'll rrreturrrn with fourrr. That leaves me with rrroom forrr some supplies, too."

"Talon can fly," Florence reminded them. "I can talk to him about going." Talon was a legendary, large bronze man with wings from the Island of Legends nearby. He and Florence lived there together most of the time, and Florence taught Magical Warrior Training there, though she made occasional trips back home to Artimé as well.

"Perrrhaps Talon could carrry someone," Simber mused. "Spike could take a few people as farrr as the waterrrfall, and we flyerrrs could ſerrry people acrrross the gorrrge to the land of the drrragons."

Aaron sat forward. "What's the situation like over there? The terrain, the climate, the distances we have to travel over land? Where is Thisbe, exactly? And how do we find her?"

"I'll sketch a map," said Carina, reaching for some paper and a pencil from Alex's desk. Thatcher leaned in to help, though he'd been very ill when they'd reached the new world, so his memory was fuzzy. "It's mountainous at first approach," Carina said as she drew, "but not unpassable on foot. Then there's a forest, which we could use for cover as we travel toward the city center of Grimere. Is that where Thisbe was snatched up, Simber? About how far from the castle?"

Simber nodded. "The Rrrevinir took herrr undergrrround in the city centerrr squarrre, which hosts Drrragonsmarrrche—a place wherrre goods arrre trrraded and sold. It's severrral miles frrrom the castle."

Thatcher smoothed his black coiled hair, then paused and tapped his chin thoughtfully. "The princess's servant boy, Dev, told us a vast catacomb stretched underneath the city. It would take a couple days on foot to get there once we cross the gorge

LISA McMANN

and reach the cliffs of Grimere. Less time if we fly, of course."

"Hmm," Aaron said. "That's a lot of area to cover. I was also wondering if we would want to bring Seth with us since he knows things."

Carina startled, then glanced at Sean. "I don't know about that."

"And," Aaron continued, looking at Alex, "what about Fifer?"

"No!" Alex said firmly. "She nearly died."

Aaron looked at his brother. "She's already starting to get better with Henry's magical medicines. And we're not ready to leave yet by any stretch."

"Not for weeks," said Florence firmly.

"Weeks?" Alex sputtered. "It doesn't matter anyway—Fifer doesn't know how to do anything. That's how she got into this mess in the first place. Besides, I promised myself I'd protect her from now on so nothing like this could ever happen again. She stays in Artimé."

"Perhaps," said Florence gently, "it's time to teach her while I retrain everyone else. Even if she doesn't go on the mission, she needs to know how to defend herself, especially now that we know Eagala is alive and going after people with black eyes. She'll never be safe—not as long as she lives."

"But—" Alex wasn't sure how to respond. His mind was awhirl with frustration and confusion and fear, and his head pounded with grief. At the same time, these events had stirred something inside him for the first time in many years—something once dormant that now twisted and turned, trying to find a way to grow. He was going on a mission once again—something he'd never thought he'd do, mostly because of his disability and how that had changed everything for him.

It was scary. It made him feel vulnerable when he allowed himself to face it: *He* was the one Florence was referring to most when she insisted they had to train, though she was too kind to say it in front of the others. It was he who was in grave need of relearning his fighting spells if he was going to go on this journey and not be a total hindrance or liability to everyone. Alex must use Florence to teach *him* more than anyone, using his right arm—it would be like teaching a toddler, he knew. Did he have it in him to relearn now that he needed to so desperately? And could he do it so quickly? It had nagged at him for years that he hadn't been able to accomplish proper

LISA McMANN

magic on his own with his right hand, since his dominant left arm was out of commission. Was he being ridiculous even thinking he could and should go on this quest?

But finding Thisbe weighed heavily on his mind. He couldn't bear to stay in Artimé when she needed him most of all. Wasn't that what leaders were supposed to do? Go out and rescue their people? Especially when this person happened to be his own sister.

It crossed his mind that his sudden decision to go was some sort of reckless response to the grief over Sky that he hadn't yet processed. He'd hardly had a moment to digest what had happened to her. His heart spun, and he tried not to think about her being swept underwater into the volcano's gaping maw. She was gone. He couldn't say dead—he couldn't let his mind go there. He had to hold out hope for Sky, that there had been some way she'd survived, and focus on Thisbe. One tragedy at a time. It was the only way he could cope with everything that had just happened.

In the depths of these thoughts, Alex's face crumpled. Aaron sensed his brother's mental war and came to sit with him on top of the desk, putting his arms around his twin to comfort him. "We're going to get through this," he whispered.

Alex took a deep, shuddering breath and blew it out. Then he nodded. "All right. I'm okay. Thanks. Let's keep going."

Aaron kept an arm around Alex's shoulders and tried to stop his own tears from returning. He couldn't imagine losing his wife, Kaylee—how was Alex handling this news about Sky right now? It was a clear reminder to Aaron and everyone present that their leader was still strong, even if the people of Artimé hadn't needed to depend on him quite so much lately. Alex moved seamlessly into his role of commander despite what he'd gone through since his injury, not to mention the huge stresses on him because of the girls and their strange, powerful, uncontrollable magic. Aaron turned to Florence. "Based on the information Thatcher and Simber told us about all of the soldiers and the massive size of the catacombs they described, my instinct says we need a larger rescue team. Do you think we can ask for help from the dragons to get us there?"

Carina looked up sharply from her sketch. "I don't know if that's a good idea," she said. "It's incredibly dangerous for them over there. The Revinir isn't going to be happy we've freed them—she'll hunt them down, no doubt."

LISA McMANN

"Maybe the dragons will just give rides over the gorge?" suggested Sean.

"But how will they know when we'rrre rrready to go back home?" said Simber. "We might not be able to sit arrround in the cliffs arrrea waiting forrr them to show up. And therrre's no good place forrr them to wait forrr us in ourrr worrrld—they'd have to float farrr frrrom the waterrrfall to keep frrrom going overrr."

Carina nodded. "Simber's right. That wouldn't have worked last time, for sure, with how quickly we had to make our escape. Besides, it's a bit risky to try to travel the whole distance from the cliffs to the big city square on foot. We'd want to be very clever and have a fast getaway plan—one that allows us all to take flight at once without delay. We must be smart about it."

"But you said the dragons might not help us on this quest because of the danger," said Alex. And then he shook his head. "I'm not so sure they'd say no once we tell them Thisbe is trapped there, being held captive by the Revinir as they once were. Especially after Thisbe helped free *them*."

Thatcher, Carina, and Simber all looked at one another

with questions in their eyes. "Perrrhaps they will," said Simber finally. "I'll talk to Pan about it."

Thatcher spoke up. "Before that could ever happen, they'll need Alex and the rest of us to fix their wings for good. They're quite a mess. The kids gave a valiant effort to make new ones with the supplies they had, and the wings got them across the gorge, which is what we really needed from them, but they're a bit of disaster, to be frank."

"That's fine," said Alex. "Hux's are already done and waiting for him. We can start gathering materials for the others. So, assuming we can convince at least one dragon to help us, who's coming with me?" Alex looked at Carina and Simber. "Who among us would you say is best for the situation? Once we determine that, we can figure out how much transportation we'll need."

"I already told you I'm going," said Lani. She looked as though she wouldn't take no for an answer.

"I'll go as well," Samheed said.

"I've been thinking about it," Carina said. "As much as I don't like the idea, I believe Seth should go. Thatcher and me, too, and Simber, obviously, since we know our way around."

"I'll stay behind for obvious reasons," said Florence,

referring to her size and heavy weight. "But like I said before, Talon may be of use." She looked at Alex and Aaron. "Have you decided on whether to let Fifer go? She's really so powerful. With a little training she could—"

"She's definitely not going," Alex said, interrupting her.

Aaron gave him a look.

Alex glared back at him. "No." He turned back to Florence. "No!" he said once more.

"Okay, okay," said Florence, giving up. "I get it." She glanced at Aaron. "What about Kaylee?"

Thatcher, Carina, and Simber began nodding immediately. "Her sword skills would be extremely useful in a land like that," said Carina. "The soldiers were armed with knives and swords and some sort of projectile bows and arrows. Aaron, do you think she'd come along?"

"I'll ask her," said Aaron. "I suppose one of us ought to stay back on our island for the sake of baby Daniel and the grandfathers, but I know she'll agree that this is of utmost importance. Whichever of us seems more useful to the mission is all right by me. Alex, what do you think?" He gave Alex a meaningful look, and a silent conversation passed between them.

Alex gazed at Aaron thoughtfully. He knew why Aaron had deferred to him. Aaron had something no one else had, and not many knew about—a likelihood that he would never die, due to eating some special seaweed many years before. The seaweed was what had kept the scientists alive too, well past the age of one hundred. Not dying was obviously a plus in battle, but this mysterious ability didn't keep Aaron from being wounded. Aaron's magical ability was strong, but so was Lani's, Samheed's, and Carina's. So perhaps Kaylee was a better fit for this venture because of her melee fighting skills—that was where the rest of the Artiméans looked to her.

"I think Kaylee gives us something we need," Alex decided. "Is that enough fighters? Enough variety in skills? We don't want our group to be too big or unwieldy."

Simber harrumphed. "You'rrre forrrgetting someone who could be verrry imporrrtant."

Alex thought hard. "Who?"

"Someone who doesn't take up much space and has saved the day morrre than once in the past."

"Ahh," Florence said, nodding. "And who just happens to have seven lives left."

LISA McMANN

Even Alex managed a small smile. "Of course," he said. "We mustn't go anywhere without Kitten ever again."

"But firrrst things firrrst," said Simber. "If I'm going to ask Pan and the otherrr drrragons for help, you'd betterrr get worrrking on those wings. Having the prrromise of a futurrre gift when asking forrr a favorrr is neverrr a bad idea."

Cold and Alone

On the fifth day after Thisbe Stowe's capture, or perhaps it was the sixth—it was hard to remember which—she woke up in her crypt full of bones feeling chilled and more tired than she could ever recall feeling before. And like the previous mornings, the memories of the past couple of weeks came like a stampede. The questions throttled her and left her breathless. Was Fifer dead? Why hadn't Simber come back for her? Was the Revinir going to keep her down here forever, dragging giant dragon bones for miles every day?

For that was what she'd been tasked to do. Each day she

LISA McMANN

and several other black-eyed children, who were slaves like her, pulled enormous dragon bones from their individual crypts through the wide, seemingly endless passages of the catacombs to the testing room, where others would extract the dragon magic from them. It took hours to get there through a maze of hallways, following faded red arrows that had been painted long ago on the chiseled walls. By the time Thisbe returned each night, dragging an already tested bone back to her crypt, it was late. She'd get her meal, collapse on the dirt floor, and be locked up again until morning.

On the first day Thisbe, bewildered and afraid, hadn't dared speak to the other children. As she'd hauled the bone from her crypt, trying to find her way through the maze to the testing room, she'd missed a particularly faded red arrow and had gotten hopelessly lost. She didn't make it back to her crypt until after midnight, and hadn't gotten her meal.

The second day, weak with hunger, she'd followed the faint arrows with the utmost care. She'd tried keeping up with one of the other children, and that's when she first discovered they had black eyes like her. But when Thisbe asked her a question, the girl seemed unable to understand her and unwilling to be caught trying to communicate. Thisbe fell behind. It had been terribly disheartening.

The third day had been the worst, for that was the day Thisbe finally lost all hope and admitted to herself that no one from Artimé was coming back for her. She'd stopped and had a hard cry along a lonely stretch of the passageway, where only one person, a tall boy a year or two older than Thisbe, passed her and gave her the tiniest look of sympathy before continuing. By the end of the day, her hopes had fallen deep into the pit of her stomach and suffocated. With them went the anger. Things had stayed the same after that.

Today she was too tired to move. When she heard a noise at the lock in her door, she squeezed her eyes shut tightly, letting a tiny tear leak out before she pushed her sluggish self up. Mangrel, the crypt keeper, had arrived to order her around. The whey-faced old man appeared weak and frightened, but he wasn't—not in the slightest. Thisbe had found that out the hard way soon after her arrival when she'd still had some anger left rumbling inside her and she'd tried to use her sparks of magic on him. It didn't work, and he'd knocked her headfirst into a pile of bones.

LISA McMANN

Mangrel opened Thisbe's crypt and entered with some water. Three of the Revinir's soldiers, wearing blue uniforms, pushed their way inside too. One of them was armed with a branding iron. Before Thisbe knew what was happening, two of the soldiers tackled her and held her face against the dirt floor. The third jabbed at the back of her neck with the iron. The force of it pressed her nose flat in the dirt so she couldn't breathe without sucking in bone dust. She felt a piercing fire on her skin, and she struggled and coughed and cried out. "Stop! Let go of me!" Sparks flew from her eyes, but they merely hit the dirt and did no damage other than to bounce back up at her and singe her own eyebrows.

The soldiers released her, and Mangrel yanked her to her feet. When she stopped yelling and wiped the snotty, tearstained dirt from her face, he gruffly pointed out the bone he wanted her to deliver to the testing room that day. He let go of her arm and retreated with the soldiers, leaving the door open for the day. Wild with pain, Thisbe lunged after them into the hallway, trying to call up the courage to strike one of them dead. As in the past, she didn't do it, but her reasoning was different this time. She'd reached the point of being desperate enough. And she could hardly care anymore about taking some horrible person's life. But after all she'd been through, Thisbe realized her ability to kill people was more than a little complicated, especially when she didn't have a way to escape this place filled with soldiers once she unleashed a spell.

Thisbe stopped herself in the hallway before they could catch her coming after them, and retreated to her crypt. After she cooled off a little, she knew her actions had been for the best. There were many more soldiers stationed out there at the nearest intersection of hallways. Sure, Thisbe might've managed to knock off one of them before the others got to her, but she'd spent a lot of time thinking about her magic in her solitude over the past days. She didn't know if she was capable of firing more than one boom spell at a time—she'd never done it before. If she couldn't, she didn't know what the other soldiers would do to her. And what if she could? She still wouldn't be able to get them all. They'd eventually overpower her. And then where would she be? Dragged back to the castle and thrown into the dark dungeon, chained to a wall and sitting in a puddle of cold water for the rest of her life, like the old

LISA McMANN

woman she'd been with? Or maybe the Revinir had someplace even worse than that here in the catacombs to punish her evildoing slaves. Here among the bones, at least, Thisbe was dry and could move around.

The back of her neck throbbed with heat and pain. She fingered the edges of the burn gingerly as she walked toward the enormous pile of bones but couldn't stand anything touching near the painful spot. She drank her water, pouring a little bit on her neck, but the liquid wasn't cold enough to stop the burning sensation and only made it hurt worse. After a long moment of staring nowhere at nothing, Thisbe wearily started climbing up the bone pile to the large one Mangrel had pointed out. When she reached it, she began to work it from side to side, trying to wrench it free from the stack. She put every bit of strength she had into it and ignored her neck pain. Once she loosened the bone and pulled it out, she sent it skidding down the skeletal mountain to the floor. She made her way after it.

Next she picked up her harness and fastened it to the dragon bone, then looped her arms through the other end, careful not to let the straps rub across her neck. She leaned forward and dragged the heavy load to the doorway, and looked left and right to see if anyone else was coming around the corner from the other crypts yet this morning. There wasn't a soul in sight. She glanced at the faint red arrows among the other symbols on the walls, pointing slightly uphill, and wondered what the people of Grimere were doing above her head in the huge square, or in the mountains beyond. Were they going about their business as usual? Selling produce and strange creatures from aquariums, totally unaware that there were a dozen black-eyed children being kept as slaves underground by the evil Revinir? Or did they actually know what was going on? If so, why didn't they care? Why didn't they do something? What power did this woman have over them? Was it just the fact that she'd taken the dragons captive that made her more powerful than the king? It seemed like she and the king must have some sort of relationship—after all, the king was keeping the Revinir's dragons in the castle. Maybe their combined power was more than the townspeople could fight off.

Thisbe pulled her dragon bone into the hallway and started her uphill trek. From what she could tell, her crypt was near the center of the catacombs, below Dragonsmarche, where the Revinir had snatched her up and brought her underground through a large, moving tube. And as far as Thisbe knew, that was the only way in and out of the warren of tunnels. She'd overheard one soldier call the tube an elevator, and there were always six or eight guards stationed outside it.

None of the other children seemed to even think about escaping. Their eyes were dead, and no wonder. Thisbe could see why they wouldn't attempt to flee through the elevator, because it would be futile—there were too many guards. Mostly the other children roamed on their own, obediently completing their task as quickly as possible so they could get their meal of the day. Thisbe thought about all these things as she plodded along, trying to keep her mind from going to the dark place where she relived the horror of what had happened in the market. Wondering endlessly if Fifer was alive or dead. Wondering why no one had come back for her.

As she trudged, she pressed her fingers into the corners of her eyes to stop the burning tears that threatened. She'd been abandoned. Did Thatcher and Simber think she was dead? Would they ever come back to search for her? And if they did, how would they possibly find her in this maze?

When Thisbe heard a scraping sound growing steadily

louder behind her, she looked over her shoulder. There was one of the other black-eyed prisoners like her. He seemed tall for his age. She'd seen him the other day when she'd been crying, and he'd appeared at least a little sympathetic. Her heart leaped at the thought of not being alone on the trek, but then it fell again when she remembered the girl who didn't speak the same language Thisbe did. This boy probably didn't either.

He eyed her, his expression flickering when he caught sight of the fresh brand at the nape of her neck. He glanced around, then said something quickly and softly in a different language.

Thisbe searched his face, wondering if somehow she could miraculously decipher the words by interpreting his expression. But it was useless. "I don't know what you're saying," she said helplessly. "I'm sorry."

He seemed surprised. "You speak . . . the language . . . of the dragons," he said in halting words.

Surprised, Thisbe stopped walking. "Yes," she said, remembering that Dev had said the same thing to her. "Do you? I mean, obviously you do, but can you understand me? Why does the Revinir keep all of us here? Is there another exit?"

"I can understand if you speak slower." His lips were full and ruddy red, and they curved into a small smile. He held a calloused finger to them and whispered, "Let's get past the guards at the next intersection. I'll catch up to you." He urged Thisbe to go ahead, then waited to follow until she was a good distance in front of him.

Thisbe entered a large intersection where several branches of the catacombs met in an open circular space. There were several like this along the way to the testing room, so she looked carefully for the arrows. Moving by a small group of guards, she kept her head lowered and forged down the correct passage.

Ten minutes passed before the boy caught up to her.

"We're safe now," he said. "What is your name?"

"Thisbe," she said. "And yours?"

"Rohan," he said. "I'm sorry about your brand. It only aches wildly for a day or so, and then the thrum eases."

Rohan's word choices were peculiar, Thisbe thought. And lovely, as if he'd chosen them from one of Lani's poems. In a distant way he resembled Dev, with his black eyes and wavy hair, but his skin was more gray than brown, like driftwood dried on the shore of Artimé. It made Thisbe wonder how long it had been since he'd seen sunshine.

"You and I are neighbors in the tombs," he said. "We share a back wall. My crypt is behind yours." He saw Thisbe's surprise and explained, "I saw you come out of yours as I rounded the corner. No one has lived in that crypt before."

It was somehow comforting to know there was someone friendly on the other side of Thisbe's back wall, though she was wary of trusting anyone in this world after her experience with Dev. Besides, as hopeless as she felt, she didn't plan on staying here for long. "Is there any way out of here?" she asked. "Besides the . . . what's it called? The tube thing?"

"The elevator," said Rohan. "Yes, there is one other easement that I know of. But luck comes with wings, and I'm afraid we're without luck."

"Oh," said Thisbe, puzzled. She felt sad, but then her heart surged as she thought of the dragons. What if she could make herself some wings? She'd nearly done it before, and she'd made an inanimate object—the bamboo prison grid—come alive. So surely she could meld wings to her own back almost as easily and bring them to life. She stopped suddenly, then reached around herself in a hug, trying to gauge how she'd be able to place heavy wings on her back and magically adhere them to herself. It seemed . . . difficult.

"Do you need me to adjust your harness for you?" asked Rohan, stopping too. "It can be irritating if it doesn't sit just right. Or is it your neck that's hurting?"

"Oh!" said Thisbe, and she felt her face grow warm. She dropped her hands quickly. "No, it's nothing—I was just thinking about something else. Thank you." She began moving again. "Where is the exit that requires wings to reach?"

"It's near the top of the climb, deep inside the mountains and near the lake, where the extracting room is situated. If no one's around, I'll show you." He held up a hand to caution her and said more quietly, "Here's another intersection. I'll go first this time and wait for you."

Thisbe nodded. When she passed the soldiers and caught up with him on the other side, she asked, "Why are all these dragon bones down here? And what are they doing with them in the testing room?"

Rohan looked at her, seeming surprised that she didn't know. "These are the bones of the ancient dragon kings and queens of Grimere," he said. "From when our black-eyed ancestors and the dragons ruled the land above us together in peace." He looked around to make sure no one was in listening distance, then whispered, "The workers pull the magic out of the dragon bones for the Revinir. The story is that she was once magical, but her magic was stripped from her by a black-eyed child."

Thisbe's eyes widened. "What do you mean?"

"The Revinir found her way here and invaded the under-world of these ancient crypts. She started rebuilding her magical abilities by stealing the dormant properties from these bones. Once she took in the magic of the dragon bones, she lured young dragons and captured them, making them her slaves. Her power and notoriety grew, and slowly she recruited and built her army of soldiers. The king felt threatened by her power and decided to work with her, offering to house the dragons since they wouldn't fit down here, and she took him up on it, letting him use the dragons now and then. But their relationship is . . . What's the word? Tenuous. Not very strong, I guess you'd say."

Thisbe didn't know what to think.

Rohan went on. "She hates children, especially ones like

us, who are descendants of the rulers." He looked grim. "In this society it's great sport to keep a black-eyed slave. But for the Revinir, it's revenge on the little girl who stole her magic in the first place." He paused and smiled. "Not to mention, I suppose she doesn't want to break her ridiculous fingernails doing manual labor."

Thisbe's lips parted, and her breath came in short bursts. "Revenge against the little black-eyed girl?" she whispered. "That's why?" She could hardly believe it.

As they continued on in silence, for some reason the stories Lani and Sky had told about the final battle with Artimé flooded Thisbe's mind. At first she didn't know why, and she couldn't make sense of them. Then she remembered where she'd first heard about a woman with long curling fingernails. The one who'd hurt Alex. The one who'd sent those horrible ravens during the final battle. *The Revinir . . . and Queen Eagala . . .* Thisbe stopped walking suddenly as she pondered it. Could it be? *The Revinir is Queen Eagala—who is supposed to be dead.* She looked up at Rohan, and the blood drained from her face when she realized that the child who had stolen Queen Eagala's magical powers . . . was Fifer.

Luck Comes with Wings

Thisbe continued walking alongside Rohan without saying anything about what she'd just figured out. They approached the next intersection, her mind awhirl. She knew from the stories Lani had written that Queen Eagala had died—she'd been sucked down by the volcanic Island of Fire. How could she possibly have survived that? And how had she gotten across the huge gorge that separated the worlds, especially without any magic? Had she latched onto the young dragons before they'd even left the world of the seven islands? Had they flown her across?

Thisbe had known her whole life that Fifer had destroyed

LISA McMANN

Eagala's ravens with her scream. But from what Rohan had just told her, Fifer must have completely obliterated Eagala's magic at the same time. The thought of Fifer having that much power was breathtaking.

Back when Thisbe, Fifer, and Seth had arrived in the land of the dragons, Dev had told Thisbe that the black-eyed people were worth a lot as slaves because they had once been rulers. Apparently the Revinir had an additional reason to pick black-eyed children specifically—to get revenge on Fifer. Did the Revinir know who Thisbe was? Surely she'd seen Simber outside the elevator tube when she'd taken Thisbe captive—he was so recognizable, there was no way she could have missed him. Had she figured out her identity? Thisbe hadn't seen the woman since the day of her capture, but she was growing more and more certain that the Revinir must at least suspect who she was. What did that mean for her?

When Thisbe and Rohan met up again after the next intersection and were on their final leg of the journey to the testing room, Thisbe was filled with questions. "How many people with black eyes are there?"

"In all of Grimere? Or down here?"

LISA McMANN

"Both, I guess," said Thisbe.

"Not many," said Rohan. "There are eleven of us in the cat-acombs, plus you. Many of our parents are dead or being held as slaves in various palaces and other kingdoms, both within and outside of Grimere. There are other lands beyond the for-est that I've never been to, but I know some of our people and at least a few dragons, too, are hiding from the Revinir there."

Our people, thought Thisbe. Rohan considered her to be one of them. "So the Revinir has only taken over Grimere so far?"

"Yes." He glanced at her, as if puzzled that she wouldn't already be aware of that information. "What about you? You seem to know shockingly little about us, and you don't speak the language of the commoners, which is strange. What part of Grimere are you from?"

"I'm not actually from here," Thisbe said a bit cautiously as she tried to figure out what things were safe to tell Rohan. Could she trust him? She'd been evasive in the past with Dev, but that was to protect the dragons. But the dragons didn't seem to be part of the picture anymore. Still, Dev had burned her. Would Rohan be different? Thisbe didn't see any reason

LISA McMANN

to hide anything now. She was stuck down here with no allies—not a single friend. She shrugged and confessed, "I came from the land of the seven islands."

"Oh, you did? Intriguing!"

"Have you heard of it?"

"Yes, of course. The pirates come from there. It's in all the history books."

"Books?" said Thisbe with a hopeful surge—perhaps there'd be something to do after all in the evenings. "Are there books here?"

"Not here. In the village schools. I had them before the Revinir caught me."

"Oh." Thisbe's heart settled into disappointment. "That's a shame. I like books. I don't know what to do all evening except look at all the awful bones, or make up stories in my head and act them out. But there's no place to write anything down."

Rohan smiled as if he'd like to see that play out inside a crypt. He pounded Thisbe with questions. "Tell me more about your world. It's magical, isn't it? Some of it, anyway? That's where the Revinir came from too. I wonder how people do it—magic, I mean. It's amazing to me. If only I could do something powerfully magical to break us all out of here. . . ." He trailed off.

"How?" asked Thisbe. In the distance she could hear rushing water, which meant they were nearing the testing room.

"However magic's done. You'd know better than me, I'd guess." Rohan shrugged and put a finger to his lips. "I'll wait for you," he whispered, then proceeded to the testing room to deliver his dragon bone.

Thisbe waited a while, then went in after him.

The cavelike room was set up as a big laboratory. The tables and machinery reminded Thisbe a little of what Ishibashi and the other scientists had in their greenhouse, only this was much bigger. The tools here were sharp, like picks, and used for extracting magic from bones for the Revinir. The workers wore ragged, loose clothing, more like the slaves than the soldiers who guarded the elevator exit and the intersections. Perhaps they were held against their will too. Thisbe tried to see if any of them had black eyes, but they kept their heads down.

As Rohan exited without a glance her way, Thisbe brought

her bone to an empty station and removed it from the harness, leaving it on the floor for the examiners to hoist up. Then she went to the pile of finished bones, chose the smallest one, and harnessed it to herself to drag back to her crypt. Before she left the room, she stopped for a ladleful of water from a bucket near the door and drank it down. It stopped her stomach from growling, at least for a few minutes. She was halfway to her meal.

When she exited, there was no sign of Rohan. She ventured the way she'd come, this time following faint green arrows which pointed the way back, and tried not to appear like she was looking for anyone. She rounded the first corner, where the rushing water sound was most distinct, and heard a noise behind her. She turned and saw Rohan beckoning to her from a side hallway that had no markings but went steeply uphill.

Making sure no one was around, Thisbe went toward him.

"Swiftly," he said when she reached him. The two went together up the passage as fast as they could go while dragging enormous dragon bones.

The noise grew louder. Rohan moved fast with Thisbe huffing and puffing behind him, trying to keep up. He turned another corner, and Thisbe dug in after him. When she went around it and looked up, she stopped short. Her lips parted. Several yards in front of her, slicing across the passageway and appearing to cut straight through the rock walls and floor of the catacombs, was a wide, rushing river with stacks of buckets like the one in the extracting room nearby. But beyond the river was what took Thisbe's breath away. It was the sky.

"Oh my," said Thisbe, her words lost in the roaring of the water. It seemed like ages since she'd seen the sky. She could see that there was a short bit of passageway on the other side of the river that led to a gaping opening in the rock wall, which wasn't guarded by anyone at the moment. She took a few more steps. "How do you get across the river?" she shouted at Rohan. "And then . . . what?"

"You don't," said Rohan, pointing to where the river disappeared below the wall. "The river never slows down, and look—if you tried to swim it, it would carry you away and slam you against the wall unless you were fully submerged. But no one knows where it leads or how far it travels under the stone. You could get trapped with no place to surface and drown in no time."

LISA McMANN

"Yikes," said Thisbe. She eyeballed the distance across. It was way too far to try to jump. It was clear now why Rohan had said luck of escaping came with wings, for just like the space between the worlds, there was no other way to get to the exit. "No wonder the Revinir doesn't bother to guard it. There's no need."

"Precisely." Rohan nodded. He tore his eyes away from the mesmerizing rush of water and glanced at Thisbe. "Even if we could get across, I think it's a long way down the mountainside, considering how far uphill we travel to this part of the catacombs. The city is back where our crypts are—but we're inside a mountain now. And I'm not sure if you can see it, but the crater lake is just out there. I can only see the tip of the volcano from here."

Thisbe frowned. Rohan was a few inches taller than her. She stood on her tiptoes and could barely see what looked like the top of a volcano.

"Here," said Rohan, hastily checking to make sure no one had come their way. He unhooked Thisbe's harness, then knelt and held out a hand. He tapped his knee with the other. "Step up here and see."

Thisbe quickly grabbed his hand and hopped up, and now she could see the lake surrounding the volcano. As she stood there marveling at it, and fretting over their distance and height from it, the volcano belched and exploded a giant ball of water into the air. A second later came a great *boom* that shook the floor. The ball of water separated and fell all around the volcano, slapping its sides and the surface of the lake. It was followed by a ball of fire that shot up and turned to smoke. Then the volcano shook and shot down under the water, disappearing.

"Wow," said Thisbe under her breath. It reminded her of the Island of Fire. "So that's where that booming sound comes from?" She and Fifer and Seth had all heard it.

Rohan nodded, and Thisbe stepped down.

"Thanks," she said, letting go of his hand and picking up her harness again. Her mind whirred with thoughts—if Simber could only find this entrance, they might have a chance! But was the opening big enough for his broad wingspan? Certainly this hallway wasn't wide enough for Simber to glide in here. She stood for a moment as her hopes sank. Why was everything so impossible?

LISA McMANN

She buckled the harness ropes to her chest, then turned around and gasped. Behind them stood the Revinir. Before Thisbe could try to stop herself, angry sparks shot from her eyes and struck the bone in her harness, breaking it in two.

Forbidden Friendship

Rohan froze, a look of bewilderment and fear on his face. His eyes darted between Thisbe and the Revinir. But the Revinir's icy stare rested on Thisbe. Arms crossed, she moved her fingers, the long curling fingernails like weapons tapping against the rich velvet of her garment. "What is this?" she hissed. "Some sort of magic? So my hunch was correct about you. You're the little tyrant—"

"No!" shouted Thisbe. Based on the Revinir's reaction, disclosing her abilities seemed like an incredibly bad idea. "This bone was . . . well, it was cracked already from the extraction procedure. And it just broke."

LISA McMANN

The Revinir narrowed her eyes at Thisbe. "Hmm," she said. "And a liar, too."

Thisbe recoiled. The Revinir had seen right through her. Flustered, she opened her mouth to reply, but the Revinir had turned to the boy.

"Rohan!" snapped the woman. "What are you doing here with her?"

"I—I—" he stammered.

"It's my fault," Thisbe said, stepping forward. "I told him I wanted to escape, and he showed me this exit to prove to me that it's impossible. That's all. I understand now, and we're going back."

The Revinir studied Thisbe, as if trying to sense her motives. Then she raised an eyebrow. "You are an evil child," she said matter-of-factly.

Thisbe gasped.

The woman continued. "Are you the one who destroyed my ravens? Or was that the dead one?"

Thisbe's heart flew to her throat. Was Fifer truly dead? She couldn't be. Thisbe would know it—she would feel it somehow. They were identical twins, after all, and they had a special connection just like their brothers, didn't they? The Revinir had to be trying to scare her. Clearly the woman had figured out that Thisbe and Fifer were the twins from Artimé—probably because of Simber, as Thisbe had suspected before. As much as she wanted to cry out for information about Fifer, she knew she couldn't. What was she supposed to say now? Pretend the woman was mistaken?

"I don't know what you're talking about," Thisbe said as boldly as she could.

The woman laughed. "Right," she said. "Magical. Your age and that flying creature with you gave you away—I know exactly who you are."

"Then why would you ask?" Thisbe said hotly. She could feel Rohan's eyes boring a hole in the side of her head, but she didn't dare look at him. She didn't want to get him into any more trouble.

The Revinir didn't respond. She stepped closer and continued to study Thisbe. "More evil than good, and magical, too," she murmured. "Interesting."

Thisbe's blood ran cold. "What did you say?" she said.

The Revinir laughed again. "You may have stripped me of

LISA McMANN

my magic once, but you won't do it again. I'm stronger than any of you now—your awful brother, too. I can't wait for your people to come back for you so we can have a proper fight. Though you'd think they'd have come by now." She tapped her pursed lips, looking troubled, but in a fake way. "Maybe they don't want you back because you are such an evil thing."

"Stop saying that," Thisbe warned. She could feel her anger building. Her fingers buzzed with heat and static.

Rohan put a hand on her shoulder and leaned in. "She has to be bluffing. Don't let her get to you," he whispered, close enough for Thisbe to hear over the rushing river.

The Revinir turned to Rohan. "You will not speak to this child ever again!" she spat out. Then she softened. "Stay away from her, my good boy—she's more evil than good, and you know well enough not to associate with slaves like that."

Rohan flinched, but he didn't respond.

"How do you know I'm more evil?" Thisbe demanded. She didn't like the way it sounded at all, and she didn't believe it was true. "You're making it up. Only dragons can tell that."

Just then there was a bit of commotion behind the Revinir as a squad of soldiers rounded the corner and came up to her.

LISA McMANN

Quickly Thisbe focused on tamping down her anger—she couldn't take on the lot of them with her fiery magic and had no idea what would happen to her if she tried.

"You are a stupid child," the Revinir said to Thisbe. "What do you think I do with the magic from the bones—throw it away? I *am* a dragon now, you fool. More of a dragon than the dragons themselves!" She turned to address the boy. "Rohan, I'm disappointed in you. Continue with your job and don't let me catch you speaking to this one again. Go."

"But—" Rohan said, hesitating.

"Now," the Revinir said forcefully, and looked to the lead soldier of the group. He and the other soldiers reached for their weapons.

Rohan gave Thisbe a helpless look. Without a word, he turned away in defeat and retreated down the passageway with his dragon bone, past the Revinir and the soldiers, and went around the corner to the main hallway.

"Soldiers," the Revinir said, still staring at Thisbe, "this girl has pointed out a very important issue to us. We will need to guard this entrance now that she's here. Who knows what that flying statue can do or what sort of magic her people might have to enable them to climb up the cliff side and get across this river. Or what sort *she* has." She looked at Thisbe's broken dragon bone, then turned to the girl. "Drag these back to your crypt. Tomorrow you'll be tackling a different project . . . with me."

Thisbe's expression flickered with surprise. She worked her jaw and said nothing.

"And don't try anything with your little sparks," warned the Revinir. "It's only fair for me to tell you that you can't hurt me. And I'll fight back with all the strength I've been saving up to kill your brother once and for all." With that, she lifted the sleeve of her garment. Instead of skin on her bare arm, she had thick scales like a dragon. Thisbe recoiled and stared. Then a curl of gray smoke drifted from the Revinir's nostrils and floated to the ceiling. She turned sharply and walked away.

Pounded with such shocking revelations, Thisbe numbly obeyed. She fought to keep her wits about her, then rigged her harness to carry the two halves of the bones and made her way slowly past the soldiers and back to her crypt.

As she walked, she dismissed the idea entirely that Fifer was dead. She refused to believe that manipulating woman. Instead she debated what else about her was most devastating—the Revinir's obvious new magical dragon powers? Or that she'd said Thisbe was evil? Or maybe it was the fact that Thisbe wouldn't be allowed to talk to Rohan ever again. Losing her new friend was a sharper blow than Thisbe expected—it left her alone once more.

That night after her meal, as Thisbe whiled away the hours locked in her crypt, she found herself looking at her short, ragged fingernails and thinking about her anger-induced magic. "You think I'm evil?" she muttered under her breath. "I'll show you evil." She sat up and pointed at a nearby bone. Then she closed her eyes and concentrated, thinking about the Revinir and trying to make herself more and more angry at the horrid woman. When she could feel her blood about to boil, Thisbe flung her fingers in the direction of the bone and shouted, "Fire!"

Her fingers and eyes sparked. She leaned forward, thinking of how the Revinir had said so callously that Fifer was dead. And then how she'd threatened Alex and the people of Artimé. "Fire!" she said again. More sparks came out, but they didn't hit the mark.

Thisbe growled under her breath. She had to be able to

do this. There was no other choice. She thought hard about the books Lani had written, about how the Revinir, as Queen Eagala, had fought against Alex and injured him so badly it had changed his life. "You wrecked my brother," she stewed, picturing the fight scene. "You'd better stay away from my family!" She leaped to her feet, took a few steps back, and struck out with her hands at the bone before her. "Fire!" she cried.

Fiery arrows burst from her fingertips and slammed into the bone, making it fly back against the wall. It bounced off and rebounded, hitting Thisbe's head and knocking her to the ground, senseless. The bone landed next to her and broke into pieces. Thisbe groaned and rolled to her side. Everything went black.

Moments later, three sharp taps came from the other side of her back wall. But Thisbe was out cold, and she didn't hear them.

In the morning, Mangrel came to get her and bring her to the Revinir's chambers.

Private Lessons

F ifer woke with a start. Where was she? She blinked a few times as the ceiling of the hospital ward came into focus. Then she pushed herself up on one elbow and looked around. Seth had gone to bed at Crow's urging, and Henry wasn't around. Only Crow was sitting in a chair nearby.

"Hey, Fife," he said. Because Alex was busy preparing for the rescue, and Scarlet was comforting Crow's mother on Warbler, Crow had decided to stay in Artimé until he was convinced Fifer was okay. Here at least he could keep tabs on what was happening, because once he left for Warbler, communication

LISA McMANN

with Artimé would be limited. He smiled and got out of his chair to stand nearer to Fifer. "How are you feeling?"

"I'm . . . okay," she said. She looked beyond him as Florence came into the hospital ward.

The warrior approached the bed and stood next to Crow, towering over him. "Oh good, Fifer, you're awake. You look a lot healthier with your eyes open."

"I suppose that makes sense," Fifer murmured. Her mind still felt a bit fuzzy, and her body ached all over. She looked down at herself and saw dozens of wounds that were in various stages of healing.

The only thing Fifer recalled about being home was a momentary face-to-face talk with Alex, and she had no idea how long ago it had taken place. Before that, she could remember being tied to a post in Dragonsmarche, seeing Simber flying toward her, then being pelted with shards of glass. Everything after that moment was blurry, but she knew Simber had swooped in with Thatcher to take her away, and she had a distant memory of the giant glass aquarium in the market square growing small and dark as they soared off. She could recall nothing of the journey home, which wasn't all bad, since no one really enjoyed the long stretch of days flying over the sea.

Her stomach growled, and she recalled how awfully hungry and wet and tired she and Seth and Thisbe had gotten on the way to the land of the dragons. Suddenly some of the conversation she'd had with Alex returned to her, and her heart plummeted. Seth had been here too, but . . . She looked up sharply. "Where's Thisbe?"

Crow and Florence exchanged a concerned glance. Didn't Fifer remember what Alex had told her the previous day? Crow gently sat on the edge of her bed and explained everything to her from the beginning.

By the time he was done, Fifer was crying inconsolably. Nothing anyone could say brought her comfort. Eventually she grew quiet and remained that way, staring at the ceiling for a long time while Crow and Florence stayed nearby, worrying over her.

Some time later, Fifer struggled and sat up. "I'm going to help find her." She threw the bedcovers off.

Crow objected. "You're still pretty weak to be getting out of bed. Take it slow. Nobody's going anywhere right now. Not for a while. They need to prepare."

Florence pressed her lips together and frowned. "Fifer, I'm afraid you're staying home when they do go after your sister. Alex won't allow it."

"Too bad for Alex," Fifer said. Her eyes turned steely. "I know Thisbe best of anyone. I'll be able to find her."

Crow shook his head. "It's already been decided."

"Without me?" Fifer reached out and put a weak hand on his arm. "Crow," she pleaded, "you know Thisbe and me better than even Alex does—she and I do everything together. We've never been separated like this. I'll be able to find her. I'm not joking around."

Crow lowered his gaze. "It's not my call."

Fifer turned to Florence. "Please. Just teach me some basics and give me a component vest and I'll be a better mage than all of them. You know I will be!"

Florence closed her eyes and sighed. "I don't know if I should do that without Alex's okay. But . . . I'll see what I can do. Don't count on anything. Alex is very stubborn. And he's worried about losing you on top of Thisbe and Sky. But I'll talk to him again."

"When are they going back to find her?"

"A few weeks. We're taking some time to prepare and train first."

"But isn't Thisbe in danger?"

"We don't think the Revinir will hurt her. And we know where she is."

Fifer leaned back into her pillows, already exhausted from the argument but not giving up. "This is ridiculous. You need me to go."

Crow looked at Florence too. "She's right," he said quietly. "She knows Thisbe best—and she's powerful. With a little training she'd be a huge asset to the rescue team, if only Alex would let her."

Florence shook her head in frustration. "I wish I could convince him of that. Like I said, I'll do what I can. Just . . . just focus on getting better, Fifer. Okay? I've got to go check on the dragon-wing progress and set up some training time with Alex and the team. And now that Fifer is looking stronger, we'll see about Simber and you heading to Warbler—perhaps tomorrow?"

Crow nodded. "That would be nice if Simber can get away."

» » « «

Later that day, as Fifer sat up in bed talking with Crow and eating heartily to help herself grow stronger, Florence reappeared at the hospital ward doorway and beckoned to Crow. He slipped out and joined her in the mansion's massive entryway while Fifer looked on curiously. "What's going on?" she called out. But Crow and Florence were having an intense conversation and didn't hear her.

Shortly after, Fifer saw Alex come down the stairs and join them. Florence and Alex went outside to the west side of the mansion, opposite the lawn, which was generally secluded and very private—almost no one frequented that side since it was small and bordered the former Quillitary grounds, which didn't offer pleasant reminders to the people of Artimé even though they were at peace with Quill now.

Crow returned to the hospital ward. "Florence wants us to go to the west window," he said quietly. "Are you feeling up to it? I'll carry you."

"Sure!" said Fifer, eager to do something less boring than lying in bed. "What are they doing?"

"You'll see."

Fifer set her plate on her bedside table. Crow scooped her

up and carried her out of the ward and across the entryway to a window that faced the west lawn. "Stay hidden now," he said. "We don't want Alex to see you. But watch closely. Florence told me she's starting training from scratch with Alex so she can teach him how to strengthen and use his right arm as deftly as he once used his left."

"Are you serious?" Fifer breathed. "That's wonderful! I'm surprised he's willing to do it." She'd only seen Alex do a few spells in her lifetime because he'd discovered the hard way that Fifer and Thisbe could learn magic just by watching, unlike others who had to try things multiple times to have success. Not to mention Alex refused to do much because of his injury. He'd tried on his own to do magic right-handed, but had eventually given up in frustration because he knew he'd never be as good as before. Now he looked like a young Unwanted sent from Quill, learning how to use his creativity to perform magical spells.

"He must really want it for Thisbe's sake," murmured Crow. "I mean, to let go of his pride in order to train like this— like he's brand new at it—it's quite a shock. But it's because he loves you two so much. I know he doesn't always show it. But he's showing it now, isn't he?"

Tears sprang to Fifer's eyes, and she nodded.

They continued watching, fascinated, as Florence stood outside in the shadow of the mansion with Alex. She worked with him on using his right arm, bringing it through the complete range of motion necessary to release a proper throw. Over and over she led him to complete it, without holding any spell components. He stopped once and argued, making Fifer and Crow wonder if this would be the premature end of his training, but then he let out a frustrated sigh and went at it again. After a while, Florence had him do it on his own while she cast a critical eye and corrected him over the most minute errors.

Fifer watched intently, then gingerly mimicked the action, trying to do exactly what Florence was teaching Alex.

An hour passed and Alex got upset again by Florence's nitpicking. But again he apologized and continued, determined.

"What's gotten into him?" said Fifer. "He must be so tired by now. And he's not giving up, even though he's not very good."

"He doesn't want to mess up the rescue mission," Crow surmised. "He's bent on going, and he can't bear to be the one who flubs up everything."

"He should let me train and go along with them," Fifer grumbled. "I won't flub up."

"You're training right now, aren't you?" asked Crow. "I know that's why Florence wanted you to watch—so you can learn the basics. She's going to be doing a training session on the lawn later with the whole team and you can watch then, too, as long as Alex doesn't see you."

"Not on the Island of Legends?"

"No. Florence made some excuse that they don't have time to waste traveling back and forth."

Fifer smiled. "I know Florence is doing this secretly for me, and she could get into trouble with Alex. But I want people to *know* I'm old enough now and see that I'm training. I want to wear my very own component vest, like Seth, and walk around without people being scared I'm going to make dishes explode in their faces or birds rain down on them. I want to know how *all* the spells work, and I want to use them to save my sister!"

"You'll get there soon enough. Thirteen is only months away."

"A lot of months." Before Fifer could fire off more of a retort, they heard a footstep in the hall and saw Seth coming toward them. "Hey," he said, a smile breaking out on his face.

"There you are. I saw your bed in the hospital ward was empty, and I've been looking all over for you." He wore his freshly cleaned component vest, its pockets bulging.

Fifer eyed him, feeling a twinge of jealousy. "Hi," she said. "Shh. We're watching Alex learn to do magic."

Seth snorted, as if the idea were preposterous. "He's the head mage. He's supposed to be the most powerful magician we have. I don't think he needs to learn anything."

Fifer raised an eyebrow. "Of course he knows the spells, but he can't cast them very well. He's relearning that part."

"Finally," said Seth. "I'm glad." Then he grew troubled. "With Thisbe and Sky gone, he must feel really terrible. Worse than any of us."

Fifer blinked back tears. The news that Thisbe was still back in the land of the dragons had been shocking enough, but learning of Sky's tragic disappearance had been horrifying. Nobody would say out loud that she had to be dead, but everyone suspected it.

"Did you hear?" Seth asked her. "Simber says the Revinir is Queen Eagala."

Fifer nodded. Crow had told her that morning.

Seth went on. "Maybe that's why Alex wants to go so badly—so he can get revenge." He watched out the window. Florence had Alex doing strength and resistance exercises now to build up his muscles. He was getting a full workout.

"I don't know," said Crow. "But I think he really just wants to rescue Thisbe. He feels responsible for you three running away. That's the way he is about everything." He paused thoughtfully. "Though no doubt you're right too, Seth. If Eagala had done that to me . . . heck, *I* might even be taking magic lessons right now."

Fifer studied Crow, who often clued her and Thisbe and Seth in to the more nuanced things about Alex that they might have overlooked from their perspective. Crow had lived in Artimé since before Mr. Today, the previous head mage, had died, and he'd seen Alex in a very different light.

"At least I get to go along and help," said Seth, picking a bit of lint from his vest.

Fifer whipped her head around to look at Seth. "What?" she shrieked. The window they were standing at popped and shattered.

"Aw, crud!" muttered Crow. He grabbed Fifer and dove for

LISA McMANN

cover; then he scrambled to his feet with her in his arms and ran, tripping and laughing, back to the hospital ward. A flock of birds soared into the mansion through the broken window.

"Fifer!" shouted Alex from outside.

"At least she's alive!" Seth shouted back to him, then ducked and ran after Crow.

The three of them huddled on Fifer's bed, a feeling of doom replacing the ridiculousness of their mad dash to safety. What would Alex do if he knew they'd been watching him? Hopefully he wouldn't suspect that—not with Fifer supposed to be stuck in bed. And it wasn't unusual for her to be able to break a window from a distance. Perhaps he was feeling generous toward her today after all she'd been through.

They waved away the birds that had gathered around. One of the larger ones, a falcon colored in beautiful jewel-toned feathers of red and purple, fluttered and landed on Fifer's bedside table. It looked up expectantly.

"Hi, bird," said Fifer in a dull voice. She was tired of the useless flocks always appearing. Somehow this one's presence had her missing Thisbe even more just because she wasn't there to object to them.

The bird bobbed its head, which made it appear like it was bowing. Fifer reached out gently and ran a finger down its long neck, admiring its shiny crimson and indigo feathers. It seemed to shimmer even more at her touch.

"That's the prettiest bird I've ever seen," said Crow.

Fifer nodded. "It's big for a falcon, isn't it? And the coloring is so unusual."

"Ishibashi told me these kinds of falcons have bunting feathers," said Seth. "He said they just started showing up on his island and around here in the past several years—they'd never seen one before then. Now they have a big flock of them that live over there."

There were a few more of the large colorful falcons among the flock. Some of the other, smaller birds made their way back out of the mansion the way they came in, but the initial red-and-purple one remained on Fifer's bedside table. With Thisbe not there to object, Fifer shrugged and stroked its feathers some more. The bird shimmered again. Then it began preening.

"I think it likes you," said Seth.

Fifer fancied the idea of having it stay. "It's my new pet," she declared. "If it wants to be, I mean." She turned to it and

LISA McMANN

said earnestly, "You can come and go if you like. At least until someone fixes the window. And there's always the door—if you stand there long enough, it's bound to open eventually."

"Aren't you going to name it?" asked Crow.

"We'll see if it stays," said Fifer. "And I'll think about it. But I'm not sure Thisbe will like me adopting a bird while she's . . . away. It wouldn't be nice for her to come home to that." None of them wondered aloud if Thisbe would indeed ever come home, but the thought crossed their minds.

After a minute Fifer gave Seth a pained look as she remembered what he had announced before the incident with the broken window. "So they're leaving me here and taking you with them," she said. It was more of an accusation than a question.

"Yes," said Seth, appropriately abashed.

"I can't believe you actually want to go," said Fifer, "considering our experience. I mean, you didn't exactly enjoy yourself."

"But this time we'll have *real* mages. And Simber."

Fifer gave him a withering look.

"I won't have any fun without you, though." Seth didn't say more, and the three slipped into an uneasy silence. Fifer moved the small stack of books on the table so the bird had more

LISA McMANN

room, and then she got under the covers. "Looks like Alex isn't too mad about the window. If he's not coming to holler at me, I think I should take a nap so I can get better."

Seth and Crow took that as their cue to leave. They said their good-byes and went out of the hospital ward, leaving Fifer quite alone with the falcon and her thoughts. She turned to face the wall, but she didn't sleep. Her mind mulled over Thisbe, and birds, and magic, and Sky, and component vests, and mostly about how Seth was allowed to go on the rescue mission but she wasn't. And her heart didn't know which way to go with it all.

A Major Clash

Thisbe waited in the Revinir's outer chamber for more than two hours, alone except for a couple of soldiers. She'd had plenty of time to roam around the vast, parlorlike room, looking at a variety of artwork and sculptures made from bones. There were carvings out of individual bones and larger works constructed from multiple bones. And there were picture frames constructed from bones connected at the corners by golden thorns.

In the center of the room there was a small dragon skeleton completely assembled. It must have been from a young hatchling, and it upset Thisbe more than she expected. She couldn't look at it without growing emotional. What had happened to the poor young thing? And why would someone ever want to put that on display, as if they were proud that it had had an early demise?

By the time the Revinir called Thisbe into her inner chamber, she'd decided she wasn't going to blindly do whatever the woman wanted just because she was worried about what could happen to her. She was going to speak her mind and oppose the ruler at every turn.

"So," said the Revinir, her clothing today revealing dragon scales around her collarbones. "Here I am, face-to-face with my match from my weaker days. I hope you don't think you can destroy *this* magic."

Thisbe's face burned, but she wasn't going to let the woman intimidate her. Instead she asked sharply, "How can you hate dragons so much when you want to be one?"

The Revinir looked surprised. Her face turned angry. "You don't know me at all. I revere dragons."

"Then why would you use them as slaves?"

"I'll ask the questions, thank you," she retorted. "How did you do it?"

LISA McMANN

"Do what?"

"Destroy my magic?"

Thisbe sighed. "Look, lady, that wasn't even me, okay? Get your facts straight."

The Revinir stared at her. "You will respect me," she said evenly. "Or you'll suffer."

"I'm already suffering quite a lot," Thisbe pointed out.

"You don't know what suffering is," the woman seethed. "You've had a very good life, I suspect. Unlike some." She sniffed.

Thisbe frowned. Was the Revinir trying to get Thisbe to feel sorry for her now? She wasn't having it. As the woman droned on about her great reverence for enslaved dragons, Thisbe folded her arms across her chest and began plotting the woman's demise.

First Thisbe would have to learn how to control her magic. Now that her bone runs were going faster, she had a few hours every night to do that. It might take a while to master it, but if she had anything, it was time. Then she'd have to figure out how to take out the Revinir's personal guards and probably Mangrel and the soldiers at the intersections near her crypt.

LISA McMANN

Oof. That was a lot. And even then, if she was able to disarm and disable that group, including the Revinir, it didn't mean the rest of the soldiers would do what she wanted. They'd certainly go after her. So, if there weren't any who would pledge allegiance to Thisbe, she'd have to fight them as well. And she still didn't have a way out, unless she injured the elevator guards too, or could get across the river.

It felt like an impossible task. She certainly couldn't do it alone—maybe some of the other slaves would help her if she could figure out how to communicate with them. Could Rohan help with that? If only there were a way to get a few of the soldiers to trust her, she might be able to deceive some of them long enough to get the other slaves and herself to the exit.

But then what? All jump into the river and be swept under? Or miraculously manage to fight the current and get across, only to reach the exit and fall to their deaths trying to climb down the mountainside?

It was a jumbled mess of ideas. She'd have to figure everything out later. For now, she tuned in to what the Revinir was saying.

"And besides," the woman said, "I like the idea of having

LISA McMANN

someone else magical around to help me manage the other slav—I mean servants. I think you can be an asset to me. Since you are more evil than good, you'll be a good fit as my assistant. You won't have to drag bones anymore. And together we can work toward a common goal."

"What?" Thisbe's eyes widened. What had she missed? "Work together?" she said, feeling suspicious, not to mention repulsed by the idea. "To do what?"

"To take a stronger hold over this land. And others, too."

"Others?"

"Other lands," the Revinir said a bit impatiently. "Weren't you listening? You are more stupid than I thought."

"I'm not stupid. I—I just want to be sure I understood you," said Thisbe. She thought for a moment, trying to make sense of it. "*What* other lands, exactly?"

The Revinir scowled and didn't answer. "You'll start now."

Thisbe blinked. She was pretty sure she knew what other lands the woman was talking about—the lands where other dragons and black-eyed people were hiding, which Rohan had mentioned. And she probably meant the world of the seven islands, too. "No I won't," she said adamantly. "I don't want to be your assistant. I'm not going to help you." Her eyes sparked without warning, so she seized her chance to lean forward and look dangerous. "And if you try to make me," she warned, "I'll destroy you, like my sister did once before."

The Revinir laughed. "You can't." But she seemed uneasy. She stood up and began to pace. "I'm presenting you with a great opportunity. Perhaps you need some time to think about it. I know it's a big step. But we'd be much better working together than fighting each other. And since no one seems to care that you're here, well, maybe you'll change your mind in time."

"That's not true!" Thisbe said, getting up. Then she lowered her voice. "Don't count on me changing my mind, ever."

The soldiers looked to the Revinir for direction. Frustrated, the woman waved at them to let the girl out. "Make her carry two bones a day," she said. "Maybe that'll help her decide that a job as my assistant won't be so bad."

Thisbe frowned and tried not to let the Revinir see the tears that sprang to her eyes. Two bones a day? She hadn't done anything to deserve this fate. And now things were getting worse. Her work had been doubled. How was she going to do that?

There weren't enough hours in the day to do them one at a time. She'd have to pull them both at once. "You're mean!" she shouted as she left, pulling out of the grasp of the soldiers who tried to control her. "And you're the stupid one if you think making me do more work is going to convince me to be your assistant. It only makes me hate you more!"

Later, struggling with two bones, Thisbe got a few sympathetic looks from the other children, who'd ignored her until now. Rohan passed her early on, hesitating like he wanted to help her. But Thisbe was upset, and she didn't feel like being helped at that moment, not even by Rohan. Plus, she didn't want him to get caught after the Revinir forbade him from talking with her. She held his gaze, then looked away. After a moment, he whispered, "I'm sorry," and continued on.

By the time she'd reached the testing room and was on her way back to her crypt, again with two bones, Thisbe's shoulders ached. The harness cut into her skin. How she wished she could be home in Artimé, going to dance and theater and learning mechanics and gardening from her nice brother, Aaron. But she was here with the evilest person in the world.

She felt her anger simmering just below the surface, and occasionally tiny sparks shot from her eyes or her fingers. It was past time to embrace the destruction inside her and let it out.

That night, after she nursed her aches, she practiced directing her magic. It came a little easier this time, and she managed not to knock herself out. She destroyed a small bone to pieces, missing it only twice before backing up a little and hitting it right where she intended to.

When she'd used up the last of her energy after the long day, she prepared to sleep. And that's when she heard the three sharp knocks on the back wall.

Her eyes flew open, and then she realized who it must be. Despite feeling exhausted, Thisbe climbed up the bone pile, all the way to the small space along the back wall, near the ceiling. She picked up a bone—a dragon toe, it must have been— about the size of her forearm. She pounded the wall with it three times, and was surprised at the loud sound it made. She hadn't expected that with solid rock.

A moment later came the response. Two knocks this time. A warm feeling came over Thisbe. Two knocks—it felt like Rohan was saying "good night" in a secret language. It

LISA McMANN

reminded her of the secret language Lani and Samheed had made up when they'd been captives on Warbler, only they'd been together and had used their fingers to tap in each other's cupped hands.

Pound, pound, Thisbe replied, and whispered, "Good night." It might not be what Rohan had intended. It might be nothing but a way to feel human by communicating. But it was very comforting to Thisbe to think it, so she did.

Secret Training

By the next day in Artimé, Henry's magical medicines had done their job quite thoroughly, and he declared that Fifer was well enough to leave the hospital ward. No one but the falcon was around to celebrate it with her—Seth and Alex were in the middle of Magical Warrior Training on the lawn, and Crow had left to be with his mother and Scarlet on Warbler. Aaron had gone back to the Island of Shipwrecks by now so that Kaylee could be here to train.

Fifer took the bird outside in case it wanted to fly away, but it stayed on her shoulder most of the time, only fluttering to

LISA McMANN

the ground now and then to catch bugs or sip from dew on the grass. It seemed to want to stay with Fifer. But she still wasn't sure it was a good idea to keep the poor bird trapped inside the mansion. So she set it down and urged it to fly away. Even as fond as she'd grown of it, she wanted it to be free to make the decision to stay with her or move along.

Eventually the colorful falcon flew to a tree. Fifer, growing tired, went back inside. Noting the time, she took the tube to her theater class and sat in the shadows of the auditorium. Onstage Samheed and Ms. Claire Morning, who lived in Quill now but still taught music in Artimé, directed some of the dancers for a new musical Lani and Samheed had written together. Thisbe was supposed to be in it, but her spot on the stage was glaringly empty.

Before class ended, Fifer slipped out and went unnoticed back to the mansion's entryway, then outside again to see if the bird was sitting there, but it wasn't. Fifer saw Carina with Seth's younger siblings, six-year-old Ava and five-year-old Lukas, starting to gather flower petals for the dragon wings. She sighed. If only she and Seth had had proper items to work with, Alex and the others wouldn't have to remake the wings.

LISA McMANN

It put Fifer in a foul mood. She felt like nobody really under-stood what she and Seth had gone through to make the new wings—all the pressure they'd faced with so little material. She went back inside and caught a glimpse of Alex and Florence through the west window, working outside on the private lawn again. Fifer pulled a stool from the kitchen so she could sit and watch the proceedings.

Just like he'd done the previous day, Alex was practicing his throwing technique. Sweat poured down his temples as he concentrated on an imaginary target. Ms. Octavia was out there today too, and Fifer watched, fascinated, as Alex gradu-ated to using actual components. After some time doing that, Ms. Octavia bravely volunteered to play the part of the enemy, as many more-advanced mages of Artimé often did for the sake of the ones in training.

Alex wound up and flung a handful of scatterclips at Ms. Octavia. They veered wildly to one side and seemed unsure what their target was, then appeared to lose momentum. The thin pieces of metal sailed to the ground, doing nothing. "Buckets," muttered Alex. He tried again and again, working hours to develop his skills.

LISA McMANN

As Alex did so, Fifer paid vast attention and memorized everything. She took in the way Florence taught him to stand and wind up and flick his wrist and hook his elbow just so. Fifer soon slipped off her stool and imitated the movements.

Every now and then, Florence glanced through the window to see if Fifer was there. But Fifer stayed back in the shadows. At one point she lifted her fingers and waved them, and Florence nodded satisfactorily. Florence was teaching her, too. On purpose. At least Fifer would be able to defend herself . . . if she ever got any components. Which wouldn't happen until Alex said so, or until she turned thirteen. But she was using her time wisely now in preparation.

After a while, when Florence switched to working with Alex on building his strength, Fifer went up to her room, where she hadn't spent any time since before she and Thisbe had left. It felt empty without Thisbe there.

Fifer practiced her scatterclips throw a few times, mimicking what she'd seen Florence teach Alex. Then she found some loose buttons from a sweater that no longer fit her and ripped them off so she could pretend they were components. She threw them across the room at the wall, aiming for the center of her blackboard. They hit dead on.

Desdemona surfaced, pushing her face from the screen. "What was that?" she said, trying to look all around.

"Nothing," said Fifer, hoping the buttons had fallen out of sight. "Sorry I bumped you."

"I heard you were back. I'm glad you're okay. I'm sorry about Thisbe."

"Thanks."

Desdemona raised an eyebrow, warning Fifer not to throw things at her again, then melted into the blackboard. Fifer picked up the buttons and put them in her pocket. She'd have to practice somewhere else.

She went into her bedroom and looked out her window— the one that she and Thisbe had climbed out of—and watched as a small group of people and creatures gathered on the big lawn for what appeared to be a special session of Advanced Magical Warrior Training.

Fifer placed her hand on the window. "Release," she whispered, wanting to be able to hear what was happening. The glass pane melted away, and Fifer turned her ear toward the outside, hoping some of the verbal instructions

LISA McMANN

would be carried on the wind all the way up to her room.

Florence led the team in practicing their spells as they got ready to rescue Thisbe, and Fifer absorbed everything she could.

Seth was down there with the more advanced mages, and that made Fifer feel bad again about Alex not letting her go with them. He was trying out a small red heart-shaped component for what seemed like the first time. Fifer guessed it was a heart attack spell—Seth had told her and Thisbe that the heart attack spell wasn't something the beginning mages usually got to try, and he hadn't had any of those components before today. She was sure Florence and Carina and Alex had made an exception for Seth since he was going on the rescue. Fifer's expression flickered. No exceptions were to be made for her.

Just then Samheed sent off a handful of scatterclips with a wild throw, leaving him yelping in pain and holding his shoulder. The scatterclips struck Florence and sent her careering backward into the mansion wall, making the whole building shake. When Florence pulled herself out of the giant dent she'd made, she looked sternly at Samheed.

"Sorry," said Samheed meekly. "I think I pulled a muscle."

"You all need to do strength training too," Florence declared. "Everybody drop and give me twenty push-ups."

Seth groaned and flopped to the ground, and Fifer could see he was already tired and sweaty by the way his blond hair stood up. He hated exercise. Fifer took a tiny bit of satisfaction from it, but not too much.

Then Florence turned to Alex. "You see? This is why we have to take the time to train. There's only one person I can think of who needs less training than any of you, but you won't let her go. So. Get moving."

Fifer's lips parted. Florence was talking about her. Tears sprang to her eyes, and she strained to hear Alex's response.

"Okay, I get it," Alex said begrudgingly. "We're all really out of practice. We want to get this right." But he didn't say anything about changing his mind to let Fifer go with them. Instead he frowned and eased to the ground to attempt twenty one-armed push-ups, and was already faltering by the time he finished the third one.

After a moment Fifer stopped watching. She replaced the glass and sank onto her bed, her chin quivering. Across the room, Thisbe's bed was empty and unmade from when they'd

LISA McMANN

snuck out. Carina, Seth, Lani, Samheed, Alex, and Thatcher were all outside training. Even Talon and Kaylee were out there with their swords, all of them getting ready to rescue Thisbe. And Fifer would be stuck here alone, with only a little knowledge and a handful of useless shirt buttons. And a bird, maybe—unless it had decided to leave her too. It wasn't fair.

She fell into a restless sleep and was awakened by the sound of Desdemona calling to her. Bewildered, Fifer fought her way out of her sheets and rolled out of bed. She glanced out the window and saw that the training session was over, then staggered to the living area feeling woozy. "What is it?"

The blackboard personality wore a puzzled look. "Seth sent a message. He says you should go outside the main entrance—there's something on the front lawn you've got to see."

A Change of Heart

Feeling a bit better after her nap, Fifer made her way down the grand mansion staircase, past Carina and her little ones in the entryway, who were back to collecting and stacking items for the new dragon wings. Fifer opened the huge entry door and went outside to look for Seth. Instantly a small flock of large red-and-purple falcons squawked and fluttered about, then settled around her. The one that had stayed with her earlier was front and center, strutting a little, then going right up to Fifer's feet and flying up to land on her shoulder. She winced as its talons gripped her right where her wounds were healing. "Well, hello there. I see you've brought friends."

LISA McMANN

Seth came walking up behind the flock, an amused expression on his face. "I think your new bird wants to show you off."

"Weird, isn't it?" said Fifer, but she was pleased. She turned to look at the bird. "What's going on with you, Shimmer?" she murmured. The name seemed to fit. She petted it, making it shine brightly, then knelt in the grass, being careful not to startle the falcon on her shoulder. The other birds crowded around her, their necks darting out like pigeons going for seeds, trying to get Fifer to pet them, too. She did, and each of them shimmered extraordinarily brightly as well.

Just then Alex rounded the corner of the quiet west side of the mansion with Florence. Had they done a second session today? He was training hard. Alex waved but kept going—he seemed like he didn't want anyone to ask what he'd been doing. "It's great to see you up and around! I've got to help with the wings," he added apologetically, and slipped inside. But Florence stopped when she saw Fifer and Seth surrounded by birds, and went over to them. "How are you feeling, Fifer?"

"A lot better. Just a little tired."

"You've been watching the side yard, haven't you?" She

nodded in the direction of where she and Alex had been working.

Fifer nodded. "Yeah. Thanks," she said quietly. "It means a lot that you trust me."

"As the Magical Warrior trainer, I made an executive decision. I want you to be able to defend yourself. But let's not mention that to your brother just yet."

"Okay."

Florence took a closer look at the birds, who hadn't scattered when she approached, which seemed odd since she was such a large presence. "And . . . these birds? Why are they shining like that? Did you make them do that?"

"I didn't do anything but pet them, I promise," said Fifer a bit defensively, since she was used to people in Artimé accusing her and Thisbe of doing magic when they weren't supposed to.

Florence flashed a sympathetic smile. "It's okay. I think you did something to them, though. Nothing bad." She knelt and observed the birds. "Have you ever petted the birds before when they've come to you after one of your screams?"

"I—I don't know," said Fifer. "I don't think so. I've never really thought about it. I usually just shoo them away because

Thisbe is afraid of them. But since she's gone, I've let them stay . . . and now they don't seem to want to leave." She looked down at the birds. Thinking of Thisbe, Fifer was reminded of all the things she was worried about. She turned her face to Florence's concerned gaze. "Any chance you've been able to convince Alex to let me go on the rescue?"

Florence sighed. "Not yet." She didn't seem hopeful that she would succeed. "I'm trying."

"I know. I'm going to ask him myself," she said. "I'm feeling better every day."

"I'll go with you if you want," Seth offered.

Fifer shrugged. She was still feeling a bit jealous of him, but maybe he could help. "Okay." She lifted the bird off her shoulder and set it on the grass, then went inside with Seth right behind. They followed the noise to Ms. Octavia's classroom, where Carina and Alex and a few others were just starting to assemble the first of many gorgeous wings for the dragons, sculpted from thick jungle vines and the finest cloth and prettiest flower petals in Artimé.

Seth and Fifer looked at the beautiful creation, then glanced at each other, shook their heads, and laughed ruefully. "It's so beautiful," Fifer said, thinking of the horrid tree-branch-and-burlap-feed-bag wings *they'd* made back at the castle.

"I'm almost embarrassed about what we did to those poor dragons' wings," said Seth.

"I'm not," Fifer declared. "We freed them. Who cares what they looked like as long as they worked." She looked at her friend. "We did magic that only Alex had done before. You and me."

"That's true." Seth and Fifer made their way through the various workstations to where Alex was standing, looking over Ms. Octavia's sketches for each of the five young dragons.

"Hi, Alex," said Fifer.

Alex smiled and looked up. "Hi. Feeling better? It's nice to see you walking around."

"Yep. I'll be good enough to go with you to rescue Thisbe in a few weeks."

Alex squeezed his eyes shut and sighed deeply, ending it with a slight shake of the head. "Here we go," he muttered. "Don't you ever let up? The answer is no, Fife. You're staying home. No more discussion." He turned back to the sketches.

Fifer looked at him and suddenly felt exhausted. It wasn't

LISA McMANN

that she hadn't expected this response. And she'd planned to cajole and plead like she always did. She'd planned to list all the reasons why she was capable of going, why she'd be an asset to the team, why she of all people would be the absolute best person to have along because of her relationship with Thisbe and her experience in the land of the dragons and her magical strength. But for some reason, all those arguments became unbearably tiresome to repeat. Because this was Alex she was talking to. And the truth was that her reasoning wouldn't work anyway. It would only result in a fight.

Fifer couldn't explain why, but right now she couldn't stand the thought of another heated argument with Alex. She narrowed her eyes and muttered something unintelligible, almost like she was having an argument with herself. It wasn't worth it.

After a moment Alex glanced at her, surprised she wasn't saying anything.

Fifer remained silent as something inside her twisted and ached and groaned in its unsettledness. Her lips parted and closed. And all she could do was stare at him, her eyes growing shiny, but this time she willed the tears away. She was done with those—done with that way of trying to convince her

LISA McMANN

brother to let her do things. Sick and tired of the arguments that never changed his mind. Her whole body seemed heavily weighed down by this mundane method that wasn't working, and she couldn't carry it anymore.

Maybe it was because she was still recovering and feeling weak and tired. Maybe it was because Thisbe wasn't there this time to help her. And maybe it was because Fifer finally found her own inner strength after what she'd gone through, and she'd realized that the harder she begged, the more Alex dug in his feet to oppose her. He didn't understand that she had changed in the short time she'd been away. And he wasn't trying to either—he'd hardly asked her any questions about what they'd accomplished, choosing to focus only on how they'd failed. And that wasn't fair. But Fifer was done waiting for Alex to catch up to figuring out her level of ability. She was done being shot down. Forever.

"Okay, Alex," said Fifer quietly. She looked away, not wanting to see his look of victory. "Okay. I'm finished trying to get you to see my way. I am so much stronger and more capable than you think I am, but I'm done trying to convince you to see what you don't want to see. And I'm tired of fighting you. You're wrong. And you're selfish and stubborn and you won't admit it. And I've had enough of that. So go do your thing with your team and leave me out of it, just like you planned. You'll realize once you get there that I could have helped you. But by then it'll be too late." She hesitated, then added, "And if you mess this up and it costs me my sister, I will never, ever forgive you. And I will focus on your failures just like you focus on mine."

Alex's eyes widened in shock and pain, and for a moment he was too taken aback to reply.

Seth poked Fifer's arm to show her that others had paused in their work and turned to listen to their discussion.

Alex set the sketches down and looked squarely at Fifer. "Of course I won't mess up," he said softly. "And Thisbe is my sister too," he said. "I know you don't think I can run things properly, but I can assure you we'll be going in extremely pre-pared. That's why we're taking all this time."

Fifer frowned. Is that what Alex thought? That Fifer didn't think he was capable? She didn't care to find out. Ignoring everyone, she whirled abruptly. Then she walked back the way she'd come, with Alex and the whole room staring after her in shock.

River of Tears

The next few days Thisbe threw herself into the task of dragging two bones a day. Her muscles ached, and she was sore where the harness cut into her skin, leaving her bruised and bloodied, but she didn't let up. She knew that the faster she went, the more time she'd have in the evenings to work on her magical abilities.

Every day she saw Rohan twice in passing—when he came up behind her on the way to the extraction laboratory and when he passed her again as he was coming back. He always offered a sympathetic smile, and at first he tried to help her, but she consistently refused. She didn't want him to get caught,

LISA McMANN

for one. But there was something else driving her refusal as well. Thisbe didn't want help because she knew she could do it herself. Sure, it hurt. Sure, it took her longer. But she wasn't incapable. And she didn't want to feel like she owed anybody anything. And besides, she was growing stronger muscles all the time from it. That would help her when she took on the Revinir and the entire blue army once she was good and ready. It was like she was in training.

Every night, after hours of concentrating on directing her magic accurately, Thisbe heard Rohan's knocks on the back wall. He always began with three knocks and waited for Thisbe. She responded with three, or sometimes four. Then he with two, and she with two. Thisbe often made up words to match the initial three knocks. "How are you?" she imagined him saying, and she would respond with five knocks. "I am doing well." Sometimes she imagined him saying, "I am here." She'd respond with four knocks. "I am here too."

They'd always end the same way, though, with two knocks each. "Good night." "Good night."

Often, after the satisfying final knocks, Thisbe would close her eyes and fall asleep imagining asking Rohan about their ritual the next day in the passageways. But the next day, she wouldn't do it. For some reason it embarrassed her. What if he was just doing it out of boredom and thought she was making too much of it by imagining conversations to go with the knocks? What if he laughed at her? What if, out of the context of her lonely crypt, her imagining him saying "I am here" sounded as dumb as it did when she said it out loud in the passageway. It was enough to bring heat to her face. "Ridiculous," she muttered. "Of course you're here. Where else would you be?"

A few days later, as Thisbe passed the steep side hallway near the testing room, she realized no one was around. She hesitated, then took the risk and went up it toward the exit so she could have a closer look at the river—and have another glance at the sky she missed so much. She peered around the corner and saw a group of soldiers standing near the rushing river, guarding the path.

One of the soldiers saw her. "Hey!" the woman shouted, then said something else in a different language.

"I don't understand you," Thisbe said falteringly.

"I said come over here. Did you understand that?"

"Yes." Thisbe was surprised to be called over, and a bit suspicious, but she really wanted a closer look. She didn't think the soldiers would do anything bad to her without the Revinir's command, so she felt safe enough to obey. She strained against her harness, dragging the bones up the steep incline, and approached.

"Yes, ma'am?" Thisbe said as she got closer. None of these soldiers looked familiar.

"What are you doing up here?" asked the soldier. "This hallway isn't on your designated path."

"I know." Thisbe looked up with as much respect as she could muster as she tried to come up with a plausible reason. "I'm . . . I'm just really thirsty. So I thought maybe I could stop for a drink at the river." She tried not to appear like she was gauging the distance across the river and looking to see what it would take to get across it. It was far, that was for sure. Too far to swim with the water moving so fast.

The woman waved her away. "Get on with you. Drink your water in the testing room or your crypt."

Thisbe dropped her gaze. "I'm sorry, ma'am. I will." Her eye caught on a tarnished gold plaque on the rocky ground along the river's edge. There were two words on it.

"Aw, let her get a drink," said one of the other soldiers, a man this time. "She's just a pea, dragging twice her weight in bones. That isn't fair, if you ask me. We can at least afford her some water."

Thisbe hesitated, strangely touched that he'd noticed her heavy load, and kept her eyes down, glad for the extra time it bought her to check things out. She focused on the plaque. It said RIVER TAVEER.

"Watch it," the female soldier warned her fellow guard. "Don't be going soft."

"It's only water," muttered the man. "Forget it, then. Get on with you, kid."

Thisbe nodded and turned away. "Sorry."

"Aw, hang on," said the woman impatiently, apparently softening herself. "Hurry up and get your drink. If you try anything, we'll shove you in the river. Those bones will sink you in an instant."

"Thanks." Thisbe quickly moved to the river's edge as the two soldiers hovered over her. She knelt on the golden plaque and slipped her hand in the cold clear water, watching it rush over her fingers for a moment as it chased along. She closed her

LISA McMANN

eyes, feeling an unidentifiable pain of longing rip through her. It made her limbs tremble, and it almost took her breath away.

"Hurry up!" said the woman again, and shoved the toe of her boot into Thisbe's side.

Thisbe gasped and opened her eyes. She began scooping water to her mouth as quickly as she could, letting some of it splash on her face. She sucked it down, refreshingly cold and clean and delicious, like the water in Artimé. An unexpected sob escaped her, but the noise was covered by the roar of the river. She splashed more water on her face to cover all evidence of her sorrow. Then she rested her hand on the golden plaque, her fingertips slipping into the chiseled grooves of the letters, and another wretched sob came from out of nowhere. Thisbe's insides were breaking, and she had no idea why.

"That's enough," said the woman, not as harshly. "Let's go."

Thisbe choked and sobbed as she got to her feet. Tears and water blinding her, she shuddered in her overwhelming sorrow and stumbled blindly over the dragon bones, tangling up in her harness and nearly falling. The soldiers caught her by the elbows and set her on her feet.

"Thank you," she choked out.

The soldiers, not knowing what to think, quickly released her and stood back awkwardly, their expressions conflicted.

Thisbe dried her face on her sleeve and took a deep breath, trying to get her bearings. Then she yanked the bones around so they'd properly follow her. She fled as fast as she could, hurrying away with her head down and wondering how on earth she'd be able to escape this maze with that river so ominous. Why had the soldiers even let her get a drink in the first place? And what was happening to her insides that would force those sobs out at such an inopportune moment?

The soldiers were silent as they watched her go, their faces flickering in ways they hadn't flickered in years under the Revinir's rule. But Thisbe didn't have the faintest clue.

Breaking Down

That evening was long and lonely. Somehow Thisbe had missed Rohan on his way back from the extraction room—he'd probably gone past while she'd been by the river sobbing like a two-year-old. She still didn't know what had come over her. But there was a gnawing emptiness inside that wouldn't go away and seemed to be growing larger.

Of course she missed her sister and prayed she was alive, but she couldn't stand to dwell on Fifer, because it made her feel helpless and hopeless. And Thisbe felt so distanced from everyone else in Artimé—where were they? Why had they

LISA McMANN

left her here? She wished she could send a seek spell, but she didn't have anything with her that was created by someone else—Fifer had the bit of script written by Seth. She was losing hope of ever knowing the answer. It made her feel numb all over. Perhaps that was how her body was protecting her—the numbness giving her the ability to survive and carry out her strenuous tasks. But today at the river a gaping wound had surfaced, and she hadn't been able to tamp it down. Would the edges of it heal eventually? Would her numbness ever wear away? Or was Thisbe supposed to be grateful for it?

She didn't have it in her to work on her magic tonight. Instead she lay listlessly on the floor in the bone dust, eyes on the ceiling, wondering how many feet of rock stood between her and the moonlight. Wondering what would happen if she tried to break through the ceiling. Would it fall in on her? Crush her? It seemed likely. Did it matter? Thisbe's eyes widened. Yes. Of course it mattered. She was not going to give up.

She thought about her options of escape. Would she be better off trying to overcome the soldiers at the elevator? But she had no idea how to control it. Even if she could kill all the guards there, could she figure out quickly enough how to make

LISA McMANN

it shoot upward and out of the catacombs before more soldiers came running?

And what about Rohan?

Thisbe blinked. She sat up. What about Rohan? And why did she even care? This escape was about her, and only her. She couldn't worry about anyone else. Unless he could help somehow. But there was no way to really talk with him. No way to discuss a plan for any meaningful length of time. And she didn't know if she could trust him to keep her secret. All they had were her imaginings of things said through knocks on the back wall. Not exactly reliable.

And speaking of knocks on the back wall, there hadn't been any tonight. Thisbe looked up at the place where she usually pounded, as if that would magically tell her why there was no sound coming from it. It felt late—late enough that Thisbe should already be asleep. But maybe time was passing more slowly than usual this evening. It was hard to tell.

After a few more minutes, Thisbe felt sure it was much later than when Rohan usually pounded. Had something happened to him? She recalled that she'd seen him only once that day, when he'd passed her early in the morning. She got up, alarmed, and climbed up the bone hill. At the top, she picked up the dragon toe and pounded the wall three times. Then she waited, sure she'd hear a response.

Several minutes passed, and Thisbe grew more worried. She pounded again, hearing an echo as if there were a hollow spot in the wall between them. There was no answer. Thisbe wanted to call out his name, but she was scared to do that in case anyone else might hear. Was Rohan okay?

Maybe he was asleep—but why wouldn't he have pounded the wall first like always? Maybe he didn't want to be her friend anymore. But that was ridiculous. They'd had a connection—they just couldn't be seen acting like friends.

Maybe he was injured. What if the Revinir had done something to him today? Or . . . what if he had escaped?

That was ridiculous too. If he'd escaped, everyone would have been talking about it, rules tossed aside.

As the minutes passed, Thisbe grew more and more worried that Rohan had been hurt or punished. She pounded a third time, and again there was no answer.

Thisbe swallowed hard. She slipped and slid down the mountain of bones to her door and tugged at the cracks around the opening—there was no handle on the inside of her crypt. But it was useless trying to get out. There was no way to get the door open except from the outside.

She whirled around, sparks soaring from her eyes as her anger heightened. "If she's done something to you . . . ," Thisbe muttered, a warning. She didn't know what she'd do, but the Revinir would suffer.

Thisbe aimed her gaze at the doorjamb and began to pummel it with powerful sparks. Little chunks of the door flew every which way. But after a minute she stopped. Even if she could get out of here, she'd have to chisel her way inside Rohan's crypt too, and the soldiers would certainly get to her long before she succeeded. Plus, they'd hear her breaking down the door now and stop her from getting anywhere.

Slowly she turned and looked at the back wall. "Of course!" she muttered. She slapped her forehead, wondering why she hadn't thought of this before. Then she aimed her laser eyes on the back wall and thought about the Revinir. Fiery arrows flew and landed almost exactly where she wanted and left big divots—bigger than the kind she'd been making from close range, which seemed odd. She scrambled up the bone mountain and began to pelt the wall with sparks, but they appeared to have less power and less effect than when she'd been standing farther away. She went down again and backed all the way up to the door. Then she aimed for the wall.

Little chunks fell away, and then one particularly well-aimed shot split the rock wall and left a wide crevice over a two-foot space. "That's the way," Thisbe murmured. She kept summoning up her fury, pounding at the wall for several minutes until there was an indent more than a foot deep. But by then her sparks fizzled. She'd run out of energy and collapsed to the floor, exhausted. After she caught her breath, she climbed back up the bone mountain and used the dragon toe to pound inside the growing hole in the wall. A few pebbles and some dust gave way, but nothing more than that. She'd have to continue tomorrow when her strength returned and her magic recharged.

She piled a bunch of already-extracted bones in front of the hole so the crypt keeper wouldn't see what she'd done and slid wearily back down to her sleeping spot for the night. Worn out, she slept hard and woke up with a start when Mangrel opened the door in the morning. He gave her some water, pointed out the two bones she was to deliver that day, and left the door standing open as usual.

Thisbe took longer to get ready this morning. She stood and watched out the doorway as some of the other children walked past, but her back-wall friend wasn't among them. "Rohan—where is he? Do you know?" she'd whisper to the others, hoping they'd recognize his name, but they all shook their heads. The last one to go by was the girl who Thisbe had tried talking to early on. Her eyes widened in response. She whispered something in the common language, then brought her fingers to her neck and sliced the air across it.

"What?" cried Thisbe, loud enough to make one of the soldiers at the nearest intersection turn to give her a warning look. She lowered her voice. "What did you say? What does that mean? Is he . . . dead?"

But the girl, frightened by the soldiers, didn't reply. She hurried on.

Thisbe stared after her, more confused than ever. With a heavy heart, she set out.

A Shocking
Revelation

Thisbe's late start left her straining to pull her load faster to make up time. Her mind was plagued with thoughts and worries about what could have happened to Rohan. She imagined all sorts of things: Rohan being taken away forever. Or maybe he was still in his crypt, ill or injured or something? He couldn't possibly be dead. Or could he? Somehow, without him here, Thisbe became even more determined to figure out how she was going to get out of here and plot her escape. And to do that, she needed to be extra diligent and work on her magic even more. She was getting better and gaining control—she could tell that

117 « Dragon Bones

LISA McMANN

much. She wished she had more variety in her abilities, but her inner magic seemed to be very focused on destruction using sparks and explosions. That didn't give her a lot of options.

As she dragged her bones through the catacombs, she planned her day. She would move as quickly as she could, and then as soon as the crypt keeper brought her dinner, she'd gulp it down and start working. One thing she wanted to accomplish was to be able to do her magic without having to work herself into an angry lather first. And she wanted to find out even more about what she was capable of—what was the scope of her power? Just how big an explosion could she create? She also needed her spells to be automatic, well placed, and lethal. It was the only way she might be able to get out of here.

Last night she'd figured out that the closer she was to her target, the weaker the effect of the spell, which seemed odd, but it was true. Being farther away made the spell more powerful and more accurate. She was limited by the size of her crypt in testing that out and didn't know if there was an optimal distance—she knew that there had to be some point where she was too far away from a target to hit it, right? But with no space to test it, it might be a while before she could find that out.

Perhaps if she reached a long stretch of passageway in the cata-combs where there weren't any soldiers or slaves she could try it out. Maybe if she snuck out in the other direction from her crypt, toward the castle, she could find a passageway less trav-eled. But would the soldiers suspect she had no business going that way? She'd have to risk it. And she had a decent chance of being able to protect herself now. Her aim was improving. Though she didn't want to have to resort to that until she was ready to make her ultimate escape—it would most certainly get her captured if the Revinir found out just what she was capable of too soon. She needed to hide her abilities to keep the suspicion at a minimum.

A big part of Thisbe wanted to fold up inside herself when she truly thought about having to hurt anyone—even the ones who had hurt her. She didn't think it was in her nature to kill a person, even though she'd done it before by accident as a child. Indeed, there was a big part of her that denied she'd really have to go through with it. Perhaps there was another way to get out without having to leave any carnage behind. But if there was, she hadn't thought of it yet. So she was determined to pre-pare. Also in the back of her mind was the unsettling reminder from the Revinir that she was more evil than good. Could it be true? Thisbe had lied multiple times, and it seemed like the Revinir could tell. Maybe being able to lie so easily really did make Thisbe an evil person—and here Thisbe had thought it was just her ability to be a good actor. But it seemed true—the Revinir had been somehow taking in dormant dragon magic for years, and that was one thing the dragons could tell about humans. Thisbe remembered how Hux had said Dev was exactly half and half. It didn't seem surprising that the Revinir would be able to pick up that ability from the magic in the bones. Which made it more unsettling.

Her mind lingered on Dev and their time together. Their relationship had been rocky, but they'd needed each other. They'd annoyed each other, done some rude things to each other, but there was something inherent in Dev that Thisbe had really liked. Then, abruptly, their relationship had ended without notice or fanfare. She'd probably never see him again. Now she'd made a friend who was nice and caring, and he was gone. Or dead. Or something horrible like that.

She was so deep into her thoughts and plans that her journey to the extraction room seemed to go more quickly than

LISA McMANN

usual. She was surprised when she reached the rushing sound of the river. Being nearly half done energized her, and she made the last leg of the journey at top speed. She deposited her bones next to empty stations, picked the two smallest of the ones that had already been worked on and hitched them to her harness, gulped downed a cup of water, and rushed out, nearly knocking someone flat in her haste.

It was the Revinir. Behind her were her soldiers.

"Ah, there you are," the old woman said, keeping her balance nimbly with the help of the doorway. "I've been looking for you." She narrowed her eyes. "Are you ready to work as my assistant yet? Opportunities abound. Mercenary options, no less."

"No way," Thisbe said with contempt, though she didn't know what mercenary meant. "Not in a million years."

"Ah well. It's a pity you're going to miss out. I'll have to make do with my newly acquired servant, then, though unfortunately he's not magically inclined. I would have preferred you." She hesitated, then leaned forward, her fingernails clicking together. "What sort of magic can you do, exactly?" The Revinir sounded slimy, and it made Thisbe want to avoid her even more.

"Nothing." Thisbe shrugged, then tried to push past her.

LISA McMANN

The Revinir put her scaly arm out to stop her. "I know you're lying. I've seen your sparks. Are you the one who killed the pirate captain? I think you are."

Thisbe said nothing, but her conscience twinged. She'd lied again like it was nothing. That was definitely something an evil person might do.

"Also," the Revinir went on, "I heard something very troubling about you. Sneaking around the river the other day, were you? Don't do that again. You're forbidden. And I've instructed my soldiers that if they catch you trying that again, they're to take any means necessary to stop you."

Thisbe's heart sank, but she tried not to let it show. "I won't. I was only thirsty."

"You know I don't believe you."

Thisbe looked at the woman with contempt. "You don't have to believe me." She started forward again, then stopped. "Where's Rohan?" she demanded, not expecting an answer. "What did you do to him?"

"Oh, he's busy elsewhere in the catacombs."

"He's alive?" Thisbe held her breath and failed miserably at trying to look like she didn't care.

The Revinir raised an eyebrow. "Hmm. Interesting. My hunch was correct. You seem to care a great deal. I'm glad I separated you two."

Thisbe scowled but didn't argue, and she tried more successfully this time not to let her intense feelings of relief be evident. "Did you make *him* your assistant or something?"

"Rohan? Please. He's only sixteen percent evil. Not nearly bad enough to work directly for me. Not like *you*. You're special." She laughed, and a puff of gray smoke came out of her nostrils. "I just needed to keep you away from him. I prefer you only be around other children with whom you can't communicate. That boy is just too educated and good to stay on this side of the catacombs. It means his work is much harder, certainly, but that couldn't be helped. I'll tell him you said sorry, since it's you're fault he's been moved—oh wait, no I won't. I'll tell him nothing of the sort. Perhaps I'll tell him you're dead." She cackled. "And he'll believe me, because he's so good. Oh, it's fun to play with the good ones."

Thisbe looked at her in horror, feeling the rage boil up. The Revinir was an awful, horrid person. She glanced at the soldiers, feeling terribly tempted to strike the woman down—did they think she was horrible too? She couldn't tell. Their faces were blank. It was too risky. Plus, hadn't the Revinir said that she was somehow indestructible now? That had to be something to do with the dragon-bone magic. But obviously dragons could die somehow, or there wouldn't be tons of their bones here. And Arabis and the others wouldn't have been threatened. Thisbe eyed the woman, wondering where to direct the spell once she was ready to do so. Her throat, perhaps. There weren't any scales there.

"You're thinking about trying to hurt me, aren't you?" said the Revinir, searching Thisbe's face. "I wouldn't try that if I were you. You won't succeed. It'll only get you thrown into the dungeon."

Thisbe's heart leaped to her throat, but she narrowed her eyes and tried not to let on. "What dungeon?"

"The one at the palace," said the Revinir. "I'm told you enjoyed your time there, though, so I'm not terribly keen on sending you back."

Thisbe was so angry she could hardly breathe. She lifted her chin and held back from letting any emotion show. After too long of a pause, she said through gritted teeth, "May I pass, please? I have work to do."

The Revinir smiled. "Of course, dear. Enjoy your day, and do tell a soldier whenever you are ready to work with me as my assistant. I assure you we'll make a good pair."

"It won't ever happen," said Thisbe. She pressed forward, leaning into her harness.

"All right," sang the Revinir, "if you say so. But you know what that means. Tomorrow you can start delivering three bones. Nice big juicy ones. The heaviest, which are overflowing with dragony magical goodness. It's past time to make another bone broth." She smiled condescendingly. "I'll convince you eventually."

Three bones? Thisbe felt like her brain was boiling. She closed her fists and her eyes to stop anything tragic from happening before she was ready and pushed past the soldiers, walking as fast as she could go and blinded by fury. But she couldn't escape the woman's laughter, which rang in her ears.

At least Rohan was alive. But how was she going to find him?

A Breakthrough

Thisbe didn't have time to wallow in her sorrows or wonder about how she was supposed to drag three bones to the extraction room the next day when she'd hardly been able to drag two. She didn't have time to whine about how her shoulders and back and knees ached from her job.

She took the time to eat, of course. She was slowly growing thin on one meal a day, though her tray today seemed to have slightly more food than normal. Perhaps when the crypt keeper had heard about the Revinir's insane order, he'd felt

LISA McMANN

sorry for her. If so, she'd take his pity and the extra food. She needed all the fuel she could get.

Once she'd finished eating and was locked into her crypt for the night, Thisbe moved the stack of bones away from the hollow she'd made in the wall. Then she stood in the farthest corner away from it, near the door, and concentrated for several minutes, remembering the moment the Revinir had told her she had to take three bones tomorrow as punishment for not being willing to become her assistant.

Thisbe knew three bones wouldn't be the end of this punishment. The woman was trying to break her, to convince her to be her assistant, and so far it wasn't working. That wouldn't make the woman pleased at all. She'd keep adding more bones until Thisbe couldn't get the job done anymore and she'd have to give up.

But the Revinir didn't know Thisbe very well. She wasn't going to give up. As the food fueled her body, Thisbe's anger fueled her magic, and soon she could feel fire pulsing through her forearms. She opened her eyes, electricity sparking at her fingertips. She needed to test some things. First she tried the

LISA McMANN

most minimal move she could think of. She flicked her fore-finger against her thumb, sending a line of sparks shooting toward the hole in the back wall. They hit a little left of center and made small divots. A bit of dirt trickled out. "Okay, so a flick of the fingers probably would hurt someone but not destroy them," Thisbe noted.

Next Thisbe decided to test her strongest move to see what the difference would be. She pulled her arm back, then took a few steps for momentum and flung her arm forward, pointing her forefinger at the hole and yelling "Boom!"

A fireball shot forth and slammed into the hole, making a small explosion that shook the walls and left a cloud of smoke and dust so thick Thisbe had to drop low to the ground to keep from choking. A piece of rock that had once been embed-ded in the wall came rolling down the bone pile at her, just missed, and slammed into the door behind her. Her sleeve was singed and smoking, and her forefinger burned in pain. She could see a blister forming on its tip. She cringed and sucked on it. "Well," she murmured, sitting on the floor and waiting for the smoke to clear, "that was pretty powerful."

After a moment she picked up a candle and climbed up the

bone pile through the haze. At the back wall, she felt around the hole and peered in. She couldn't tell how deep it went.

It was twice the diameter it had been before, easily wide enough for Thisbe to fit into if she curled up a little. She wrinkled her nose and shoved her head inside it, arm outstretched with the candle, trying to see what her magic had done. The candlelight flickered and shone in a circle, bouncing off the uneven walls of the hole. Thisbe crawled in and waved the smoke away.

Just then she heard a noise behind her at the door. She froze, then quickly backed out of her tunnel. She dropped her candle and began shoving the bone pile back in place to cover the hole.

Her door opened, and the crypt keeper looked inside. "What's going on in here? Did you make that explosion? Where did all this smoke come from?"

Thisbe stared down at him, hoping desperately that he couldn't see the gaping hole in the wall from his angle on the floor. "What?" she said weakly, stalling so she could think of an excuse. There was no use denying the smoke—it was obvious. "Oh, you mean this?" She waved her hand through the air and laughed a little. "It's . . . really . . . nothing. . . ."

"It doesn't look like nothing." He took a step inside and

tried to wave some of the haze out of the room so he could see better. "What did you do?"

"I—I accidently set my clothes on fire with the candle," said Thisbe sheepishly. "I've been trying to sort the dragon bones. Used ones over here, you see, and the ones that haven't been extracted go down toward the floor so they're easier to get to. Anyway, I knocked over my candle when I was moving today's bones up here and set my shirt on fire. Burned my finger, too. It hurts pretty bad."

"That wouldn't make that explosion sound," the crypt keeper said, looking suspicious. "It rocked this whole section of the catacombs."

"Oh, that! I have no idea what that was," said Thisbe. "I felt it too, but I didn't have anything to do with that. Maybe it was an earthquake. That's . . . actually . . . what made me knock over my candle." She coughed and waved the smoke aside. "Very startling."

The crypt keeper looked frightened, which puzzled Thisbe. But then his expression changed, and he narrowed his eyes at her. "The Revinir said you were more evil than good, which means you probably lie a lot."

Thisbe stared at him. He'd voiced her fears, and she didn't like the sound of them. She gathered her wits. "With all due respect, sir," she said, "perhaps the Revinir, who is the evilest person we've all met, is the one who is lying about my level of evilness. After all, you know she seems to have it in for me, don't you?"

The crypt keeper's mouth opened but then closed again. He frowned, then said, "That's true. And . . . it may be the smoke fogging my sensibilities, but I don't think it's fair what she's doing to you." He ducked his head and backed out of the crypt, then closed the door behind him.

Thisbe stood silent, letting his sympathetic words exist and ring about the room, almost as if they became stronger because they were the last ones spoken. She picked up the candle.

As time ticked forward without another interruption, she relaxed a bit and went back to rebuilding the bone pile, but she didn't quite dare to explore the tunnel again in case Mangrel returned.

She could hear little pieces of the wall continuing to break off and fall inside the hole behind her, but she ignored the noise and focused on swiftly finishing the bone pile. Since the door had been opened, a lot of the smoke had dissipated, which Thisbe realized in retrospect had probably been what had prevented the crypt keeper from seeing the gaping hole before she could finish hiding it.

Soon Thisbe had constructed a significant cover in front of the hole. "There," she said, placing one last bone. She took her candle and got ready to head back down, when she heard a sudden rushing sound of dirt and pebbles from inside the hole. She bent down and peered inside. When her eyes adjusted to the darkness, she realized she could see a tiny crack of light from the other side.

After a moment, the crack split wide and someone pounded the rest of the wall away, revealing a candlelit face peering back at her. Rohan smiled wearily through the tunnel. "My goodness," he said admiringly. "What a beautiful sculpture you've created while I was away. It almost appears as if you might have missed me a little."

A Heart-to-Heart

Throwing caution to the wind and her candle to the bones, Thisbe dove into the tunnel and helped Rohan clear out his end of it. "You should build a pile too, so the tunnel can't be seen from your door," she said. "I'll help you."

Together they made quick work of it. When they were finished, they climbed back inside the tunnel and sat with their backs curling to the curve of the wall, facing each other in the short passageway that connected their rooms. Thisbe retrieved her candle, relit it, and set it between them, then peered at her

LISA McMANN

friend. The shadows under his eyes seemed pronounced, and his eyes were weary.

"Are you okay?" Thisbe asked him.

"I'm pretty tired," he said.

"Do you want to go to sleep?"

"I'd rather talk with you."

Thisbe's face burned, and she shifted the candle away from her so Rohan wouldn't be able to see the color rise to her cheeks. He had such a strange way of talking, unlike Seth or any other boy Thisbe had known. Definitely not like Dev. The way he said whatever he meant with no hesitation was as intriguing as some of his word choices.

"Where have you been?" Thisbe asked.

"Have you missed my rapping on your wall?" A smile played at his lips. "I was so glad you responded. I thought you might be angry with me."

"No, I wasn't angry. I just didn't want to get you in trouble by talking to you. But it seems like you got punished anyway. I'm sorry. So . . . where have you been?" she asked again.

Rohan's eyes glistened in the candlelight. "To the castle."

"On foot? All that way? How?" Thisbe remembered

the lengthy ride she and Fifer had had from the castle to Dragonsmarche. It would take a tremendously long time to go that far on foot—at least a day.

"Yes, on foot. And in fact, these catacombs lead all the way to the castle dungeon. I'd never gone that far before in that direction."

"What's over there? Why did the Revinir have you go so far?"

"The crypts of the ancient human rulers are over there. Our ancestors."

"Oh." The statement weighed heavy on Thisbe. She'd never spent much time thinking about her ancestors before her time in the catacombs. She'd known little about her family's past, other than that her parents had died when she was a toddler. Her mother had black eyes, which was where she and Fifer had gotten theirs. Had their mother come from here? Or perhaps her grandparents? There was no record of such things in Quill. No history. No writings or stories—it hadn't been allowed. The only record of her parents' life and past had died with them.

Rohan touched Thisbe's singed sleeve. "Are you all right?"

LISA McMANN

Thisbe pulled away from her thoughts and looked up. "Yes," she said. "I'm just thinking about what you said. About your . . . our . . . ancestors being buried a day's journey away." She swallowed hard and looked at him. "I don't know any history of my family. Do you . . . I mean, are you sure . . . that I'm descended from rulers like you? I just don't really feel like my family was . . . you know. Strong and noble like that. They . . . they weren't. I'm pretty sure." All she could think about was how her parents had sent their creative son, Alex, to his death. How they might have done the same with her if that practice in Quill had continued. That didn't seem noble at all. It seemed cowardly.

Rohan pressed his lips together. "There was a time about forty years ago when our people were worried about being tortured and killed—the uprising was already happening. Some of our grandparents tried to save their children by sending them away from here. Perhaps your mother was one of them."

"But how would she have gotten over there? Across the gorge?"

"The worlds were connected back then."

Thisbe blinked. "They were?"

"Do you remember seeing the narrow waterfall that drops to nowhere off the side of the cliffs of Grimere?"

Thisbe nodded.

"It used to be a river that ran to the sea in your world. And your sea didn't end in a waterfall spinning around your world. It butted up against our cliffs."

"What split the worlds apart?"

"An earthquake. We have them now and then. Not to be confused with the volcano in the crater lake that rattles Grimere, of course." Rohan's voice was teasing.

"Of course," Thisbe said with a smile. "No wonder the crypt keeper looked freaked out when I suggested the big explosion earlier was an earthquake."

"Yes, you might get that stunned reaction from the older folk who remember the massive one. Sometimes they even react when the volcano in the lake erupts, even though they hear it all the time. According to my studies, a lot of people lost their lives." He yawned and rested his head against the wall. His eyelids drooped.

Thisbe wanted to know more about his studies, but she could tell he was exhausted. "When did you sleep last?"

LISA McMANN

He murmured sleepily. "Two nights ago. My journey takes fifteen hours each way."

Thisbe stared. "With no sleep in between?"

"The soldiers at the castle end offered to let me take an hour's nap before I returned, but I said no."

"Why wouldn't you want to rest in between?" asked Thisbe. It seemed crazy to not at least put his feet up for a while.

Rohan opened one eye and looked at her with a lazy smile. "I needed to get back so I could knock on your wall."

The Birds

Back in Artimé, Fifer's abrupt change in behavior had Alex more than a little puzzled, but he kept himself as busy as possible in the following weeks to lessen the time he spent worrying over Sky and Thisbe. He and the team that was preparing to go on the rescue mission spent their days with Florence doing extensive Magical Warrior Training and exercises, and their evenings continuing to build the new larger wings for the dragons.

After delivering Crow, Simber spoke to the dragons about helping their effort, leaving them with much to think about.

LISA McMANN

They promised to have a decision by the time they came to get their new wings.

Then Simber spent a couple of days circling the area around the Island of Fire, knowing his search for Sky was probably futile but somehow feeling like he had to do it in order to be sure for himself. He even dove under the water and discovered Spike still combing every inch of the depths of the sea, looking for her too. But there was no sign of their beloved Sky. Eventually Simber made his way home, and Spike did whatever she usually did in the great sea while waiting for Alex to call upon her.

And then there was Fifer. She was rapidly regaining strength by the day until she was as good as new. Fifer's interest in the falcons had her venturing out in the mornings to the private area of the lagoon. With Crow on Warbler Island unable to keep an eye on her, and with Alex and Seth busy preparing for their quest, Fifer found herself left very much alone. Except for the birds, of course. They went with her everywhere, and their numbers grew as the days went by. She began to talk with them about her worries over Thisbe, her frustrations over Alex, her sadness over Sky, and her deep desire to be treated like a real mage. The creatures seemed sympathetic and always

LISA McMANN

appeared to be listening, which gave Fifer some comfort, even though she knew it wasn't normal to think birds could understand her. Still, she wondered.

Whenever Florence trained the veterans and Seth on the lawn, Fifer watched secretly from the edge of the jungle and learned the various components and how to use them. And when Alex and the others worked on the wings, Fifer began experimenting with training the birds and soon discovered they were fast learners. The first thing she taught them was to stay outside when she went into the mansion. Using spoken words and the Warbler sign language, of which most mages in Artimé knew at least a little, Fifer commanded them to stop and put out her hand in a signal to the birds, and then she ventured to open the door. If they tried to follow her, she'd reprimand them and do the hand signal and verbal cue again. They soon caught on, and when they did it right, Fifer praised them.

The rest of Artimé was just glad the birds stopped trying to get inside the mansion, and they paid little mind to what else Fifer was doing.

Soon Fifer had the grand falcons flying to and away from her at her command. Next she taught them to fetch things—a

LISA McMANN

leaf, a small branch, or anything Fifer could find to toss in the jungle. The birds eventually learned to act only when Fifer was speaking directly to them, and soon she was able to get a specific group of birds to do what she commanded while the rest waited, straining and eager to be addressed too.

She taught them to fly in a pattern following her hand movements. Sometimes she'd spend hours waving her hands like a conductor, directing the birds to swoop and soar and circle around. She got them to create shapes in the air—a circle, a triangle, a heart—and taught them all the hand signals and verbal cues that meant go, come, fetch, and more.

When she grew bored with those commands, Fifer taught the birds to take hold of her by her clothing and fly her around the lagoon close to the ground. It was great entertainment, especially when Fifer was feeling bad about everything. It never ceased to cheer her up at least a little.

In the evenings Fifer would leave the birds to roost in the trees. She'd go inside and retreat to her room, where she'd take her dinner alone because she didn't want to sit with Alex or hear Seth and Lani and Samheed and the others go on and on about the rescue mission.

She felt bad about it, but the truth was she just couldn't face Alex, especially after the way she'd left things with him. She knew he had to be hurting more than anyone about Sky, and of course he was worried about Thisbe. But Fifer couldn't seem to get beyond his refusal to let her join them. She just couldn't understand it. She'd already learned so much in her first trip away from Artimé, and she had so much magical potential, but Alex was treating her like a baby. Hadn't he noticed how much she'd grown since she and Thisbe and Seth had left? Didn't he grasp the amazing things they'd done while they were away? Clearly he appreciated what Seth had done, but Seth would've accomplished none of it without Fifer. Alex was being impossible. And she couldn't stand to be around him or Seth right now.

On the day the young dragons returned to get their new wings, much of Artimé gathered around to witness the transformation.

The first thing Alex did when they arrived was take Arabis aside. He had a question from the distant past that had been weighing heavily on his mind lately. "When you left our world ten years ago," he said to her, "did Queen Eagala somehow travel with you to the land of the dragons?"

"No," said Arabis. "We went alone. Her ship had sunk weeks before we left. When we were captured and until you told us, we didn't know Eagala was the Revinir—we'd never really had a good look at her before and hadn't realized the connection all these years."

Alex nodded, but appeared confounded by the answer. "Okay, thank you." He looked over the water toward the west for a long moment. "It doesn't make sense," he muttered to himself. "How did she get there?" Then he turned abruptly back to Arabis. "Have you had a chance to think about joining us? Can you risk coming along?"

Arabis nodded. "I've chosen to go with you. My brothers and sisters and mother and I have decided that one of us must go back and warn the ghost dragons in the land beyond Grimere."

"Ghost dragons?"

"That is what they are called," said Arabis with a bit of mystery. "They are in danger from the Revinir now that she has lost us. So I will help you get to your location and continue on a few hours' journey from there. I'll deliver my message and return to the forest outside of Grimere as quickly as possible to hide until you are ready to return to the seven islands."

It wasn't a perfect situation, but it was close enough. Alex poured out his gratefulness to Arabis, and she in turn voiced her thanks for the three children who'd freed them and given them the wings they needed to escape.

Only one, Seth, was standing nearby, and Alex called him over. Seth flushed bright red. "You're welcome," he said.

"Shall we put on your beautiful new permanent wings now?" Alex asked the dragons, standing aside so they could inspect them along the shore. The orange dragon nodded regally and moved closer so Alex and the others could start the job.

Fifer watched the gathering from afar, sitting on a log in the lagoon, her birds surrounding her. She couldn't hear what was being said, but the crowd seemed to be very excited about the new wings. It made her a bit glum to think about how everyone had been spending so much time on constructing them and making such a big deal over these beautiful new wings and cringing over the ugly ones Fifer and Seth had made. If Alex and the others had only had sapling branches and burlap

LISA McMANN

and a few scatterclips to pin the whole thing together, they would've made ugly wings too. It was an amazing accomplishment under really difficult circumstances, but nobody understood what they'd gone through. Maybe Fifer should start writing books about it like Lani had done so she could point out all the things everyone else thought were unimportant. And reveal the truth about Alex, who was nothing like the boy in Lani's books.

Kaylee, who had come with Aaron to see the event, noticed immediately that her young sister-in-law, Fifer, was nowhere to be found. She left baby Daniel with Aaron and sought out Lani near the edge of the shore.

"Have you seen Fifer?" Kaylee asked her.

"I spied her earlier heading along the shoreline in that direction," said Lani, pointing toward the lagoon.

They could just barely see a human blob shape sitting there, with birds fluttering about. "Thanks," said Kaylee. "I'm going to go talk to her."

"I'll come with you."

Kaylee strolled along the sand, and Lani rolled alongside

her. Aaron had designed and crafted Lani's sleek magical vehicle ten years before, after her legs had become paralyzed in the final battle, and he'd constantly made improvements to it in the years since so she could travel over a variety of terrains. The contraption embraced her around the hips and held her upright, giving support to the lower half of her body and keeping her hands free. Powered by concentration, it moved magically in compliance with her unspoken wishes unless she was particularly tired—then it sometimes veered off track. Now the vehicle struggled a little in the deep sand, but Lani powered it forward anyway, hopping up out of the sand to ride on the grass instead. Kaylee realized what was happening and stepped up on the grass too.

Before long they reached Fifer.

The girl looked up at them quizzically. "What are you doing out here?" The birds fluttered and settled.

"May we join you?" asked Kaylee.

"Sure, I guess," said Fifer.

Lani adjusted her wheeled vehicle and put her hands back to allow her to ease into a sitting position on the log next to Fifer. Kaylee sat on the other side of her and gazed out to where the crowd had spread in front of the mansion.

"I haven't seen you around much lately," said Lani.

"I've been here," said Fifer with a sniff. "Busy with my only friends."

Kaylee pressed her lips together to squelch a smile. "Aw, come on, kiddo. That doesn't sound like you, feeling sorry for yourself. Are you doing all right? You must be so anxious about Thisbe. I know I am. We're going to find her, though. I won't leave there without her, I promise you that."

"I should be going with you," said Fifer bitterly. "It's not right. I'll be sitting here helpless."

Lani put her hand on top of Fifer's. "I can only imagine how bad that feels."

Kaylee nodded. "Just so you know, I've talked to Aaron about it. He said Alex gets to decide these things because he's the one taking responsibility for you. He thinks Alex is saying no because he can't bear to lose anyone else, and I gotta be honest, I can't fault him for caring. Still, Aaron tried to convince Al to let you go, if that makes you feel any better."

"Thanks, but not really." Fifer blinked hard. "If you even manage to rescue her, I won't find out for days and days. It's not fair." She pressed the heels of her hands to her eyes to stop them from leaking, but it didn't work. "Who took responsibility for you, Lani, when you were twelve?" she asked, knowing the answer.

"I did," said Lani softly. "But that was a different time and a different situation. I would have loved to have had my parents and Henry in my life then. I know it feels like Alex is smothering you, but at least be glad you have him. At least he cares and would do anything for you. He had no one. When we were purged from Quill, he lost everybody. Everyone, Fifer. And his parents—your parents—didn't do anything to stop the governors from taking Alex away. It was horrible. I think he made a vow to himself to not stand idly by if you are in danger. To not be like your parents. So when you and Seth and Thisbe left, he fell apart. He thought he'd lost you. Now that he has you back . . . Well, he's going a little overboard in protecting you, but like Kaylee, I honestly can't say I blame him after what he's been through. Do you know what I mean?"

Fifer hadn't thought about it quite like that. She often forgot how real the Purge was—it was more than just a story in a book. And it made her feel softer toward her brother—at least a little. But then she grew frustrated again. "The thing is," she said impatiently, "I'm a great mage. I know how to do things now, only Alex didn't witness any of those things. It's because of *us* that those five dragons are here right now! Don't you get it? I'm not just able to do things—I'm also really powerful! But nobody sees that. Nobody understands. They're letting Seth go—why not me? Thisbe and I saved Seth's life like seventeen times!"

Kaylee, who was watching Fifer's impassioned speech, wore a troubled expression. "I suppose if Alex were in charge of Seth, he'd make him stay home too. But he's not, and Carina thinks Seth will be useful."

"Not for the Dragonsmarche part," Fifer argued, "which is where Thisbe is! Neither Seth nor Carina was there. But I was. I saw what happened." Fifer stood abruptly and whirled around to face the women, making the birds scatter. The leader falcon fluttered to Fifer's shoulder and began making a worried-sounding clicking noise by her ear, obviously sensing that she was upset. Fifer absently petted the bird and winced at how its claws pricked her skin, but she only felt more frustrated. "I can't stand arguing about this anymore. I should have my component vest—I've earned it. I should be training with all of you instead of sneaking around learning all the spells behind Alex's back—and yes, that's exactly what I've been doing, and I don't care who knows it. This whole thing is completely senseless, and you're all making a huge mistake by not bringing me with you." She blew out a furious breath and dropped her arms to her sides. "Thanks for trying to help. I mean it. But I give up."

With that, Fifer stormed into the jungle. Her flock of birds squawked and followed her, leaving Lani and Kaylee sober and thoughtful.

After a while, when the dragons had left to test their new perfect wings and the crowd had dispersed, the two young women went back to the mansion and found Alex. "You need to go after Fifer," Kaylee said to him. "And talk to that girl. She's distraught and you're not helping. Do it before we go. She needs you. Like, yesterday. So get a move on it."

LISA McMANN

Continuing Clashes

All right," Alex told Kaylee and Lani, though he looked like he couldn't do one more thing. The hard training and wing making and stress of the losses were taking a toll, and he wasn't sleeping well. But this was important. "I'll go look for Fifer."

Alex had been coasting on fumes for a few months, ever since Fifer and Thisbe had snuck off, and now he carried his weary body toward the jungle in search of his sister. His heart had been ripped from his chest and stomped on. First Thisbe, then Sky. He was having a hard time coping. He'd resorted to doing what he'd done in the past when things were

LISA McMANN

overwhelming—put his head down and work. Try to overcome another enormous obstacle. That was the way it always went.

The last time something so personally tragic had caught him this unprepared was when Mr. Today had died and Artimé had vanished. But at least then he'd had Sky. Now . . . well, she'd dragged his heart with her under the sea.

He hadn't been able to face the fact that she was dead. Despite all the evidence, there were a few puzzling details that kept him from losing all hope. Perhaps his mind was trying to protect him from totally breaking down while he was dealing with Thisbe's abduction. But there was something concrete that left him with a shred of belief that Sky had somehow survived. A belief that stemmed from his archenemy, of all people—Queen Eagala.

Ten years ago, the giant squid who lived under the Island of Legends had followed Queen Eagala's ship and had watched it, with Eagala herself onboard, get sucked into the plunging volcano. Yet she was alive. If Queen Eagala had survived that, could Sky also survive? Or was she doomed without magic to help her?

Alex had always known that Queen Eagala was magical, but

he didn't know the extent of her abilities. What he knew of her—the ability to cast a silence spell over her island and send a flock of ravens to try to peck out the eyes of the Warbler children who'd found refuge in Artimé—seemed relatively tame compared to the magic of Mr. Today, or Alex, or the other mages in Artimé.

He also knew that despite being nonmagical, Sky, like many of Artimé's mages, could survive underwater for several minutes thanks to Ms. Octavia teaching them all how to utilize underwater breathing. So that added at least a little hope in her favor.

But even if she'd survived the plunge, where had she gone? Simber, Pan, and Spike had all been searching the area for weeks with no sign of her.

To the best of his knowledge, the ship Eagala had gone down in had never resurfaced. Even if it had, eventually it would've been seen by Pan or Spike, if not Simber. And they would have reported it. Perhaps the ship had been obliterated. It was the only explanation Alex could think of. But if it had been, how had Eagala survived that kind of beating? Especially when she couldn't swim?

Somehow she'd done it, which left the possibility that Sky could do it too. If the world's most evil person could survive, it seemed wrong that the world's best soul mate couldn't. Sky was pure goodness. When Alex was emotional, she was steady. When Alex was frustrated, Sky had quietly found solutions. When Alex had wanted to give up on the Island of Fire and consider it a disastrous place to live, Sky had wanted to figure out why it moved the way it did and do something about it. Well . . . maybe Alex had been right about that one—it had been disastrous. Though Sky had been so close to figuring out its systems.

"But how . . . ?" muttered Alex as he entered the jungle and began walking toward the depths to where the rock and Panther and the sharp-toothed dog lived. "*How* did Eagala survive *that* and get *there*? She'd had absolutely no means to do it. And, for that matter, didn't the pirates do it too? Didn't they say years ago that they traded sea creatures somewhere else?"

Alex was so lost in thought he walked within ten feet of Fifer, who'd been training her birds in a little clearing.

With no place to hide, Fifer watched him and overheard part of his muttering, and it made her think of something.

LISA McMANN

"There was a giant aquarium in Dragonsmarche," she said, startling him.

Alex looked up and spied her. "Oh," he said. "There you are. I've been looking for you. An aquarium? What of it?"

"You said something about pirates trading sea creatures, and that reminded me of the aquarium full of creatures in Dragonsmarche. Somebody else there said something about pirates trading sea creatures too. Do you think they're the same pirates who used to live inside the Island of Fire?"

Alex came over and sat down heavily next to her. "I don't know—we killed a lot of them in the last battle. But I'm really starting to wonder if there's another way to get to the land of the dragons other than by flying."

The mention of that brought something else to mind for Fifer. She recalled when she and Thisbe and Seth had been preparing to leave Artimé, they'd overheard Pan and Hux talking quietly about it. "I think there might be," said Fifer thoughtfully. "Before we left, Hux asked Pan if she would search for them. 'Like I told you?' he said. 'There has to be another way.' Then Pan told Hux if there is another way, she'd find it. Maybe we should ask her."

"That sounds like a good idea," said Alex. "Though she'd

LISA McMANN

probably consider that one of her many secrets." He leaned back against a tree and looked at her.

Fifer eyed him back. His face was scruffy and his eyes red rimmed. "So what do you want?" she asked. "You said you were looking for me. I'm not doing anything wrong. I didn't go deep into the jungle or anything."

Alex allowed a grim smile. "I know. It's not about you being out here. It's just . . . I feel like we need to clear the air a bit before I leave. I noticed you haven't been talking to me or eating dinner with me. And I . . . I miss you. And I know you're upset, and I understand why."

Fifer narrowed her eyes. "And so you've changed your mind? You'll let me come with you?"

"Oh, no. Not a chance. But I love you and I want you to know that. I can't bear to lose you and—"

"Alex, please. Knock it off."

Alex raised an eyebrow. "Wh-what does that mean? 'Knock it off.'"

"It means stop. It's a Kaylee phrase."

"Clearly." He folded his hands in front of him. "Anyway . . . I'm sorry. But I'm doing this for your safety."

"No, you're doing it because you don't want to feel guilty if something happens to me. Tell the truth, Alex. You're being selfish."

Alex's eyes burned. "I'm being selfish because I don't want to feel any more *pain* if something happens to you! It has nothing to do with guilt."

"People have to feel pain sometimes, Alex!" Fifer got to her feet, furious. "You can't keep me locked in Artimé forever!"

"I'm not going to! But you're *twelve*!"

Fifer sighed loudly. "Not this again."

"It's a factor!" said Alex. He got up too. "You don't get it right now. But someday, when you've experienced pain like I have—I hope that never happens, by the way, but if it does—you will understand. And we'll talk it over then."

Fifer fumed. "You. Are. Impossible!" Her yells startled the birds, and without thinking she yelled, "Attack!" and pointed at him.

To Fifer's great shock the falcons obeyed, and before she realized what she'd done, the birds were soaring at Alex, pecking him and grabbing at his clothing with their claws. "Aaargh!" Alex cried, flinging his arm over his face. "No! Release!"

"Ack! Stop!" shouted Fifer. "Retreat! Birds, come back!"

The birds obeyed again.

Alex cautiously lowered his arm. He straightened his robe and ran a hand over his disheveled hair. Then he gave Fifer a withering look. "So that's what you've been doing out here. Training birds to attack me."

"No, that's not—I'm sorry!" Fifer said. "I didn't mean it. I called them off. Are you . . . okay?"

Alex worked his jaw. Then he shook his head, like he couldn't stand to continue the conversation. They cared so much about each other, but they were miles apart in how they looked to the future. They were on complete opposite sides, and there was no backing down for either of them. As much as Alex hated to leave her on a sour note, he had little choice. "I love you," he said again gruffly. "I just wanted you to know that in case anything happens to me on the journey."

"I love you too," Fifer growled, kicking her foot against a tree root. "I just wish you weren't so stinking annoying."

"Likewise," said Alex. He shook his head, giving up, and turned back toward Artimé. "I'm going to talk to Pan like you suggested. I hope you'll be out in front of the mansion in the morning to say good-bye. If not for me, then at least for the others. This isn't a game. Some of us might not come back."

Fifer worked her jaw and didn't answer, but her stomach flipped. She knew it wasn't a game, but she hadn't really thought about *that* before. As she watched him walk away, she fought the urge to follow him, to jump on his back or hug him tightly. She wanted to tell him how sad she was. How scared she felt. But she and Alex had grown very far apart from all their conflicts, and she felt lost.

Just then he stopped walking and turned around. Fifer's heart surged. Had he changed his mind?

"I forgot to tell you," he said. "Aaron is going to stay behind so there's someone to take care of you and Daniel."

Fifer sighed heavily. "Believe it or not, I can take care of myself." All Alex had seen was her coming home bloodied and unconscious, and that wasn't even her fault—it was Simber's, for crying out loud. Alex hadn't witnessed how well she'd managed to take care of herself without anyone's help most of the time before that. She thought briefly about arguing, but the idea of starting that again just made her queasy. It was over, and he was leaving.

"Once we're gone," Alex continued, "if you could pack up and go to his island, that would be great. You can stay with him over there. It'll be fun—you can play with Daniel and help out with Ishibashi, Ito, and Sato. And hey—maybe they'll even teach you how to respect your elders."

Fifer's face fell at the slight. "Wow," she said. She sat down and reached for the nearest bird as her anger clouded up behind her eyes.

Alex dropped his gaze as if he regretted saying it. "Sorry," he muttered. He turned and walked away.

Maybe the best thing that could happen for them was to be apart for a while.

A Consolation Prize

Fifer hadn't kept track of everyone who was going on the rescue attempt, besides watching some of them practicing their magic and sword combat on the lawn now and then. In the morning, she reluctantly came downstairs and went to see them off.

The crowd was large, and Fifer could barely squeeze out of the door. Florence, standing just outside at the back of the crowd, saw her and helped guide her over. "Want to climb on my shoulders so you can see better?" the statue asked.

Fifer's eyes widened. Florence wasn't the "ride on my shoulders" type of warrior, so this was a rare treat. "Sure," she said.

Florence removed her bow and quiver of arrows and propped them against the mansion wall. Then she lifted Fifer up. Fifer scrambled to her shoulders and looked out high over everyone's heads. She was surprised to see Arabis the orange floating in the water near the shore. "Arabis is going?"

"Yes," said Florence. "There aren't enough seats on Simber, and she offered to help get them there. She's got to deliver a message to some other dragons in a neighboring region. Then she's going to hide out and wait for them to return. It's generous of her under the circumstances."

"Hmph," said Fifer. "What we did for them was pretty stinking generous too."

"Arabis said that—she thanked you yesterday. Didn't you hear?"

"I wasn't here—I was in the lagoon," Fifer admitted.

"She said later to Simber and me that she wanted to do this in your honor, actually. She was horrified to find out what had happened to you and to Thisbe after the dragons left."

That made Fifer feel better. "That's nice of her." When Arabis spotted Fifer sitting high above the crowd, the dragon bowed her head to the girl and offered a slow blink.

LISA McMANN

Fifer gave a sad smile and waved. They'd been through a lot together in the castle dungeon. "Who else is going besides Alex and Seth and Kaylee?" she asked Florence. "Samheed and Lani, right?"

"Yes, and Carina, Thatcher, and Talon. Oh, and Kitten."

Fifer smiled reluctantly at that. "Of course, Kitten. She's in someone's pocket, I'm sure. Is Fox sad to be left behind?"

"Devastated." Florence laughed and pointed to the middle of the lawn, where Fox was alone and heartbroken, howling at the blue sky.

"Maybe I should join him over there."

Florence turned her head to give Fifer a sympathetic look that became devious. "With Alex away, I suppose you could wander over to Magical Warrior Training anytime. I'll slip you some clips when nobody's looking and teach you a few things."

"Maybe." Fifer sighed. It was a great offer, and even though under normal circumstances she would be ecstatic, she couldn't muster up her enthusiasm at the moment. She watched as Alex and the other rescue team members, including Seth, looking quite proud and a little full of himself, secured their knapsacks, weapons, and supplies to Arabis. Then they climbed on, with

Samheed carrying Lani aboard since her contraption couldn't really navigate a dragon's back. Seth pointed out where the hollow was at the base of the dragon's neck, which was quite obvious in daylight, and they all settled into it.

On shore, Kaylee kissed Aaron and baby Daniel and hugged them both tightly, then climbed onto Simber's back.

Alex hugged his brother, patting him hard on the back, and the two spoke earnestly and quietly for a moment. Then Alex scanned the crowd over Aaron's shoulder, looking anxious until he spotted Fifer. He released his brother and fought his way through the crowd over to Florence, then reached up to grasp Fifer's hand. "Stay safe," he said. "And please don't do anything . . . dangerous."

Fifer sighed. He still didn't trust her. "Bye," she said.

"Bye, sweet sister. I love you."

Fifer's heart was heavy. "Me too," she mumbled. Of course she loved him, but she didn't *like* him very much lately.

"I'm going to find her," Alex promised.

Fifer nodded, a lump rising to her throat. "I'll be the last to know."

With a pained look and a squeeze of Fifer's hand, Alex

LISA McMANN

worked his way back through the crowd. He climbed on Simber and sat behind Kaylee, and after a moment of discussion with the team, Arabis and Simber took mightily to the sky, leaving Fifer and Artimé behind.

Fifer watched them for several moments, then dropped her gaze and rested her chin on the top of Florence's head. They'd done it—they'd gone without her. She sighed wearily, then slid off Florence's shoulders and thumped to the ground. With a word of thanks and a half-hearted wave, Fifer went against the flow of traffic and headed toward the jungle to mope before she had to pack up and go to the Island of Shipwrecks.

Birds flew in from all directions as she went, and they fell into step behind her. She didn't see Florence watching her go or disappearing inside the mansion with a consternated look on her face. She just went to her comfort spot in the lagoon and sat on her log and thought about life.

She tried hard to look at the bright side—sneaking into Magical Warrior Training would be fun. And finally getting to try out all the spells she'd learned by watching Alex would be a decent consolation prize. She might need a little coaching from Florence to really finesse her throw, but Fifer had all the components and their verbal commands memorized, and she'd been practicing the particular throw motions for each. Being one of the most naturally talented mages Artimé had ever seen had its benefits—she didn't have to go through months of practice in order to perfect the art of a spell like other new mages had to. At least she didn't think so—she hadn't actually tried very many so far. But she'd made dragons fly. There wasn't much out there that was harder than that.

"I just want to go," she moaned, and buried her face in her hands. As she sat there, the warm sun inched up her back through the trees, and the birds trilled and squawked around her. Fifer had become accustomed to their flutters and hardly noticed them anymore, but soon they grew louder and more insistent. She lifted her head to see what was going on.

The falcons were dragging brush from the jungle to her and laying it in a curious crisscross pattern on the beach in front of her. Fifer studied their work, wondering what on earth they were doing. Soon the project took on a netlike appearance. The lead falcon, Shimmer, came up to Fifer and chattered at her,

LISA McMANN

while dozens of others joined in to pull more vines to the sand. Some of them pecked at the intersections and looked expectantly at Fifer, like they wanted her to do something.

"What in the world are you doing?" she asked them.

Shimmer squawked at her.

Fifer didn't understand.

Finally Shimmer began chattering to the other falcons, and soon at least twenty of them were flying up to Fifer and grabbing at her clothes. Before Fifer could realize what was happening, they had lifted her into the air like they'd done before.

Staying low, they flew a bit jerkily over the sand while the lead bird lectured Fifer.

"Okay, okay!" said Fifer. "I think I get it—you're making me a net hammock so I don't have to hang by my clothing. That's really nice, thank you. And, um, I mean, having you fly me around was fun and all the first time. But I'm not sure I want to spend the time tying all the net pieces together just so you can do that. I already have a winged creature to fly on if I want. I mean, when he's here, that is. But thanks. You can set me down now."

They let her down roughly and squawked and chattered,

making quite a racket trying to get Fifer to understand them.

And then she replayed what she'd said in her mind, and it dawned on her what they were doing. "Wait a second," she said, waving her hands to get the birds to settle down. "You heard me say I want to go with the rescue team?"

The birds reacted loudly—she was on the right track.

"And now you want to fly me places? Not just around Artimé, but faraway places?"

"Yes," the birds seemed to say.

"Like, to find *Thisbe*? But you have no idea how far that is. It's a super-long journey! It takes days! You'd never make it."

At that, the lead bird let out a high-pitched *spirrrr*. Within a minute, hundreds of purple-and-red falcons flew in and landed, standing almost in rank form in front of Fifer.

Fifer blinked. Was this really happening? Did she have a way to help find Thisbe after all?

A thousand fears rushed in. What if the birds couldn't fly that far? What if they dropped her in the sea, miles from anywhere? What if they got lost or attacked, or they starved to death before they got there?

But Fifer pushed all those questions aside. "Just . . . hold

LISA McMANN

that thought," she said to the birds. She got to her feet and started quickly toward the mansion. Soon she was running at full speed and dodging Artiméans who were on the lawn enjoying the morning.

She ran inside and up the staircase, then darted down the not-very-secret hallway. At the Museum of Large, which was across from Alex's living quarters, she stopped and recited the spell that would let her in—she'd heard Alex say that one enough times. She pushed the grand door open and stepped inside.

To the left was the vast library, with all the books neatly categorized and alphabetized. Straight ahead was a pirate ship that had seen better days, and beyond it was the gray shack that would be the only thing left if Artimé disappeared again—which only happened when the head mage died. To the right was Ol' Tater, a mastodon statue who was currently magically asleep, being too dangerous a creature to roam the island.

Beyond these massive items was an area that Fifer and Thisbe had spent plenty of time playing in when Alex and Lani had undertaken the great task of organizing Mr. Today's personal library. It was an area where people stored their useful things that they didn't need very often. And one of the useful things Fifer remembered being in here was a sort of hammock that had been made many years ago and used to transport Seth's stepfather, Sean, home after he'd broken his leg on their journey. They'd constructed the hammock out of thick ropes and sturdy canvas sails, and they'd tied it to Simber's body so Sean could rest as easily as possible in his uncomfortable state.

Fifer remembered it now because that was a story Thisbe had always wanted to reenact when they were younger. Thisbe had loved the drama of the injury, and she always wanted to play the part of Sean, while Fifer got stuck playing the part of Simber, dragging Thisbe around the Museum of Large on this hammock.

Fifer ran to find it, and she pulled it out from under a bunch of other stuff that had accumulated over the years. The canvas was wrinkled and the ropes were a bit tangled, but other than that, it seemed as sturdy as ever.

Her hands shaking a bit with excitement, Fifer checked the thing over, making sure all the knots and connections were

LISA McMANN

solid, and laying it out to see how big it was. It was large enough for two or three people, and there was room for supplies, too.

Fifer smoothed out the canvas, her mind moving a mile a minute as she thought of the possibilities Shimmer and the other birds had presented to her. But could she trust the falcons? She had no reason not to—they adored her. They obeyed her. And together they made a fierce army.

Folding the hammock, Fifer blocked out all the doubts that crowded her mind. She picked up the unwieldy thing, letting a few of the ropes trail behind her, and fled the Museum of Large. Peeking carefully out of the hallway to make sure nobody was around who might get suspicious of her, Fifer ran to the girls' hallway and down to her room. She called out to her doorway so that it would open, and she rushed in, past Desdemona before she could surface and see what Fifer was carrying. Then she threw the giant hammock onto Thisbe's bed and sank onto her own, huffing and puffing and sweating from the exertion.

After a moment to catch her breath, Fifer went back to her living area, and to her tube, where she was planning to place a room service order so she could collect food for her trip. There, on the floor of her tube, was a package tied up in colorful paper and string.

"What's this?" Fifer whispered.

Desdemona pushed her face out of the blackboard. "It came up a little while ago," she said. "Anonymously. I guess you'd better open it."

Florence Sends a Message

Desdemona kept her head pushed out far enough from the screen to watch Fifer pick up the package.

"It's heavy," Fifer said. She pulled the string to release the bow. The wrapping paper fell open, revealing a note on top of a big lumpy cloth sack. Fifer lifted the piece of paper and read it.

Dear Fifer, you've earned it, the note read. *Do what you need to do. If you need more lessons, you know where to find me. Your friend Florence, Magical Warrior trainer.*

Fifer stared at the words in wonder. Then she opened the sack and peered inside. She reached in and pulled out something soft and brown. It shimmered a bit when she first touched it. She dropped everything else, the package hitting the floor with a *thunk*.

Fifer shook out the gift and stared at it. "My component vest!" she said, then shouted, "YESSS!" She hurried to put it on, her fingers trembling with the buttons. She smoothed it down the front and whirled around to face Desdemona. "How does it look?" she asked, breathless.

"Very smart indeed," said Desdemona, and she actually smiled to see Fifer's excitement. "It fits you perfectly. And did you see the shimmer? That's the magic protection activating. Mr. Today began adding that many years ago, and Florence continued it. You're very lucky to get yours early. And I feel lucky to have witnessed it. It's a big moment in a blackboard's career to see their human get a component vest." She almost looked misty-eyed. "You're growing up."

Fifer nodded, unable to speak. She ran to the mirror to admire it. She looked absolutely wonderful. "I'll never take it off," she said.

"Don't forget there was something else in the package in that mess on the floor."

"Oh!" said Fifer. "Right." She darted back to the living area, kicked away the wrapping paper, and picked up the heavy cloth sack. Reaching inside, she felt around and pulled out a handful of stuff. "Spell components!" she cried. Scatterclips, clay balls for shackles, little moss bits for magic carpets, yellow high-lighters for light and to blind enemies with, backward bobbly heads, and real fire-breathing origami dragons, among others. There were tons more where those came from.

Fifer hopped up on her sofa and started jumping and danc-ing for joy and shrieking and laughing for the first time in forever. It was the best possible gift she could imagine.

She went back to the note and read it again. "Do what you need to do," she read out loud. Her heart rose to her throat. Was Florence somehow giving her permission to go after Thisbe? Fifer knew that Florence had disagreed with Alex, even though the statue hadn't ever disparaged the head mage. But Florence was openly defying his wishes by offering to let Fifer join in on Magical Warrior Training—she took her job seriously and acted as the final word on who was ready. "If you need more lessons . . ." Fifer stared at the words. "If." Florence knew very well that Fifer didn't really need lessons to make the magic work. She'd been teaching Fifer secretly while she taught Alex. But was Florence really saying what Fifer thought she was saying? Florence knew about the birds and their magical presence. Did Florence also know that Fifer would figure out a way to use them to go after Thisbe? And was she trying to help her?

It seemed to be so.

With that kind of permission, Fifer felt even better about her decision. She'd leave Florence a note and be off this very evening. Maybe she could even catch up to the others. Alex would have to let her join them, and if he didn't, Fifer would just continue on her own anyway. On second thought, there was little chance Fifer could catch Simber and a dragon at the speed of a hundred birds. How fast could falcons fly, anyway? It might take her weeks to get there.

She had to gather supplies and get it right this time.

With a final word of congratulations, Desdemona shrank back and disappeared into the blackboard. Fifer changed her mind about ordering food up and decided to go down to the kitchen to sneak some food. She didn't want to tip off the chefs by requesting two weeks' worth of meals all at once. She needed to be smart. Stealthily, she gathered as much sensible food as she could carry, like nut butters and fig jam and some fruit and cheese and crusty bread and slipped back to her room through the room service tube when no one was looking. She managed two more trips like it without being noticed and was able to hide everything in the bedroom with Desdemona only poking her head out and sounding suspicious once.

Next Fifer went back to the Museum of Large to find a big travel bag so she could carry everything. Her mind whirled. Was Florence really and truly giving her permission? Or was Fifer twisting the warrior's words to make them seem so? When she returned to her room, she picked up the wrappings and string and the sack full of components. A small slip of paper fluttered to the ground. She hadn't noticed it before. Fifer stooped to grab it. It was a drawing—an absolutely terrible stick-figure drawing—of Florence herself. Written alongside the picture: *If you ever need me, use my fabulous drawing with the seek spell.*

The seek spell was something Fifer was extremely familiar with since Alex used it constantly to try to track down her and Thisbe. It only worked if the spell caster held an item created by the person they were seeking. Florence wasn't particularly artistic, so her crude drawing made Fifer smile, but it also made it even more special to know the extra effort she'd put into it.

And seeing the gift and the note solidified in Fifer's mind that Florence wasn't going to stop her if she decided to strike out on her own. With a surge of fear and excitement, Fifer went into the bedroom and began packing her bag. She was going to avoid all the problems they'd had last time by taking plenty of food and water and extra clothing. And now she had all these spell components, too.

Florence trusted her. Now Fifer had to show her she hadn't made a mistake. She took a moment to write two letters. One to Florence, thanking her and explaining what she planned to do. *I'll stop at Warbler to see Crow so you'll know I made it that far at least. That'll keep you from worrying too much. I won't do anything dangerous until I'm safely with the others. Thank you for trusting me. Your friend, Fifer.* The other letter was for Aaron to assure him she was okay and there was no need to go after her. *I'll find the rescue team, and I'll stick with Alex no matter how much he annoys me,* she wrote. *I promise. I love you!* She signed her name at the bottom.

While Fifer waited for dusk and for the lawn to clear so she could sneak off unnoticed during the evening meal, she thought about other things that could be useful to have with her. She found a new rope that would help her out the window and down to the ground, and might come in handy on her journey, and added it to her bag. Then she remembered how Dev had fished for food, and she went in search of fishing tackle and flint to make a fire—though she had the fire-breathing origami dragons to help with that part now. Still, she didn't want to use her precious components if she didn't have to.

By the time most of Artimé was inside the mansion for dinner, Fifer was packed and almost ready to go. She ordered up her favorite meal through room service and ate, then sent the letters to Florence's room through the tube—she'd be sure to give Aaron's to him. Then she went back into her bedroom and closed the door.

Her breath came in short, excited bursts as she thought about what she was going to do. It was a thousand times scarier to do this alone than it had been to have Thisbe and Seth by her side. She calmed her nerves by reminding herself that she wouldn't be alone once she found the others in the land of the dragons. But doubts kept poking at her. What if she never found them? It was a huge land—much bigger than any of the seven islands. And what if she and the birds didn't make it? No one would ever know what happened to her. An uncomfortable chill raced through her.

"Stop," she chided herself, and released the glass spell from her window. It melted away, and she sucked in the cool evening air. She spotted several of her falcons on the lawn or in trees. "Ready for an adventure?" she murmured. She grabbed her travel bag full of supplies, hoisted it out the window, and let it drop. It hit the ground with a *thud*, and Fifer cringed. She hoped nothing had broken or smashed. But if it had, it was too late now. She threw the hammock out the window after it. Grabbing the rope, she tied one end to the invisible hook outside the window and flung the other end down. Then she slipped her rucksack over her shoulders and took one last look at her comfy bed. It would be a while before she felt so snug again—at least a week. But it would all be worth it to have Thisbe back.

She climbed out, hung for a moment while she replaced the glass with a spell, and went down the side of the mansion as stealthily as possible. When she reached the ground, she coiled the rope and put it in her pack. Then she made a soft scream to call the birds. She turned and was surprised to see hundreds of eyes glowing in the dusk. The birds were already there.

"Oh, my sweet birds," she said, and bent down to pet the nearest ones. "Are you ready for this? It's going to be hard."

They bobbed their heads as if they understood, and Fifer believed they did—for some reason, with Fifer's kind of magic, they could understand her. She unfolded the hammock and spread it out. "See what I found?" she said. "Do you think this will work?"

The birds chattered softly as they moved around the edges of the hammock, tentatively testing the ends of the many ropes to make sure they weren't too big for them to take in their beaks. Shimmer slipped its head into a loop of rope and wore it around its neck, prompting the others to do the same with the other loops, which had no doubt been hooked around Simber's appendages at one point.

While the birds figured out the hammock, Fifer loaded her travel bag and backpack onto it, and then, when the birds seemed ready, she sat down in the middle of the canvas. "Should we do a test run above the lawn just in case?" Fifer asked Shimmer. She didn't want to risk being seen, but with Alex and Simber away and Florence on her side, she wasn't nearly as worried about that as she had been the first time they'd snuck out. Anyone noticing her antics now might just think she was amusing herself with her flock of birds.

Shimmer chirped out instructions to the others, and together they began flapping their wings. They lifted the corners of the hammock off the ground, and then, almost as if Fifer and her goods were weightless, the whole contraption rose into the air. With the lead bird directing the others, they flew with the precision of dancers over the lawn.

Fifer slid to her knees so she could see over the edge of the canvas. It was like a picture of a hot air balloon she'd studied once in a book, only her basket was made of a ship's sail, and the balloon was made of red-and-purple falcons. Her heart soared with the creatures as they slowly circled the lawn. It worked! She looked up at the birds and noticed that only about a third of them were holding a tether. The rest were flying alongside and in front, creating a thick cover over Fifer's head.

She wasn't sure why, but she had a lot of faith in the birds by now and knew they must have a reason for what they were doing. She'd probably find out eventually.

"If you're ready, let's go!" Fifer called out to Shimmer. "First stop, Warbler Island." She watched as Shimmer let out a sharp *spirrr*, prompting the falcons to change course. After a few minutes, Fifer rummaged through her bag of goods. She pulled out a fizzy drink and got comfortable in the hammock. Soon they were soaring over the water toward Warbler.

Fifer Rides Again

The first ten minutes of Fifer's ride to Warbler were pleasant, but then the wind picked up over the open sea and began buffeting her around. The birds soared with it, reaching speeds Fifer had never imagined they could reach and zigzagging to catch the gusts. Fifer didn't know how to anticipate which way they were going to go, and soon her stomach was flipping with each turn. She put her fizzy drink away and tried not to throw up. Next she lay back and closed her eyes, focusing on rescuing Thisbe. Eventually she tried to sleep, and she managed to get a few hours. When she woke to the sound of Shimmer's *spiiiiiirrr*, she could see in the starlight that the birds were switching out duties. The ones who had been carrying the hammock gave their ropes to the ones who'd been flying alongside. Some of the newly free group of falcons fluttered to rest on the edges of the hammock, while others flew in front and to the sides so the birds carrying the ropes could draft along with less resistance.

It was a magically smooth changeover, and it made Fifer wonder just what had gone into these birds when she'd touched them. Had she alone made them magical, or had they somehow been magical before? They weren't native to the seven islands, according to what Seth had learned from Grandfather Ishibashi. Had they come from some other magical land that no one had discovered yet?

She dozed again. By morning Warbler Island was growing close. Fifer peered over the cloth. "That's where we want to stop," she called out, hoping the birds understood. "That island there."

A few of the birds bobbed their heads. They headed for it. That's about the time Fifer first began thinking about landing.

By the time they reached Warbler, Fifer was worried. "Set me down gently," she said. They hadn't practiced this part with the hammock, and she was situated much farther below the birds than when they'd carried her by her clothing. She braced herself for a crash, but when the birds got close to the ground, Shimmer squawked out an instruction—or something—and they threw their wings up against the wind, then slowly lowered Fifer to the ground. Once she was down, they fluttered to drop their ropes in an outstretched direction so that it would be easy to lift the cargo again when it was time to go.

Fifer crawled to the edge of the hammock and slowly got to her feet. She felt a little wobbly after the ride, like the ground was moving. She stood there for a minute, taking in the lush tropical trees and white sandy beach, then made her way into the brush toward the entrance to the underground world of Warbler Island.

The opening in the ground was slightly hidden, but Fifer knew how to find it among the palm fronds. She pushed them aside and peered into the hole, then slid down into it. She landed in a hallway lit by magical orbs that some of the Artiméans had created for Sky and Crow's mother, Copper, who was the ruler of the island now that Queen Eagala had been killed. Or . . . maybe "replaced" seemed more accurate now.

LISA McMANN

The hallways echoed with the sound of voices from people working in various rooms off the main passage. Fifer didn't stop to see if she recognized anyone. Instead she went straight for Copper's living quarters, which had once been an elaborately decorated golden throne room. Now it had been toned down quite considerably to match Copper's more sensible preferences.

A young man around Alex's age, with orange eyes and scars around his neck, sat at a desk in the outer chamber. He smiled sympathetically when he saw Fifer come in. "Hi, Fifer. How are you?"

"Hi, Phoenix. I'm doing all right, I guess. Is Crow here?" Fifer asked.

"He's in the shipyard. Do you want me to take you there?"

"I know the way. Thanks." Fifer hurried back out to the hallway and kept on in the direction she'd been going before. After several minutes, she came to an exit and climbed the steep path that brought her outside on the opposite end of the island from where she'd landed.

All around her were ships in various stages of construction. Copper and Scarlet were balancing on the mast of one, repairing

LISA McMANN

something, while Crow stood on the ship's deck holding a rope attached to a block. He pulled down, and a large sail rose and flapped in the air. Copper reached out for the end of it.

"Hi, Crow," Fifer called out, trying not to startle him. "It's me. Are you doing all right?" She meant all of them, regarding Sky's disappearance, but kept the question vague in case they were weary of speculating about her. Fifer knew well enough how hard it was to keep wondering about someone.

Crow turned sharply. "Fifer," he said, seeming alarmed to see her standing there alone. "What happened? Is everything okay?"

"Everything's fine. I just promised Florence I would stop here and see you on my way to . . . um, to find Thisbe."

"You're going after all? How did you convince Alex? And hey—nice vest! What's happening? Where's the rest of the team?" Crow secured his end of the rope and climbed down a ladder to the ground. Scarlet and Copper stopped working to listen, then started down to the deck railing so they could hear better.

Fifer explained everything about the team already having left, and what had happened with the birds, and fudging a little when it came to her being officially permitted to undertake this journey alone. "Anyway," she said, "I just wanted to report that I'm fine and the journey is going well. The birds trade places when they get tired. Some even ride in the hammock with me if they need to sleep along the way. So if Florence checks in with you, just tell her I'm all good. Okay?"

Crow frowned. He glanced up at the deck where Scarlet and Copper stood, looking skeptical. Fifer squinted up at them and had a funny feeling they were going to ask a lot of questions. "Okay, well, bye!" she said, and took an uneasy step back.

"Wait," said Crow, moving toward her. "Just hang on a minute."

"My goodness, Fifer," said Scarlet, looking over the railing, concerned. "Are you sure you can go all by yourself? What if you can't find the others?" Scarlet was blond and fair skinned, and her cheeks were bright red from exertion and sun. She had scars around her neck like Crow and all of the other people who had grown up on Warbler under Queen Eagala's rule. The awful woman had used golden thorn necklaces threaded into their necks to keep them from being able to speak. Alex had long since magically eradicated the thornaments, as he'd called them, and now the Warblerans were left with scars in place of them. Some, like Sky, had hoarse voices to this day because of the awful devices.

"Yes, I'm sure," said Fifer with confidence she wasn't quite feeling. "I know my way around there better than any of them. And I have lots of supplies with me."

Crow remained skeptical. He'd spent many years with the twins, and he knew better than to believe that everything had happened the way Fifer had laid out. "Did Florence really tell you—to your face, in those exact words—that it was okay for you to go?"

"Well, no," said Fifer, shifting her gaze away, "not to my face. But she told me in a note to do what I needed to do, and she gave me a drawing so I can send her a seek spell if I need to. So that seemed pretty much like permission to me."

"Oh, Fifer," said Crow, like he'd said so many times in her life.

Fifer scowled and produced the note as proof. "Here, see?" She shoved it at him.

Crow studied it. "Well," he said, looking doubtful, "I have a feeling she expected you to maybe get in touch with her before you headed out, but . . ."

"It's too late now," said Fifer. She took another step back in case he was going to try to stop her, but he saw what she was doing.

"Look, just take it easy," he said. "I'm not going to send you home. I'm just . . . I'm trying to decide how I feel about it. I'm worried about you being alone over there. Like Scarlet said, what if you can't find them? With your black eyes you'll be in danger every moment."

Scarlet looked at Crow with a concerned expression. "Crow," she said. "Maybe you should . . . you know."

He glanced up at the women and nodded at Scarlet. "Yeah, I think so too. Mother?"

Copper nodded, and she and Scarlet started down the ladder to the ground.

Crow turned to Fifer. "Any chance you've got enough food for me in your pack?"

Fifer's eyes widened. "You're coming with me?" She wasn't sure how to feel, but surprisingly, the first emotion that came over her was one of relief. If any other person in the world had offered, Fifer might have stubbornly refused. But Crow was like a brother—not an overbearing brother like Alex, but the nice kind of older brother who takes you on adventures and lets you do things your real brother never would.

"May I?" asked Crow. "Is there enough room for me in your bird hammock? Can they handle an additional passenger?"

That was another thing, Fifer thought. Crow wasn't pushy or demanding. He asked politely. Fifer liked that in a brother. "There are so many birds," she said. "They should be fine to carry us and Thisbe, once we find her." And then she grew somber. "But we might have to fight once we get to the land of the dragons."

"Oh." Crow wrinkled up his nose as Scarlet and Copper joined him. "Boo fighting."

"I'll protect you, though. You don't have to do anything."

A smile played at Crow's lips. "Thanks, Fig. I appreciate that. Is there time for me to gather some things?"

Fifer glanced at the sun's position in the sky. "I suppose we have a few minutes. We can meet on the front beach."

As Crow turned to go, Scarlet gave him a secret sort of smile and touched his arm. He touched her hand and smiled back.

Fifer stared at them. They were acting weirder than usual. Everybody knew that Crow had a crush on Scarlet, but he'd never done anything about it. What in the world was going on here? Then Scarlet kissed Crow's cheek, and he grew embarrassed. Fifer felt heat rise to her face. A kiss? Were they suddenly in love or something? Feeling super awkward, Fifer yelled, "Okay, bye!" and turned and ran for the entrance to the tunnel, which was faster than going through the brush aboveground. Since Crow had left Artimé to spend a few weeks here, everything had become weird. She didn't know what to think.

When she got back to the hammock, she told the birds that Crow was coming, and they seemed to be fine with the news of a heavier load. Several minutes later, Crow emerged from behind the palm fronds carrying a small kit bag and a few jugs of water. He stopped to take in Fifer's hammock-and-bird contraption and shake his head a little in awe. "How did you manage this? Actually, never mind. Sometimes it's better if I don't know the answers."

Fifer grinned. "Come on. Just sit here next to me."

Crow joined her on the canvas. Shimmer *spiiirrred*, and the other birds flew in from the trees where they'd been resting. This time half of the birds found spots holding ropes, clearly preparing for the heavier load.

Fifer was pleased to see it. "These birds are exceptional," she confided as they began lifting off.

"Exceptional, really? They do seem quite, um, capable. I hope."

"I made it all the way here, didn't I?"

"Very good point."

As they went up into the air, Crow looked back at the island, straining to see the shipyard. He waved his arm wildly at Scarlet, making the hammock sway. Fifer blushed again. In her mind Crow belonged to her and Thisbe, and it was strange to see him giving so much attention to somebody else— especially *that* kind of attention. But Fifer knew that Crow had liked Scarlet forever, so she supposed she was happy that he seemed to be getting closer to her. It just might take a little while for her to get used to it.

After a minute, Crow turned back around and settled in. "Oh my," he said as the birds found their wing rhythm and began riding the wind westward. "We're really moving."

"I know," said Fifer. "I didn't know falcons could fly so fast."

"You've really trained them a lot since I've been gone." He glanced at the water below them. "What happens if they drop us?"

"Oh, they'll probably come after us and fish us out of the water," said Fifer with confidence.

Crow nodded. "I hope you're right."

"They do whatever I tell them to do."

"Somehow I believe that," said Crow. "You've always had a way with birds. It's great you finally figured out what to do with them."

"Hopefully they'll help us find Thisbe."

Crow shrugged. Stranger things had happened with the magical twins—he was the last person to doubt Fifer when it came to this sort of thing. "As long as I don't have to learn magic, I'm good."

"Well," said Fifer doubtfully. "I mean, there are tons of soldiers everywhere, so you might end up in a fight. Do you have any weapons or anything?"

"I've got my slingshot and a pocketful of stones. Oh, and Scarlet gave me these." He pulled out a handful of red heart components. "She told me how to use them in case I really got into trouble."

"Heart attack components?" said Fifer in awe. Florence

hadn't given her any of those. Using one would knock some-body unconscious. Using three at once was lethal—Fifer had learned that from Lani's book in the part where Aaron had killed Mr. Today. Fifer wondered idly if she would ever use three instead of one. Unlike Thisbe, Fifer had never killed anyone. But she didn't think she'd hesitate too much if it was really necessary. Of course, that kind of decision was a long way off, since Fifer'd only been given temporary spell compo-nents. She could worry about that later.

Crow nodded and put them back into his pocket without giving Fifer any. She pressed her lips together, almost about to inquire if she could have just one, but it seemed like too much to ask since it was the only spell Crow knew. Maybe she'd bet-ter show him that she could do a simpler spell first before she convinced him to give her some.

They talked some more, Crow catching Fifer up on how he and his mother were doing after Sky's disappearance. "It's very hard," he admitted. "Sky and I have been through a lot together. We almost died on our raft when we escaped Warbler. We thought we lost our mother for good, but then we found

LISA McMANN

her. And now, when all was finally going really well . . ." His eyes became misty. "I miss her so much it makes my stomach hurt."

He went on to tell Fifer that his mother was handling the news better now than at first. She was feeling numb, and working on the ships helped her try to get back to feeling normal, at least a little. "My mother doesn't want to accept that Sky is gone, but I can't imagine there's any way she's still alive."

Fifer nodded somberly.

"Scarlet has been a good friend to us both through all of this," Crow said carefully. He glanced at Fifer, like he expected her to need to process this change in his personal status. "She's been there whenever I needed to talk."

"That's nice," Fifer said. "She's . . . nice. I like her." Still awkward but getting easier, Fifer noted. That would have to do for now.

"Yes." He resettled himself more comfortably in the hammock. After a moment he said, "It's odd, you and me being together without Thisbe. It feels like we're missing a piece of our group."

Fifer nodded, feeling suddenly melancholy. She tried not to

let her worries bubble up. That wouldn't help anything. She looked up at him and saw his easygoing grin as the wind caught his long hair and blew it behind him. She grinned back. Crow was so calm and gentle and good—he'd been such a big part of her life. Even though they were suffering so much over Sky and Thisbe, it felt like everything would be okay now that he was here. And together they were going to find their missing piece.

A Wrench in Thisbe's Plan

Rohan and Thisbe met in the tunnel between their crypts every other night after he returned from his long trek. Thisbe told him about her work and how she feared that someday soon she'd be dragging four bones a day. She showed him the cuts that the harness had made in her shoulders.

Rohan sympathized and pointed at his shoes, which were quickly falling apart from so many miles of walking. "The Revinir wishes me to bring her the bones of the most ancient human rulers," he said. "Conveniently kept in the crypt farthest away from here."

"Of course they would be. You said the catacombs actually connect to the castle dungeon? So you could get in there if you wanted to?" She wondered if that might be the best way to escape since she knew her way around the dungeon a little.

"There's a thick old door separating our side from theirs. But it's heavily protected by sentries. The Revinir's blue-uniformed soldiers on our side, the king's green-uniformed soldiers on the palace's side. I've started making friends with our soldiers at that end, and one told me that it's so heavily guarded to make sure none of the miscreants in the castle dungeon can get out—I guess there was some sort of uprising down there recently. The Revinir's captive dragons escaped."

Thisbe grinned to herself. She hadn't yet told Rohan about the part she'd played in that.

Rohan went on, his face concerned. "The problem is, the king didn't confess it to the Revinir right away, so she just found out about it a few days ago. She was positively boiling over it, Thisbe. Spitting fire. I worry . . ." Rohan hesitated and shook his head. "I worry for Grimere, and for us. If the king doesn't give proper restitution to the Revinir for the dragons

LISA McMANN

he lost, the two leaders will be at odds. The Revinir isn't going to just forgive him. It's troublesome."

"What are you saying?" asked Thisbe.

Rohan looked up. "I suppose I'm saying this could spark a war between them." He noticed Thisbe's frightened face and relaxed a little, waving his hand to try to erase what he'd just said. "It'll probably never come to that. And the king has already started offering her things as payback, so they're sorting it out. I guess I just have too much time to imagine what-ifs on my journey." His smile was strained. "Please don't worry about it. Perhaps the king will come through with something tremendous to appease the Revinir."

"I hope so." Thisbe breathed a little easier. She wasn't sure what a war would mean for the black-eyed slaves—would they just stay down here or be forced to fight for the Revinir? Against the king?

"Anyway," Rohan went on, lighter now, "about the Revinir's soldiers stationed at the door to the dungeon— which is what we were talking about before I turned all grim and brooding—I'm sure they're trying just as hard to keep us from finding a way out as they are to keep their prisoners in."

He yawned and scratched his back on the rough rock wall, then slid into a more comfortable position. "I've heard it's a maze down there, though. Impossible to find your way through."

"I'll say," said Thisbe, a bit smugly.

"Oh, will you?" Rohan said, teasing her.

His teasing smile fell away when Thisbe told him about her time in the dungeon and about how she and her twin sister, Fifer, and their friend Seth had helped the young dragons escape . . . or at least she'd been hoping they'd escaped. "I don't want a war, but I'm glad to know the dragons made it out," she said.

"Oh yes. They're long gone."

Long gone. Like Simber. "How do you know all of this?" asked Thisbe after a time. "The dragons, I mean, and the stuff about the king?"

"I talk to the Revinir's soldiers, who talk to the king's soldiers."

"And they just tell you stuff so willingly?"

"I give them things so they like me. Bits of gold. Stuff I steal from the extracting room."

"Ah. So you bribe them with stolen items?"

"If you must call it that," said Rohan with an evil smile. "I'm not a hundred percent good, you know."

Thisbe laughed. "Okay, anyway, can you explain this gold thing to me? I never understood what the big deal was about it," said Thisbe. "The Revinir, back when she was called Queen Eagala on Warbler Island, used to make her people forge golden thorns. She would string them around people's necks to stop them from being able to talk."

Rohan blinked. "What a horror. She really did that?"

Thisbe nodded. "And she changed their eyes to orange so they'd be easily identified if they ever tried to escape."

"Like branding them," said Rohan. "She put her mark on them."

Thisbe nodded.

"And now she's put her new brand on us," Rohan said, running his finger over the back of his neck. "Does yours still hurt?"

"No." Thisbe touched her brand too. It was scratchy with dried scabs, some of which had already fallen off. "I don't understand why she has to do such violent things. I mean, she's got us captured and doing her work for her. Why does she need to brand us too?"

"She's obviously not right in the head," said Rohan. "To ingest dragon-bone marrow for its magical properties, and to delight in dragon scales growing thick on her skin? That's deranged."

Thisbe agreed, even though she wasn't quite sure what deranged meant. She wished for a library like the one in Artimé so she could look things up. But without that, she could at least guess what Rohan meant. It didn't sound like a nice word.

Rohan rested his eyes for a few moments while Thisbe thought through all she'd learned. After a while she sat up, startling Rohan awake again. "She's got a new assistant instead of me," Thisbe told him.

Rohan nodded as though he knew about it, but he didn't interrupt.

"Yet she still keeps trying to convince me to help her. She says . . ." Thisbe hesitated. For some reason she didn't want to talk about how the Revinir had told her she was more evil than good—besides, Rohan had heard her say it the first time. He knew the truth about her, and it didn't seem to bother him. Instead, she went in a different direction. "She's going to keep adding bones to my workload. I'm already struggling with

LISA McMANN

three, but I'm due for another one any day now—I can feel it. I won't be able to do four. No way. I wonder if maybe . . ." She grew quiet, thinking.

"Maybe what?" prompted Rohan.

"Maybe I should give in. I mean, she's right. It's obvious nobody's coming back for me. Will I have more chances of getting out of here if I work with her? If I can get her to trust me?"

Rohan tapped his chin, thinking aloud. "Hmm. Interesting. And why *not* give in? Why not be her assistant? Maybe that will give you some power. And perhaps you can find out her weaknesses or even her secrets if you work with her all day."

"Exactly." Thisbe wrinkled her nose. "Working with her sounds awful."

"But like you said, it might give you a better opportunity to escape. Because you still want to, right? Even after you told the Revinir you no longer did?"

Thisbe looked hard at him. Again a ribbon of doubt sliced through her—could she trust him? Was he so good that he would feel compelled to tell the Revinir about her plans?

At this point, Thisbe decided, she couldn't *not* trust him. She had no one else in the world, and without help, she might never escape. Before she could change her mind, she blurted out, "Yes, I still want to escape. Do you? Will you help me? Will you escape with me?"

Rohan looked solemnly at her and nodded. "I never thought I could get out of here alone. But I believe if we work together, we might succeed. Especially if you can make your fiery magic work properly." He hesitated. "A lot of the guards already favor me, and I'm being extra good to them lately so they trust me more. If you can get cozy with the Revinir and find out some things, well . . . I think it's worth the attempt, anyway."

They stayed up late talking about the plan, and eventually Thisbe decided it was inevitable—she wouldn't be able to continue her job with more dragon bones. So she agreed to make the most of the situation.

As Thisbe stared off, thinking things through, Rohan dozed again.

"I wonder who the new assistant is," she mused. "Maybe he could be useful."

"What's that?" said Rohan, jolting awake.

"I said I wonder who the new assistant is. Is it one of the other slaves here?"

"No. He's actually part of the king's payback for the drag-ons that I mentioned earlier—one of his slaves. My sources tell me the king's daughter, Princess Shanti, got mad at her whipping boy and said she didn't want him anymore. So the king immediately offered him up when the Revinir found out about the dragons' escape."

Thisbe's stomach lurched. "What?" she whispered. "Princess Shanti's servant boy is . . . here? *He's* the assistant?" Her mind was spinning.

"That's what the soldier gossip is. I don't know his name, but I suppose you'll meet him soon enough."

Thisbe blinked, trying to figure out what it all meant. "Dev," she said softly, and then she looked at Rohan. "His name is Dev."

A Dark Venture

The next morning when Mangrel opened Thisbe's door, the Revinir was standing there with him. The woman didn't bother asking Thisbe if she'd be her assistant this time. She simply said, "Four bones."

Thisbe had to think fast. She hadn't prepared for the Revinir to show up at her door—she'd just intended to tell Mangrel she was giving up and have him show her to the ruler. Now she scrambled to make her plan work. She kept her chin up and gazed at the woman's pale, wrinkled face. "I can't do four," said Thisbe. "It's too heavy. It's too much." She dropped her gaze.

The Revinir didn't try to hide how pleased she was. "You could take two trips a day," she suggested. "You might still have time for a couple hours of sleep each night. Though you'd miss dinner. You wouldn't last many days that way."

Thisbe stared at the dirt floor and was quiet, as if she were considering it.

"Or you could work with me," said the woman. "Those are your options. Which do you choose?"

Thisbe glanced at Mangrel, who stood at attention, his face showing no emotion. Then she looked at the Revinir again and despaired. "I guess I have no choice. I won't live long without any meals."

"Precisely," said the Revinir. She grew more reserved and clicked her long fingernails against each other. "Come along, then. Bring three dragon bones with you. We're starting a new project today. How convenient to have you to help me and my new assistant just when we need you. I timed that quite well, didn't I?"

When no one answered, the Revinir glanced at the crypt keeper. "Didn't I, Mangrel?"

Mangrel frowned slightly, then answered, "Yes, ma'am."

Thisbe took her morning pitcher of water and drank it slowly, staring at the Revinir over the rim the whole time, which she hoped was unnerving. When she finished, she wiped her mouth with her singed sleeve and handed the pitcher back to Mangrel, then turned away and harnessed three bones to herself. She dragged them into the hallway and followed the Revinir in the opposite direction she'd normally go.

Thisbe watched the symbols on the walls, wondering which one of them pointed to the Revinir's quarters. Eventually she determined that a crown symbol next to a purple directional arrow was the one to follow. She noted that the red arrows that pointed to the extraction room would return her to the hallway where her crypt was, so she wouldn't have to worry about getting lost on her way back.

The path to the Revinir's quarters twisted and turned, and the woman walked briskly. Thisbe followed, falling several steps behind because of her heavy load. Eventually they came to a group of soldiers who were guarding the entrance to a side hallway. When they saw the Revinir, they parted to let her and Thisbe through, and the woman spoke to them while Thisbe caught up. This side hallway had gold stone walls rather than the gray rock walls of the rest of the underground. The doors were covered in jewels. It reminded Thisbe a bit of the castle, and for a moment Thisbe wondered if the Revinir was trying to turn the catacombs into a showy underground palace.

The woman went through one of the bejeweled doors and Thisbe went after her. The place shone with gaudy baubles and golden trinkets. Thisbe grimaced, finding it ugly. They passed through the entry room and continued into a huge kitchen, where enormous cauldrons sat near fire pits. Smoke curled up to the high ceiling and disappeared through a metal vent. Thisbe wondered if it led to the outside somehow, and if so, was the opening big enough for a girl her size? It didn't seem likely.

"You can unhitch the bones. You'll be working in here," the Revinir declared. "But first we're going to have a little chat." Thisbe slipped the harness off. They went back out of the kitchen and into a room nearby that had a throne in it, sitting atop a short pedestal. Thisbe nearly laughed at how ridiculous it looked. Did the woman actually sit there sometimes? If so, why? To feel important? Down here, there were only some soldiers and slaves around to be in awe over her—and Thisbe certainly wasn't impressed.

The Revinir stepped up to the throne and sat down ceremoniously. The hem of her robe rose up when she sat, revealing luminescent scales of all colors around her ankles. It was creepy. Thisbe stood on the floor, unsure of what she was supposed to do.

"Tell me about your magic," the woman demanded. "How did you destroy my birds?"

Thisbe almost corrected her like she'd done before, but then decided not to bother. The Revinir might as well think she'd done that, too. "I don't know how I did it. I was two."

"What else can you do? You sent sparks at my soldiers when they branded you. How did you do that?"

"It just happens. I can't control it," Thisbe said easily, even though it was no longer true. She'd repeated that line her whole life. "It's just some little sparky thing—it doesn't do much."

"And? What more?"

"Nothing much," said Thisbe. "Not without spell components."

The Revinir frowned and stared at Thisbe, like she was trying to determine if she was lying. Thisbe stared back, convincing herself to believe everything she'd just said—she wasn't sure what the woman could do with her dragon abilities, but it seemed like dragons might be able to know if someone was telling the truth. So she assumed the same for the Revinir. It was unsettling, thinking about how many lies Thisbe had told down here. There were a lot. If lies were evil, Thisbe was starting to wonder if the Revinir's assessment of her being more evil than good might actually be true.

She didn't want to think about it. "What can *you* do?" Thisbe asked her.

The Revinir seemed taken aback by the direct question. Her face clouded. "A lot more than you."

"I didn't know it was a competition," said Thisbe, feeling like she was talking to a child. She sniffed and looked around the throne room. "What do you want me to do here, anyway?"

"First you'll be helping me develop a new product to sell in Dragonsmarche. We'll see how well you do with that. Mostly I want you nearby so I can keep my eye on you."

"You could always just let me go. Then you wouldn't have to worry about me at all."

"Oooh no, my dear," said the Revinir. "You're much too valuable."

Thisbe stiffened at the term of endearment.

"Besides," said the woman, softening her tone a bit. "We can do great things together."

Thisbe's eyes narrowed. "Like what?"

"Well," said the Revinir, "to my knowledge, you and I are the only magical people in Grimere. Isn't that fascinating? And I'm growing more powerful by the moment with my dragon magic injections."

"You're injecting that bone marrow stuff?" asked Thisbe. "That's disgusting."

"Ah, but I'm a wonderful showcase for the new product we'll be creating, and soon I'll be richer than the king. Of course, we won't be selling the same strength of magic that I use for myself—that would be absurd to let anyone become as powerful as me."

Thisbe stared. "What?"

The Revinir continued. "I believe there's a way to reap the benefits of the dragon bones on a less potent level, however, through bone broth. I'm testing it out in my kitchen, and I've already begun experimenting on my test subject. It's risky, sure. But the bones are plentiful, and there is a great amount of gold to be made if I'm successful. The pirates will pay top prices once they see what I've done, and the townspeople will be astounded and beg for more. But the timing is very important." She paused, deep in thought.

Thisbe silently freaked out.

"Once I buy the kingdom, or take it by force, we'll defeat my worst enemy once and for all. He'll never know what hit him."

"Your worst enemy?" asked Thisbe, suspecting she meant Alex, but hoping otherwise. "You mean the king?"

The Revinir eyed her. "The king is my pawn. He made a grave mistake in letting my dragons escape, and he'll pay for it. But I'll finish him off when his usefulness has run out. I'm talking about someone far more powerful. Someone from another land."

Thisbe didn't know of any other lands besides her own. "Do you mean the pirates? But you said you were going to sell this stuff to them."

"No, not the pirates." She smiled down at the girl. "I'm talking about your brother."

Thisbe stared as if she were shocked to hear it. "My brother? You mean Alex?"

"Yes. The one who left you here and never came back. That's what a horrible person he is."

Thisbe reared back at the inaccurate portrayal of her brother. "He—he's not—" she stammered. "He's not horrible."

"Then why, Miss Stowe, hasn't he come back for you? Why hasn't *anyone* come back for you? Surely *someone* would, unless the ruler of your world commanded them not to."

Thisbe fought with her words, trying to find the ones to protest what the awful woman was saying. "You don't know him at all!" she cried.

"Maybe he's trying to punish you," the Revinir said. "Teach you a lesson by leaving you here. Have you done anything wrong lately? Anything against his wishes?"

"I—I—you don't know what you're talking about!" Thisbe said. "You're a terrible person to say such things about my brother. He loves me! He's going to come for me." As she said the words, she felt doubt creep in. She'd told herself the same thing just the other night. It had been weeks, and no one had come. What did it mean? Why hadn't they found her yet? Where were they?

"There, there," said the Revinir. "I didn't mean to upset you. I just thought you'd have figured it out by now. After all, he didn't take this long to come after me with an entire army the first time we had a falling out. You'd think he'd come even quicker for his sister, but alas, he hasn't. It seems pretty obvious to me what's going on here, but if you're not ready to hear that . . . well, let's change the subject." She clicked her fingernails against the arms of her throne. "Are you ready to start working on the first batch of broth?"

Thisbe couldn't speak. Her face was hot with anger, and she feared she'd start shooting sparks everywhere if she wasn't careful. She turned away from the woman and stared at the door where the soldiers stood. "Sure," she said through gritted teeth.

"Let's get moving, then." The Revinir stood and clapped her hands. "Come with us, Dev," she called out, then turned to look behind her throne, where a small table was pushed up against it. Thisbe peered around it and gasped. Dev had been sitting there working quietly the whole time.

"Come out, Dev. Meet Miss Stowe and show her what a great assistant you are. My first glorious test subject."

Dev stepped slowly into view. He wouldn't make eye contact. Thisbe watched him, confused by what the Revinir was saying about him being a test subject. She looked harder at him, and then, with horror, she noticed that the skin below his ragged sleeves and pant legs was speckled lightly with dragon scales.

LISA McMANN

Doubt Creeps In

This listened numbly as the Revinir showed her where to find everything in the test kitchen. Dev didn't say a word. He looked like he wanted to disappear into the floor. When the Revinir had explained everything that Thisbe was to do, she turned to face the girl. "Do you have any questions?"

"No," Thisbe said. Then: "Yes. Why are you doing this here? Why not in the testing room?"

"I wish to keep this product private for now until I know how it works. Once I've determined the proper levels to provide the weakest visible effects, we'll produce a small batch to sell in the marketplace. I don't want it to be too plentiful—we want dragon-bone broth to become a craze. We want people to be searching for it. We want them to feel they must have it at all costs."

"But . . . aren't you afraid of people buying it and becoming magical and able to attack you?"

The Revinir laughed. "They won't have access to nearly enough magical product to make them anywhere strong enough to attack me. Besides, they can't get to me down here. And when I've gotten as powerful as I can be, and finished all I intend to do around here, we'll leave this place. I'll go back home to Warbler Island and take over the other islands like I'd planned all along. Especially Artimé."

Thisbe stared. "But how will you get across the gorge?"

The woman smiled. "I have my ways of getting back home. And there are the ghost dragons to the south and west of us if I should need to take them captive. But with any luck, I'll have my own dragon wings by the time I need them."

Even Dev reacted to that, repulsion evident on his face.

Thisbe could hardly take in what she was hearing. She didn't ask any more questions. Eventually the Revinir left her and Dev alone in the kitchen to start working on the magical dragon-bone broth. Three soldiers stood guard at the entrance to the Revinir's quarters, a whole room away from the kitchen. Thisbe and Dev were practically alone.

Thisbe turned to look Dev in the eye. "Hello again, thief," she said. "I didn't think I'd ever see you again. And now you've got dragon scales. How fashionable."

Dev closed his eyes and shook his head. "Shut it."

"Rude," muttered Thisbe. She hauled one of the giant pots across the floor to place on the fire, then hoisted one of the dragon bones into it. Then she began dragging buckets of water to pour over the bone. The Revinir had said it would need to simmer for many hours, perhaps overnight, in order for some of the magic to seep out of the bones into the broth.

Dev did the same with another pot and bone. He didn't talk to Thisbe.

She didn't talk to him, either—she was still reeling about him having dragon scales. Part of her thought through the idea of getting Dev on her side. He was maybe a little bit powerful now because of drinking the dragon-bone broth, which could be useful, though she had no idea what he could do—perhaps he just had the scales and that was it. The other part of her wanted to punch him in the face for what he'd done to her and Fifer and Seth. She wanted answers. But she knew she needed him on her side. She just wasn't sure how to get him there. And if she did, how would she even know? He wasn't trustworthy.

Once they both had their pots filled, all they had to do was sit and watch them, and add more water after a while to cover the portion that boiled off. The two sat awkwardly across the room from each other by their pots and stayed that way, casting veiled glances at each other.

Eventually Dev sighed and got up. He went over to Thisbe and sat down next to her. "Sorry," he mumbled.

Finding his apology surprising yet totally inadequate, Thisbe ignored him and chose instead to read the labels of the various ingredients on the pantry shelves next to her.

After a few minutes, Dev began to tremble and shake.

Thisbe didn't notice what was happening at first. But then Dev made a few weird squeaks. She turned and realized with a start that he was falling apart in sobs. She looked at him in alarm, and then she glanced out the door to make sure the soldiers weren't watching. After a long moment of uncertainty, she reluctantly reached out to him and gave him an awkward hug.

He held his body stiff, like he didn't know how to hug, but he stayed there, crying into Thisbe's dirty shirt like the world had ended for him.

Thisbe wasn't sure what to do. She stayed still and patted his back every now and then. Once she said, "There. It's okay." That made him cry harder. She didn't know what to make of it, but her sympathy for him grew as the time passed. She thought about what might have caused him to be so overwhelmingly crushed that he would fall apart like this with a practical stranger. Had he lost his precious piece of traitor gold? Or was he actually broken up about leaving the palace? This work in the kitchen seemed so much easier than the work he'd been doing—she'd think he'd be happy about that.

After a while he lifted his head and sniffed loudly. Then he wiped his face with his shirtsleeve. The uneven smattering of dragon scales on his forearm caught the light and shimmered. Maybe that was why he was crying. Thisbe hadn't fully processed how the Revinir might have administered the test product to him, but if she'd forced him to take it against his will, that seemed a strong enough reason to be upset.

"Are you all right?" Thisbe asked gently.

"I don't want to talk about it," said Dev. He pulled away and stared at his cauldron.

Thisbe made a frustrated noise, her sympathy flying out the door. "Are you kidding me? You get snot all over my shirt and you won't tell me what is so upsetting?" After weeks away from Dev, she was immediately as annoyed by him as she had been the day he'd stolen their food and eaten it in front of them.

"It's not that I won't. It's just . . . I don't want to start blubbering again." He said "blubbering" with a sneer, then frowned hard at the floor.

"Suit yourself," said Thisbe, her tone icy. "But where I come from, blubbering isn't something to avoid. It's a normal part of life to cry sometimes. And it makes you feel better. So maybe if *you* feel better, we'll both have a nicer time of it here."

Dev said nothing, but another tear dripped down his cheek. He swiped at it.

Thisbe sighed. She got up and went to check the bone

broth. "So . . . she made you drink this stuff? Is that how you got all scaly?"

"Yeah."

Thisbe peered at him. "Can you do anything magical now? Or dragonlike?"

"I . . . No. I don't think so."

"Do you feel anything different?"

Dev flashed an annoyed look. "My nose still hurts from when you broke it."

Thisbe frowned. Back in the dungeon, she'd planted a glass spell in his way and he'd slammed into it face-first. The reminder made her want to do it again. "So you don't feel anything different at all? You just grew some scales? Do they itch? They look itchy."

Dev sighed heavily and got up. He walked across the room to his cauldron and sat down on the floor over there.

Thisbe rolled her eyes. This wasn't going at all how she'd planned. She'd wanted to be friendly with Dev and try to get him to join her and Rohan in a revolt. But his bad attitude was extremely annoying, and Thisbe couldn't seem to let it go. Why couldn't he be decent?

After a while Thisbe sat down again by her pot. "I'm sorry about breaking your nose."

Dev shrugged and closed his eyes. "I lied. It wasn't broken. Just sore."

"Of course you lied," muttered Thisbe. What else was new?

Dev fell asleep, or faked it well, and Thisbe sat wrapped in her thoughts. When she grew bored, she concentrated on the fire and tried to flick sparks at it. She wanted her aim to get better from close range, but her flicks caused sparks to go in all sorts of directions. One flew up and came down on her head, causing a lock of her hair to melt and fall to the floor. She slapped the top of her head to make sure it went out. Then she scooted back from the fire to try sending sparks at it again from a distance.

The day continued with time moving extraordinarily slowly. Thisbe napped too. When she awoke to a nasty smell, she scrunched her nose and sat up. "What's that awful stink?" she asked Dev.

"It's the bone broth," he said, seeming less antagonistic after his nap. "The bones are releasing all the gunk inside them. It reeks enough to poison the gods. The Revinir said that'll make people in the marketplace want it even more. I don't get it, but she seems to know what she's doing."

"Is she going to keep making you drink it?"

Dev gazed at his forearms. His expression grew troubled again. "I think so."

Thisbe watched him. "Is there any way to make the scales go away?" she asked softly.

"I don't know." Dev blew out a breath. "It doesn't matter, I guess. Nothing that happens to me matters. We're not people. Not to her. Or to them."

"Them?" asked Thisbe, puzzled. "The soldiers?"

"Well, them too."

"But that's not who you meant."

Dev gave her a look. "You're not going to give up with the questions, are you?"

Thisbe grinned. "Not likely."

He threw his hands up. "Fine. The princess. And the whole kingdom, really. We're just . . . less than." His face screwed up. Then he stopped fighting the tears and let them go. He pressed his thumb and forefinger to the inside corners of his eyes, squeezing even more out.

Thisbe was quiet. After a while, she said, "I thought Shanti was your friend."

Dev didn't answer at first. Then he let out a shuddering sigh. "So did I."

So that was why Dev was so upset. Even though she knew some of what had happened from Rohan, she didn't want to let on. "What happened? Is she the one who got rid of you? Did she send you here?"

He stared at the floor in front of him and nodded. "She'd been mad at me for a few weeks."

"Why?"

After a moment, Dev looked up. "Because I helped your friends save Fifer's life."

LISA McMANN

Trying to Cope

Thisbe looked up sharply. "What?" she asked Dev. "Fifer's alive?"

"She was alive when I saw her," Dev said. "I showed Thatcher how to stop her bleeding. If he kept doing what I showed him, I would guess she survived."

The news of Fifer slammed into Thisbe, leaving her reeling. Over the past weeks she'd tried desperately to put Fifer's unknown fate in the back of her mind so she could get through each day. And now everything that had happened, everything she'd tamped down in order not to feel it, came rushing back. She slid her shaking fingers into her hair and gripped it, wanting to scream, but she couldn't with the soldiers nearby. She covered her mouth and tried to calm her breath until she could trust herself to speak quietly again. "Fifer's alive. You think."

Dev gave her a pained look that was not unkind. "I think so, Thisbe, but I can't say for sure. All I know is that she was alive at the point when Thatcher and that flying monster reached the forest. Thatcher and I started patching her up. She'd lost a lot of blood. And they had a long journey ahead of them, right? I told them to go right away—they weren't safe in Grimere with her."

The additional revelations rattled Thisbe again. "So they went . . . home? Without me?" She choked on the words as she pictured Simber, Thatcher, and Fifer flying over the gorge, away from her. She'd assumed it after a while, but now she knew it was true, and it hurt like a fresh stab to the heart.

Dev nodded. "Yes," he said quietly. "I watched them go. I think they *had* to—they had to do it to save Fifer's life."

Thisbe felt her body go numb. Of course they had to do

that. Of course they needed to save her sister, who was right there with them, rather than the one they couldn't get to. There was no other choice.

After a long while, Thisbe looked up. She swallowed hard. "You haven't seen them return?"

Dev's expression flickered, like he was realizing what Thisbe must be thinking—that they weren't coming back for her. "No," he said reluctantly. "I'd been watching. Before Shanti sent me here, anyway. That was three days ago."

Thisbe grew urgent. "No sign of anyone? Are you sure you'd have seen them?"

"If not with my own eyes, I'd have heard about it. Visitors from that direction don't often go unnoticed."

Thisbe felt something tearing through her chest. She couldn't breathe. Her head fell back against the wall, and she began to moan in pain like a wounded animal.

Dev looked at her in alarm. He glanced worriedly at the door, then back at Thisbe. When she continued the noise, he got up and went over to her. "Shh," he said softly, keeping an eye out for soldiers. "I know it feels bad."

Thisbe raked in a breath and started sobbing. "They should have come back by now," she cried, not caring who heard her. Her heart was breaking right there on the Revinir's kitchen floor, and she couldn't stop it.

Desperate, Dev reached out to put an arm around her shoulders. "Shh," he said again. "Shh. The soldiers will hear."

Thisbe covered her face with her hands and shook. Dev patted her back, looking terribly uncomfortable but growing more desperate to quiet her cries. "Thisbe," he said firmly. "It's going to be okay. It doesn't mean they're not coming. Maybe something held them up."

Thisbe shook her head in her hands. She knew better. Nothing could hold them up if they really wanted to go after something. She'd read Lani's books. The people of Artimé were warriors. And they didn't waste time.

After a while Thisbe lifted her head and saw Dev's concerned face in front of hers. She looked at him for a long moment. "Maybe the Revinir was right," she whispered. "They're never coming back."

"Don't listen to her," said Dev weakly. But his face gave

away his own suspicions. "How long does it take for them to get to your island?"

"A few days. They could have dropped Fifer off and turned around and been back here within a week."

"Oh." Dev looked away.

Thisbe could tell he believed what she was thinking and feeling too. They should have been back long before now. For an instant Thisbe wondered if the Revinir was right that Alex really was teaching her a lesson. If so, it was the meanest lesson she'd ever heard of. But deep in her heart Thisbe knew that couldn't be it. The Revinir was lying, making things up to get Thisbe to be on her side. Even as forgotten as Thisbe was feeling right now, she knew there had to be a logical reason for no one from Artimé coming back for her. And she refused to let the Revinir poison her mind against her brother—everything he'd ever done was out of love for her. She knew that. She began crying again, quietly this time. Because despite all that, she still had no idea where they could be.

Dev gave her a helpless look. After a while he got up to add water to his bone broth. He added some to Thisbe's as well while she sat grieving on the floor.

LISA McMANN

Hours went by in which neither of them spoke. Before they were done for the day and allowed to return to their crypts, Thisbe turned to Dev. "Thank you for saving my sister's life," she said. "And I'm sorry about Shanti."

Dev glanced at her, and for a moment they both felt the connection that comes when people are in pain together. "Thanks," he said. After a minute, he added, "She was my only friend."

LISA McMANN

Dev's Story

Thisbe spent a thoughtful evening alone in her crypt. It was a night Rohan was working, so he wasn't around. She ate her meal and worked on her magic half-heartedly, then went to sleep early.

The next morning Mangrel told her to bring three more bones to the Revinir's kitchen. She dragged them there.

The stench of the broth was permeating the nearby hallways now. When Thisbe arrived, Dev was already there with the Revinir, checking the cauldrons that they'd covered and left simmering over a slowly dying fire all night. Dev stoked the fires and added wood as Thisbe unharnessed her dragon bones.

LISA McMANN

"That's the last load you'll need to bring for this batch of product," said the Revinir, tasting the broth. She wrinkled her nose. "Disgusting," she said. "It's perfect."

Dev flashed an "I told you so" glance at Thisbe, and it was true—to the Revinir, bad was good. Scarcity increased demand. What other weird lesson would Thisbe learn today?

"Now we'll have to make the new broth equally as bad," the Revinir declared.

"New broth? Won't it all taste the same?" asked Thisbe. "It's just bones and water."

"You'll see soon enough." The Revinir took a cup and dipped it in the dragon-bone broth. She handed it to Dev. "Drink up," she said. "Let's see how strong it is."

Dev closed his eyes momentarily, as if he was resigned to doing this thing he didn't want to do. He plugged his nose, then took a few swallows. He almost gagged, but held it down. Then he took a few more breaths and finished the cup. "Blech!" he said when he finished. "That is just . . . the worst. It gives me a stomachache."

"Lift your sleeve," said the Revinir, who didn't seem to care.

Dev shoved his sleeve up, revealing the scales. As they

looked on, a few more scales appeared and blended in with the existing ones.

"Hmm," said the woman. She turned to Thisbe, her eyes narrowed, then scooped another cup of broth. "Drink it," she said, shoving it at her.

"Who, me? No!" said Thisbe, though she was curious about it.

"Soldiers," called the Revinir. Three soldiers came running. They pulled out their weapons. The Revinir turned back to Thisbe. "Drink it!"

"Sheesh." Thisbe, unnerved, took the cup in her shaky hand. She looked at Dev, who had dropped his gaze. Her heart fluttered in her chest, as if she sensed her life was about to change forever, and she gasped a little in fear. "I can't do it," she said.

One of the soldiers stepped closer, a menacing look on his face.

"Do it!" said the Revinir.

"Okay!" said Thisbe, shrinking back. She closed her eyes and pressed the warm cup to her lips. She tipped it and took a sip, swallowing it down. It was awful.

"Hurry up," said the Revinir. "I've got things to do today."

Now that she'd taken the first bit and there was no undoing it, the rest went down more easily. She took a few swallows, grimaced, and then finished it. It made her feel a little bit dizzy. Her arms and legs began tingling.

"Your arm," prompted the Revinir.

Thisbe pushed her sleeve up and held her arm out. A smattering of iridescent scales pushed out of her skin. She stared at them. "Oh my," she breathed, equally horrified and curious. They'd sprouted from her body, which was weird. But they were beautiful.

"It's too strong," declared the Revinir. "Dilute it with water to twice the volume. Then bottle it up to be sold. Don't spill any—not a drop!" With that, she dashed off.

The soldiers left the kitchen too and settled in their usual spot by the hallway. Dev and Thisbe looked at each other. Then Thisbe examined her arms and legs again and tried unsuccessfully to pull one of the scales out. "This is . . . horrifying. I think."

"I mean, you get used to it," said Dev, looking cautiously at Thisbe. "It's really sort of interesting. Unique, you know?"

But Thisbe was overwhelmed. Even coming from a magical world, she'd never seen or experienced anything like this. It was one thing to discover the larger-than-life Revinir sporting the scales, but to have felt them sprout from her own skin and to see them shining now—it was nothing less than extraordinary. She was forever changed. A human with dragon scales! And it had happened with such negativity and force, and so little fanfare or joy, which felt wrong for such a beautiful thing. It seemed like it could be so great to take on a dragon property like this, yet it had been done in such a degrading way that Thisbe was having a terrible time trying to figure out how to feel about it.

She crouched and looked at her legs, and slid her finger over her shin, feeling a surprising softness. This was so strange that she couldn't quite grasp what it meant for her. Would the scales ever go away?

"Are you okay?" asked Dev, looking at Thisbe curiously. "It's a little bit of an odd feeling, isn't it? Like . . . losing a tooth. It takes a couple days for it to feel normal."

Thisbe nodded. She definitely felt odd, not just physically, but mentally, too. Almost like she had gained an unspecified amount of knowledge, though she couldn't pinpoint any top-ics. She felt older, though that wasn't quite it either. "Wiser," she murmured.

"Yes," Dev said emphatically. He knew exactly what she meant. Then he turned quickly, embarrassed by his own enthu-siasm over Thisbe's sudden change. Perhaps he felt less alone because of it. He fumbled with a cart filled with tiny empty bottles, then remembered they needed to dilute the broth first and went after a bucket of water. "I told you it tastes awful."

"Yes. It's like dirt and mustiness," said Thisbe, wondering if her fate had been instantly changed by this. Perhaps not. All she knew was that her desire to escape was stronger than ever. Would this newfound wisdom help her understand the Revinir a bit better? Could she anticipate the woman's motives more successfully now? Maybe it could help her get out of here.

Her mind turned to that dilemma as she absently stroked her arm, trying to get used to the surprising softness of the scales. When she brushed her hand down over them, they lay smooth and flat. But when she brushed upward, they stood uncomfortably, tugging at her skin. She didn't like that feeling, so she smoothed everything downward again.

Dev's water bucket clanged against the side of his cauldron, bringing Thisbe back to the task at hand. She realized that he was doing all the work while she had just been standing there. "Sorry," she said, and began helping to dilute the broth. She could feel the scales slice the air.

"It's okay," said Dev generously, going back for more water. "I get it."

Thisbe marveled a bit longer, but her thoughts eventually returned to escaping again. She knew with certainty that she needed to work on Dev some more—and with the new scales, they had something extraordinary in common. That could serve to bring them closer. And he was being decent today, at least, so she wanted to take advantage of it. As they worked, she thought about the previous day and realized she'd never gotten the whole story behind why Dev was sent away from the castle. Maybe talking about that would also serve to strengthen her trust in him a little.

"So . . . what actually happened to bring you here?" asked Thisbe. "You said Shanti sent you away because you helped Fifer."

"Yes," said Dev. "That was part of it."

"Why wouldn't she want you to help her?"

Dev shrugged. "Shanti assumed Fifer would die. She was mad that she wouldn't get the money from selling her at the auction after she was counting on her."

Perhaps because of the Revinir's teachings about the marketplace, or because of the wisdom from the dragon-bone broth, Thisbe, who'd never spent money in any form before, was beginning to understand how and why it was used to trade for things. But she still thought money was a waste of time. "In Artimé, we don't use money. Nobody buys or sells things. We just have them. Or we give each other things if we need something. I guess we don't need gold if we have magic." She thought for a moment, landing back on what Dev had said about Shanti. "Wait. The princess didn't want you to help a severely injured person because she was losing money over it?"

"Basically."

Thisbe was incredulous. "And you went against Shanti's wishes to save my sister? You risked that?"

Dev looked uncomfortable. "Of course. Fifer was going to die otherwise." He started to fill the tiny bottles.

Thisbe wasn't quite sure what to say—Dev had been a

LISA McMANN

hero, and she'd had to drag the information out of him. That wasn't what she'd expected from him. "Then what happened?" she asked.

Dev started from the beginning and told her about how he and Shanti had been heading for Dragonsmarche to see what would happen at the auction when they noticed Simber flying toward them. After Dev had done what he could and the Artiméans flew away, he and Shanti continued to the city. "Dragonsmarche was in chaos when we got there. Carts were overturned, people trampled, the giant aquarium was cracked and flooding the square, and some of the sea creatures were sure to die. There was nothing we could do for them. Some were captured and stolen. I hope the rest of them made it to the lake."

"That's horrible." Thisbe remembered pointing out the aquarium to Fifer before they'd been tied up on the auction stage. There had been a creature inside that had looked familiar. But it was all a blur now.

"We hung around the square listening to the story about what happened to you. I tried looking for you, but of course there's no way I know of to make the Revinir's elevator come up when you're on the outside. Most of us didn't even know that entrance to the catacombs existed. She must only use it in the dead of night or something."

Thisbe had figured as much when the crowd seemed surprised to see it come up in the square. "You really looked for me?"

Dev's expression flickered. "I mean, I couldn't, obviously— you were underground, and the other entrances are far away from where we were in Dragonsmarche. But I looked around a little, in case the townspeople were wrong."

"Interesting," said Thisbe. She almost smiled, but the memory of being snatched away by the Revinir was too heartbreaking—that moment marked Thisbe's estrangement from everything she knew, or might ever know again. "Did the Revinir pay Princess Shanti for me? Or did she just steal me and get away with it?"

"I think she paid the princess something afterward. But then she got really mad when she found out the dragons had escaped."

Thisbe nodded, saying nothing to give away the fact that she'd learned some of that information already. She felt an emptiness growing inside whenever she thought about people buying and selling other people. And she wondered if Alex and the others would have to *buy* her in order to get her back. The desolate feeling led her to wonder once more if the Revinir was right about Alex not sending a rescue party for her. Why? The question pounded in her ears, unanswered. Maybe he'd had enough of her. Maybe he'd actually just thrown his hands in the air in frustration for the last time. But wouldn't someone try to talk him into going back, like Florence or Lani? Wouldn't anyone else come back for her? Not even Fifer? Maybe they didn't know how to get money.

It was all too confusing. As much as Thisbe tried to convince herself that she was being ridiculous in thinking any of those bad thoughts, she still couldn't come up with a good reason for Alex not sending someone for her. And that continued to sow more and more doubt in her mind as she began to bottle the magical bone broth.

"So you stayed with the princess?" Thisbe said eventually, picking up Dev's story again and prompting him for more.

"Yes, but she was mad that I'd defied her. I apologized, and things got a little better. Then, about a week ago, the Revinir

LISA McMANN

finally discovered that her dragons had escaped—she hadn't heard about it since she was underground, I guess, and the king wasn't about to admit it. But word worked its way underground to the Revinir's soldiers, and she came storming into the castle to talk to the king."

"If the Revinir owned the dragons, why did the king have them?"

"The Revinir didn't have a place to keep them. The original dragon entrance to the catacombs, which was used to bring in the dead ones, collapsed a long time ago with the big earthquake, and they don't fit into any of the other entrances. So the Revinir had made an arrangement with the king, which allowed him to use the dragons infrequently to transport building materials and jewels and junk like that in exchange for keeping them captive and feeding them."

"Oh."

"Anyway, when the Revinir found out the dragons were gone, she was really mad. There was a huge shouting match, and the princess got hauled into it because the king found out that she was the one who'd ordered the gate opened, which allowed them to escape. Naturally Shanti was boiling mad at me, since it was sort of my idea to release them."

"It was—you?" Thisbe was surprised again.

"Yeah. I couldn't stand that they were locked up and muzzled like that. Anyway, when the Revinir demanded payment from the king, Shanti suggested . . . me." He grew quiet. "So. That's how that happened."

Thisbe dropped her gaze. "I'm sorry." She had so much to process, so much she wanted to say. Dev was more complex than she'd ever imagined, and she wasn't sure what to think about him and how the things he'd done and all he'd experienced in his life had shaped him. He was one surprise move after another—maybe that's what happened when you were exactly half-bad and half-good. Whatever the case, Thisbe was mystified by him.

They worked the day away, scooping all the way to the bottom of the giant cauldrons and pouring the smelly liquid into tiny bottles, then capping them tightly and putting them on a cart. When they finished, they began the broth-making process all over again, each with a new bone in their pots, covering them with water and stoking the fires to bring them to a boil.

After a while, a soldier came in. "The Revinir told me to tell you that you're to stay late tonight to add water to the cauldrons for the next five hours. Then you can cover them for the night and go."

"Five more hours?" Thisbe looked up at the woman. "Why can't *you* just put some water in these pots? Why do we need to sit here?"

The soldier pointed her weapon at Thisbe.

"Okay, okay," Thisbe muttered. She wasn't happy about this development. It meant she might miss her secret evening time in the tunnel with Rohan. She was looking forward to seeing him, and she wanted to show him what the Revinir had done to her. Every time she moved, she felt the breeze slice through the scales, and it reminded her again of this incredible thing that had changed her. She still hadn't quite gotten over the shock of it. Now and then she rubbed her hand over them, always expecting them to be sharper. But they remained soft and pliable. They didn't itch.

As she and Dev continued their jobs into the evening, they chatted on and off. Things had grown comfortable between them, and they sat together in between the times they were

LISA McMANN

adding water to their cauldrons. The horrid smell grew as the bones boiled and released their bits of magic into the liquid.

Dev explained to Thisbe the parts of the dragon-freeing story that she'd missed while being chained in the castle dungeon. And he told her how he'd led Seth out. Eventually he also confessed that he'd intentionally put Thisbe in the prison chamber with Maiven Taveer because he knew the old woman would be decent to her.

The surprises about Dev didn't end. He'd done some really thoughtful things. Maybe he wasn't all bad. Thisbe laughed to herself at the joke, but then realized he could have changed for the worse or the better by now, and it seemed like he was heading in the better direction. But was he good enough to trust him with her secret to escape? He'd burned her before. She was tempted to tell him, but she just couldn't. Not yet. She needed to be absolutely certain he wouldn't betray her.

As they were about to leave for the night, there was a noise at the door. Thisbe turned and sucked in a sharp breath when she saw Rohan coming toward her, dragging a huge sack of small bones into the kitchen. He looked exhausted and ragged.

"Rohan," she whispered. Then her eyes landed on the

bones. Her sight wavered for an instant when she realized what they were.

"Who are you?" Dev asked him, looking alarmed at the delivery. "What are those for?"

Rohan glanced at Thisbe, telegraphing a warning look. Then he turned to Dev. "The Revinir told me to deposit these here."

Dev narrowed his eyes at the pile. "Those . . . aren't dragon bones."

"No, they aren't," said Rohan, looking disgusted. He unhooked his harness from the sack, which fell open and flattened on the floor, leaving the bones in a pile. "You're to make broth from these once the dragon-bone broth is done." He looked defeated. "May the gods of our ancestors forgive us all." With that he turned around and walked heavily out of the room.

LISA McMANN

Despair

That night Thisbe and Rohan huddled in the tunnel between their crypts. Rohan's mood was unlike any Thisbe had witnessed. He seemed beside himself in desperation. "Unearthing the dragon bones was bad enough. Making broth from them for profit—even worse. But now, taking the bones of our ruling ancestors who came before us . . . It's absolutely beyond the pale. I feel like filth. Like I've lost all sense of decency."

"But it's not your fault," Thisbe said. "The Revinir is making you do it."

Rohan buried his face in his hands and sighed heavily. "I complied. I didn't resist. I should have."

"She'll torture you if you resist! You're trying to stay alive. We're trying to get out of here."

Rohan shook his head. "On my walk back, I saw my future in those bones, Thisbe. And it was one of complete disgrace. What good is living under the weight of that?" He dropped his hands and looked at her, his passion evident. "Tell me if you know the answer. Make up something. I'm grasping for an excuse. For anything that will allow me to sleep tonight, because I can't rationalize this any longer." A noise of frustration escaped him. "I have too much time to think."

Thisbe looked at him with solemn eyes. A long moment passed in silence as she rolled the words over in her head. These bones didn't quite have the depth of meaning to her as they did to him, but he was right. And while discovering her history was new and strange to her, Thisbe felt the horror in her gut too, growing more powerful since she'd taken the broth, as if a stronger sense of right and wrong had begun to shred away her innocence.

"I don't know the answer," she said. "But look." She pulled up her sleeve and showed him her arm with its dragon scales.

Rohan sucked in a breath and held his candle closer, examining her arm. "She made you drink it too?"

Thisbe nodded. "She brought in the guards to threaten me."

"Oh, Thisbe." Rohan didn't seem to know what else to say. "I'm sorry."

"You can touch them if you want. I don't . . . I don't hate them."

After a moment Rohan drew his finger lightly down Thisbe's arm. "Can you still feel things?" he asked.

"Yes."

"They're softer than I imagined."

Thisbe nodded. "Do you think they will ever go away? I tried to pluck one, but it's stuck fast."

"I don't know."

"Dev has had more than me. She's been testing on him for a couple days."

Rohan shook his head and closed his eyes, a pained expression on his face. "And now the ancestor bones. We can't . . .

We just can't . . ." He let his head fall back against the stone wall.

Thisbe didn't know how to comfort him. She didn't know how to stop what was happening. But she had new information to share, so she turned to that. "Dev said the Revinir paid the princess something after she snatched me from the auction, trying to be fair about it and not stealing me. So that might be why she was so angry when she found out about the dragons' escape and learned that the king kept it from her at first. Now she really doesn't trust the king."

Rohan sighed and let his head fall forward. "That's not encouraging in the least. The stability of Grimere is about to crumble."

Thisbe didn't know what to say, but fear clutched her throat. War was such an unknown to her—she'd only known peace in her world.

After a few minutes, Rohan opened his eyes. "I'm so tired, but we have to fight this. Are you ready to escape? Can you be ready soon?"

Thisbe pressed her lips together. She'd been practicing her

LISA McMANN

magic, her aim, her concentration for some time now. She'd grown steadily better, but she knew her ability was limited. Her explosive spells would work for a time, but did she have enough in her to fight everyone they'd come across as they ran to the exit? She wasn't confident.

"How will we go?" she asked. "When is the best time? Do we try to kill the Revinir or focus only on escaping? What about Dev? And what about our black-eyed brothers and sisters? Do we leave them here? Or try to tell them what we're doing?"

Rohan blew out a breath. "This is complicated," he said. "If we tell too many, word will leak to the Revinir. Do you trust Dev?"

Thisbe closed her eyes, feeling a faint electricity buzzing over her scales when she thought of him. She was torn in half trying to decide. And as much as she wanted to give him the benefit of the doubt, she didn't have any room to make a mistake just because she felt sorry for him in a weak moment. "I'm not sure. Do you know how to swim?"

"Yes, a little. Why? The river?" He looked scared but didn't voice his fear.

"Yes. I think we two should go alone and head for the river exit. We can figure out how to come back for the others later. Shall we plan it for two days from now, when you return with your next load of ancestor bones?"

Rohan nodded. "We'll go that night, at midnight when the slaves are locked in and the soldiers are feeling at ease. You can break through the door, and we'll go no matter what happens."

Thisbe nodded.

"We can't continue on like this," Rohan said, as if to reassure himself that this was the right plan.

"And if we die in the river," said Thisbe, "at least we'll die honoring the lives of our ancestors."

Rohan agreed. "I can't bear to go on desecrating their remains—it will rest on my conscience forever. So it's settled: In two days we'll run for the river at midnight. And we won't stop for any reason."

Thisbe's eyes shone in the candlelight. She grasped Rohan's hand, and they nodded solemnly together. It was settled. They stayed up late planning and then said their good-byes before going off to sleep—they wouldn't see one another again until the escape. But no matter how tired she was, Thisbe tossed and turned. They had a plan. But how were they going to get across that river?

In the middle of the night Thisbe awoke with a start, her scales standing on end. She was panting as if she'd been running for the exit in her dreams. And in the pitch blackness, an idea began to form.

A New World

Morning was dawning when Alex and his team flew over the gorge, giving them a spectacular view of the gaping space between the worlds. Behind them the wide waterfall of the seven islands, which they'd once been swept down, rolled neatly under the world and disappeared into the mist. In front of them soon appeared the narrow waterfall that fell infinitely off the cliffs of Grimere. The sun hit the highest castle, next to it, making it sparkle.

"That's the castle where the dragons were chained up," announced Seth, sitting up a little on Arabis's back and acting as a tour guide for the others. "There's a horrible dungeon with lots of prisoners and the dragon stalls." As they reached the other side of the gap, Seth went on to describe in graphic detail how Hux nearly hadn't made it, and how he and the twins had been hanging by slipping vines above the great nothingness.

"That's a lot more than I needed to know," remarked Carina. Alex nodded in agreement.

"The twins saved me, pretty much," Seth admitted. "If it hadn't been for them, we wouldn't have been tied together. Thisbe was able to hang on to Fifer and me until Hux could pull us up." He paused, remembering, then added, "I like this way better."

Arabis, Simber, and Talon landed safely on the mountainside near where Seth and the girls had been before. The Artiméans climbed down to stretch. Kitten crawled out of Seth's pocket and began sniffing the air all around them.

Arabis turned her head to address the group. "There is an entrance to the catacombs from the castle Grimere's dungeon," she said. "I've never seen it, but I know the passageways go on for miles and miles underground. The entrance in Dragonsmarche would be near the center. There is a third entrance beyond Dragonsmarche, near the crater lake. I've flown by that one. It's a cavelike opening high on a rock wall that drops down to the lake's edge."

"A cave opening?" asked Simber. "That might be easierrr to access than trrrying to figurrre out how to rrraise that moving cylinderrr in the middle of the squarrre."

"It would be if it were big enough," said Arabis. "Unfortunately neither you nor I would be able to fit. I don't think anyone uses it except for fresh air. There's a sheer drop-off to the shore of the lake, and it's quite impossible to access for most anyone." She eyeballed Talon. "Though Talon might be small enough to enter that way."

"The castle entrance doesn't seem like our best option either," said Thatcher. He recounted to the others his narrow escape when the portcullis came down. "There are soldiers everywhere who would see us coming and close the drawbridge. Besides, I don't ever want to go near that dungeon again, much less through it, even if we did manage to get past everybody."

"Mewmewmew," said Kitten sweetly.

"So that leaves the center entrance in the middle of Dragonsmarche," continued Thatcher. "Which is going to be very difficult since we'll have to try to find it and then figure out how to make it come up so we can go in there."

"Mewmewmew," said Kitten again.

"Perrrhaps we need to collapse a larrrger arrrea of the grrround arrround that entrrrance," Simber mused. "We'd have to do that at night so we'rrre not obvious about it to the townspeople. And we'd rrrisk hurrrting people below. I don't like that." He glanced at Kitten. "Wait. What did you just say?"

"Mewmewmew!"

Simber tilted his head slightly as if deep in thought. "That's a verrry long way to rrrun for a tiny kitten, though."

"Mewmewmew."

"Trrrue." Simber looked thoughtful.

"What's she saying?" asked Alex.

"She says we should drrrop herrr off at the castle, and she can find herrr way thrrrough the dungeon and into the catacombs without anyone noticing herrr." Simber looked at Kitten. "But then what? How does that help us get in?"

"Mewmewmew," said Kitten confidently.

Simber looked at the others. "She says she'll trrravel to the Drrragonsmarrrche entrrrance and brrring the cylinderrr up forrr us."

"But, Kitten, how will you know when we're ready?" Alex asked.

"Mewmewmew."

"Hmm," said Simber. "Good point—we could send you a seek spell once we arrre quite surrre you'd be therrre. Do you have anything you've crrreated that you can give us?"

Kitten reached her tiny paw into a tiny tuft of fur and pulled out an even tinier something. She held it out. Seth opened his hand, and Kitten dropped it on his palm. It was a silver square.

"What is it?" asked Seth, straining to see.

"Mewmewmew," said Kitten with pride.

"It's a locket," said Simber. "She made it in jewelrrry class."

"Mewmewmew," said Kitten.

Simber rolled his eyes. "She wants you all to know it has a picturrre of Fox inside it."

"Aw," said Seth. "That's pretty cute, I have to admit." He looked around. "Do we have some fishing line? I can wear it around my neck so I don't lose it. It's so small."

LISA McMANN

Carina reached for the supplies and found a piece that was the right size, and Seth poked the line through the locket's miniscule ring, like he was threading a needle. Then he tied it around his neck. "Maybe Talon can be ready and waiting at the cave entrance at the same time. We could send him a seek spell too, to let him know it's time to attack."

"That's a good idea, Seth," said Alex. "Then we'll go in together." Simber nodded his approval.

Alex regarded Seth thoughtfully for a moment, his esteem for the boy rising. Seeing his sharp problem-solving skills surprised him, not having witnessed them before. It made him wonder if the girls had become that sharp too. He thought about Fifer back at home and how hard she'd tried to convince him that it was so, and felt a pang of guilt. He'd been so busy training he'd never given her a chance to show him or even tell him much about what she'd been through.

Seth didn't notice Alex. He was working through the rest of the plan. "How are we going to get Kitten to the castle? We don't want any of them to see Arabis or know that Simber is back, do we?"

"That's right," said Lani. "Let's not tip them off."

Talon stepped up. "I'll take you, Kitten. I can fly above the clouds so no one sees us coming and put you down on one of the turrets. Do you think you can figure out how to get to the dungeon from there?"

Kitten nodded.

"It'll take Kitten quite some time to travel the distance," said Arabis. "You'll want to head due west, Kitten—as much as you can, anyway. If what the guards have said is accurate, your path should be slightly uphill the entire way."

Kitten bowed graciously to the dragon. "Mewmewmew."

"She intends to sneak rrrides along with anyone going in that dirrrection," Simber interpreted.

"Good. Likely just a day's journey, then." Arabis glanced around, assessing their safety on the hillside. "Perhaps we should make our way into hiding, just there," she said, nodding and pointing with her tail toward the forest. It had been many hours of walking for Seth and the twins over rough terrain, but flying wouldn't take long at all.

"Talon, can you find us at the edge of the forrrest?" said Simber, pointing with Arabis to where he wanted Talon to go.

"Fear not," said Talon. "I shall see you there by afternoon."

LISA McMANN

With that, Talon set off with Kitten for the distant castle. The rest of them climbed onto Arabis and Simber and took off to the shelter of the forest. To their right they could see the tiny village waking up. Seth told everyone how Fifer and Thisbe had made the bamboo prison bars come alive, how he'd gotten hooked on them by accident, and how the girls had then saved him.

"Wow," said Alex. "They did all that? I—I didn't realize." Somehow seeing the place where his sisters had been brought all sorts of questions to his mind. He regretted that he hadn't thought to ask Fifer more when he'd had the chance. Had he made a mistake not letting her come? "What else happened, Seth?"

Kaylee and Lani glanced at him and then at each other. Lani rolled her eyes, but they kept quiet, and Alex didn't see her.

Seth pointed to a hill rising between them and the castle. "Over there is where Thisbe killed a poisonous snake and saved Dev's life. And Fifer helped me walk after I twisted my ankle."

Arabis, who'd heard by now that Fifer hadn't been allowed to come, sensed that reinforcements might help the girl's case for next time. She added to what Seth was saying. "Fifer and Seth were heroic in saving us. I was about to be killed. They stayed levelheaded, even after Thisbe was thrown into the dungeon, and performed the most amazing magic I've ever seen, given what they had to work with." She snorted. "Some saplings and a bit of burlap they found in the dungeon—I would never have believed they could make true working wing extensions come alive from that. And Fifer's ability to comfort and work with Drock, who was exceedingly upset as he often is, was a lesson in patience for the rest of us." She paused. "I commend them both."

The words brought tears of pride to Carina's eyes, and Seth lowered his head. "Thanks." He knew telling these stories was the least he could do for his friend Fifer, to say these things in front of Alex where he could actually see for himself what odds they'd been up against. It was his way of making up for Fifer being stuck at home. Maybe he could play a part in Fifer getting to go along in the future. Or at least getting Alex to understand that they were not just simple inexperienced kids. They were real and true mages.

Alex remained thoughtful and quiet as they descended to

the edge of the forest. They all followed Arabis into a clearing that both she and Simber could squeeze into.

They ate a meal and refilled their water jugs from the river while waiting for Talon. As the day wore on, Carina and Thatcher told more tales from the dungeon where they'd spent time in the cell next to Thisbe, and Kaylee asked for more details about everything, trying to get to the real heart of what it was like out here for the three children—not only to inform Alex but also so the team would have as few surprises as possible.

Finally Talon was a glint in the sky coming toward them. But the stories continued. In the middle of Seth recounting how Fifer had to race against the clock to make the magic wings come alive without Seth there to help, Alex let out a long, troubled sigh. "Okay, okay," he said, holding up his hands in surrender. "I know what you're doing. And I know why you're doing it. And you're right." He hesitated for a moment, struggling for the right words. "I'm deeply disappointed . . . in myself. I am. And it's hard for me to admit that. It's hard for me to not get defensive or to accuse you all of ganging up on me, even though you haven't said a word about me refusing to let Fifer come along. I guess . . ." Alex picked up a small stick and began breaking it into pieces. "Seth, I guess seeing this new land and hearing about the various struggles you and the twins overcame makes it real, and it brings me back to when we were your age. I still want to protect my sisters, but I'll admit it. I think . . . I made . . . a mistake."

Everyone was quiet, and Lani didn't roll her eyes now. Solemnly she locked her gaze with Samheed, remembering those times when they were twelve and thirteen too. Carina, Thatcher, and Kaylee exchanged glances, then nervously watched Alex's bowed head. Had they gone too far with all the stories to try to make this point?

Finally Alex looked up, resigned. "It was a big mistake. As much as it breaks my heart with worry, I should have let Fifer come with us. And . . . I hope I haven't compromised our mission by not allowing her to be here."

On the Right Track

Fifer and Crow crossed over the space between the worlds at sunset. Like Seth had done a half day earlier with his team, Fifer pointed out the various places she'd been to and told Crow all about her adventures with Thisbe and Seth. Crow was appropriately shocked and impressed. It seemed surreal to Fifer now, reliving all the close calls and near disasters. It almost made her feel like Alex had been right to be overly worried, but she quickly brushed off that feeling. Along with the familiarity of the terrain, having Crow with her gave her added comfort.

They stopped on the hillside, wanting to stretch and give

the birds a rest, but there wasn't much for the birds to eat or drink among the rocks. So soon they were off again. Fifer directed them toward the forest and river, where they could safely settle down for the night.

When they reached the edge of the forest and landed, Fifer took the supplies and Crow folded up the hammock. Fifer lit a blinding highlighter to guide them closer to the river, and soon they came upon a large clearing that had been recently and quite magnificently trampled by what had to be very large creatures. There was a spot that had held a fire, though it was fully extinguished now. The birds chattered noisily over it all.

"I'll bet Arabis and Simber and the team stopped here for a bit," Fifer said. "We're not too far behind them."

"We'll have to set out early to catch up," said Crow. "I'm sure they've stopped somewhere as well for the night." He pulled out a couple of prepared meals that Fifer had taken from Artimé's kitchen and quickly ate his.

Fifer ate too, though she wasn't very hungry. She began to feel butterflies in her stomach when she thought about meeting up with the rescue team. It would no doubt be a huge surprise for them to see her. "I wonder if Alex will yell at me when we find them," she mused as they made beds out of the brush. "Actually, there's no 'if' about it, because I'm sure he will. But how badly?"

"There's not a lot he can do about it," said Crow with a shrug. "We're here. I know it's early to go to sleep, but we can't do much else now that it's dark. We may as well rest up so we can make ourselves as useful as possible tomorrow." He lay on the grass and put his hands behind his head. "Have you thought about what you'll tell Alex?"

Fifer set the glowing highlighter between them on the grass and rummaged through her travel bag. "A little. I'll say I couldn't stand to be away from Thisbe a moment longer. And if that means he loves me less, then that's the way it goes. I'll take her over him any day."

Crow smiled wryly. "I'm not so sure that technique will endear you to him. You might want to leave out that last bit and stick with the first. I think he might understand that, especially since he's chosen his twin over some other things in the past. Try to see things from his perspective, and use what you have in common with him instead of getting immediately hot and butting heads. If you attempt to do that, and he sees your effort to understand him, maybe he'll realize you're more mature now and do the same thing for you."

Fifer pulled a thin blanket from her bag and lay down, draping it over her. "I remember in one of the adventures Lani wrote that Alex could feel it when Aaron was badly injured after the pirates captured him. That made him want to go after Aaron."

"Yes," said Crow. "I remember that. He was totally driven by that feeling that Aaron was on the brink of death. Do you have that kind of twin bond with Thisbe? Or those prickly feelings about each other when you're separated?"

"I'm not sure," Fifer admitted. "This is the first time we've ever been separated. I don't have some weird sense that she's about to die or anything, though." She paused, thinking it through. "Maybe our bond isn't as close as Alex and Aaron's."

"Or maybe Thisbe's not in life-threatening danger," Crow suggested. He yawned and rolled to his side.

"Mm-hmm." Fifer nodded sleepily. Crow's words comforted her. She was glad they'd talked this out. She'd thought worrying about it might keep her up all night, but she felt better now. Almost good enough to face Alex tomorrow.

Now all they had to do was find him.

LISA McMANN

A Tragic Turn

By that evening, Thisbe was growing nervous. The ancestor bones lay on the kitchen floor where Rohan had left them, and they'd soon be using them to make a new broth, which was unsettling enough. But adding to that, in just over twenty-four hours she and Rohan would be breaking out of here. *No matter what.* That phrase repeated in her head unendingly, like one of Fox and Kitten's songs they'd sometimes play at Artimé's annual masquerade ball—it was annoying, but you couldn't stop it. All she hoped was that she could get through the remaining time without the Revinir making her drink ancestor-bone broth. Because she wouldn't do it.

"What's wrong with you?" Dev asked her when he caught her paused in filling the last of the dragon-bone broth into the bottles.

Thisbe blinked and continued working slowly. "Nothing." She felt guilty for not telling Dev the plan, but she had to protect herself. She'd learned her lesson with him.

Dev frowned and helped Thisbe finish. They cleaned out the cauldrons and replaced them on their fires. Then they both turned slowly and looked at the pile of ancestor bones.

"I can't do this," said Thisbe.

"Me either. It's horrible."

They continued to stand there, trying to figure out what to do. "We could tell the soldiers we're done for the night," said Thisbe. "Then we wouldn't have to start this until tomorrow. Maybe . . . maybe something crazy will happen that will stop everything." Thisbe glanced sidelong at Dev.

"They won't let us go." Dev went to the door and looked at the entry room.

"Get back in there," growled a soldier. "The Revinir is coming."

Dev scooted back into the room. "She's coming."

"I heard," said Thisbe, growing panicky. She and Dev scrambled to look busy as the woman came into the room.

The Revinir assessed the kitchen and saw both cauldrons empty and the fires low. "Get started on the new bones," she barked. "What are you standing around for?"

"Well," Thisbe began, stalling for time, "I don't understand what you are trying to do with the ancestor bones. I mean, the dragon bones have magic in them. What do these have?"

"Nothing, I assume," said the Revinir. "The broth we make from them is just the placebo for after we sell out of the batch of dragon-bone broth."

Dev and Thisbe were more puzzled than ever now. "What are you talking about?" asked Dev.

The Revinir looked at the children like they were stupid. "We'll sell through the first batch of dragon-bone broth at the market tomorrow. People will take it home and drink it. They'll see the changes and show their friends. Everyone will get excited, word will spread, and hundreds of people will come to our booth next week seeking it. But we don't want anyone to have a second dose of dragon-bone broth—they could get too powerful. So we're making this fake magical broth to replace it, and increasing the price dramatically. The people will buy it anyway, but they won't know it's not dragon-bone broth when they spend all their money on it, trying to become stronger. Once we have their money, our booth disappears without a trace before we're discovered."

Thisbe was disgusted, but she wasn't surprised. The Revinir was going to knowingly give the ancestor-bone broth to hundreds, maybe thousands of people, while passing it off as magical dragon broth. She hardly knew what to say at first. Then she whispered, "I see."

"So get moving," said the woman. "We'll need a lot more of this fake dragon broth so we can sell as much as possible. Half the bones to each pot, cover with water, bring to a boil. And don't leave until you have a full cauldron simmering on a healthy fire that'll last until morning. Then we'll test it to see if there might be some ancient magical component to them. After all, the bones are intact after all these years. Something must have preserved them."

She turned to Dev. "I want you to report to my throne room an hour earlier than usual in the morning," she told him.

Dev didn't ask why, and she didn't explain. The Revinir turned and left Dev and Thisbe to get started.

"I wonder who is going to the marketplace to sell this stuff," Dev said. "I'm worried it might be me since she wants me here early. She knows I have experience in the market because Shanti told her—that's what convinced her to take me as partial payback for losing the dragons."

"Everything about this is horrible," said Thisbe, absently stroking the scales on her arm, which she was starting to get used to having. "She's horrible. And I'm not drinking this stuff."

They did what they'd been told to do. A few hours later their giant pots were completely full and simmering properly, and the fires were going strong. They left after the soldiers checked their work and went their separate ways back to their crypts.

That night, after her meal, Thisbe spent every waking moment working on her magic and her aim. Her stamina seemed to be improving a bit, probably helped by the less physical work she'd been doing lately. But she was afraid to try anything too powerful for fear it would summon the crypt keeper again. She wouldn't know until the actual escape how much the powerful spells would drain her energy—she'd only ever done one at a time before. She'd have to use her magic wisely and sparingly in case they were faced with more obstacles than they'd planned.

Early in the morning Thisbe went into the kitchen. The Revinir was there with a handful of guards. Before Thisbe knew what was happening, three of the guards stepped in front of the doorway behind her, blocking the exit. Another stood by the cauldron.

Wary, Thisbe glanced around and saw she was trapped in the kitchen with the Revinir. "What are you doing?" she asked. "Where's Dev? What's happening?"

The Revinir calmly picked up a cup. "I've tried this new broth, and it seems worthless," she said. "But I want to test it on you."

"No," said Thisbe, eyeing the soldiers and trying to remain calm. She took a step back. "I don't want to drink that."

"Oh, but you will," said the woman, stepping toward her. "It's not a big deal. I don't think it'll do anything to you, either."

"No," said Thisbe, more firmly. "I won't do it!"

The Revinir narrowed her eyes at the girl. Then she sighed heavily, annoyed, and looked sideways at one of the soldiers. Without a word, the soldier stepped up to Thisbe and grabbed her arm while the Revinir dipped the cup into the boiling broth.

"I said no!" Thisbe cried out. She wrenched her arm out of the soldier's grasp.

"Drink it!" shouted the Revinir, holding the steaming cup toward her. "Here. You can hold it. Just take your time. Just a small sip."

"I won't!" Thisbe darted to keep the guard from grabbing her again, then lunged at the Revinir, trying to knock the cup out of her hand. The soldier stuck his foot out to trip Thisbe. She screamed and flopped to the floor hard on her back. "Stop!" she yelled. The soldier backed off, but the Revinir swooped in and splashed the cup of hot broth in Thisbe's face.

Mid-scream, Thisbe gasped in surprise, sucking some of it in. She choked and sputtered and felt it scald her lips and tongue and the back of her throat as it went down. Coughing, she swiped her eyes to clear them and rolled to her side. "I hate you!" she said bitterly, and tried to spit the taste from her mouth. But it remained.

Satisfied that Thisbe had ingested at least a little of the broth, the Revinir backed off and held the soldiers at bay, watching Thisbe carefully.

Thisbe stayed low, feeling strange. Slowly she wiped her face with her shirt. Her mind spun as odd new thoughts entered it—but none of them made sense. A flash of an ancient stone road, an army of soldiers, a blaze of silver dragons in battle. A broken land, a destroyed forest, a river stretching out and falling into a sea. Bodies in heaps. A pirate ship sailing away. A barrage of meteors and a devastating earthquake. Children being sent away in the dead of night. A young woman dragged off by soldiers.

The images kept coming, flashing behind Thisbe's eyes, making her dizzy. She stared blindly at the floor of the kitchen, feeling the Revinir staring at her and knowing she couldn't let on that anything had changed. She didn't want the horrid woman to think she had felt anything at all.

Her stomach roiled, and she clutched at it. She lifted her head weakly, then gagged and retched at the Revinir's feet. The woman exclaimed in disgust, and the soldiers yanked Thisbe away from her. Still dizzy, Thisbe couldn't see anything beyond

LISA McMANN

the images flashing, too many to keep track of. Sometime during all of this, her dragon scales had risen painfully of their own accord. They stood on end as burning tears poured from her eyes, trying to flush the broth. She coughed again. "Leave me alone," she whispered when she could speak again. Her body ached.

After a few moments the flashing images subsided. Thisbe's coughing fits settled, and the tears slowed. She lifted her head and tried to focus on the boiling pot of broth nearby. Her vision steadied, and she glanced at the soldiers near the door, seeing that a few of them didn't try to hide their discomfort at witnessing the Revinir's actions. Then Thisbe turned and looked up at the woman with more contempt than she'd ever felt for anyone in the world. "Are you happy now?" she said sarcastically, her voice ragged. "You got your way again by being horrible. You must be so proud of yourself."

"Did anything happen to you?" the Revinir asked, clearly having no qualms about what she'd just done.

Thisbe clenched and unclenched her fists. Her face blazed. She spat on the floor again, then wiped her mouth, the taste of vomit overshadowing the broth. "No," she said as civilly as she could muster. She focused on remaining calm. She had to, or she could ruin her plans for escape. With all the soldiers nearby, Thisbe couldn't let a single spark escape or they'd be all over her.

"Nothing at all?" asked the Revinir, a tiny line of gray smoke coming from her nostrils. She stared into Thisbe's eyes as if she could read if she were lying.

Thisbe stared back defiantly, no longer caring what the Revinir could do with her dragon powers. "Nothing at all." She worked her jaw, then moved to clean up the mess on the floor since she knew no one else would do it. She glanced at her forearms and saw the dragon scales were lying down again.

"Good," said the Revinir. "Start bottling it up. Dev can take it to the market next week."

"Unbelievable," Thisbe muttered. Then she narrowed her eyes. "Is that where he is now? Alone?"

"Of course not alone. I sent soldiers with him."

"Why didn't you send me and leave him to drink that horrid stuff?"

"Because you don't have the first clue about money. Besides, you'd try to escape."

"Wouldn't Dev try?"

"No. He's been a servant his whole life. He wouldn't dare. He knows his life would be in danger if he's not with someone in authority." She gave Thisbe a warning look. "Yours would be too."

"Because of our eyes," said Thisbe.

"Obviously. You're safe down here. And you can gain more power over the others by sticking with me. Despite your horrendous behavior and lack of respect, I'm holding out hope to be able to trust you." She folded her arms. "I promise we can go far together."

Thisbe glared. After all the woman had done to her, she still thought Thisbe would leap at the chance to work with her over the long term. "Right." Thisbe shook her head. "What do I have that can help you?"

The Revinir began to pace. "You have the magic and the ancestry. I've got the dragons. Together we're the right combination to take back this land."

Thisbe narrowed her eyes. "You have more dragons? Where are they?"

The Revinir gave a condescending smile. "I *am* the dragon.

LISA McMANN

But we have access to other dragons if we need them. You'll find out more in time if you commit to working with me."

"How do you know I haven't already?"

"I can read your thoughts."

Thisbe knew the woman had to be lying, because if she could read her thoughts, she'd know a lot about what she and Rohan were planning to do. "What am I thinking right now?"

"You're thinking that I'm right about your brother and the people of Artimé. They aren't coming back for you."

The words struck Thisbe like a spear to her heart, and she couldn't stop her gasp in reaction.

The Revinir seemed pleased to have hit her hard. "See? I'll convince you eventually. We're better together. We could rule this entire land, beyond the depths of the forest," she said, pointing north, "and far beyond the lake." She pointed west. "But only if we work together. There's a lot to overcome."

"I'd rather die than work with you," said Thisbe.

The Revinir grabbed Thisbe's arm and said in low, sinister voice, "If you attempt to escape, you just might."

LISA McMANN

Fifer Catches Up

The birds had begun rustling early near the hammock, seeming to understand the need to get off to a good start before the light of day. Fifer shook Crow awake, and the two of them packed up and climbed onto the hammock. "We need to find Alex," Fifer told Shimmer. "You know who that is, right? And Arabis the orange and Simber." Shimmer and several others bobbed their heads, and then Shimmer called out instructions in its usual way. Soon they were rising above the trees and soaring over the forest.

"They seem to understand everything you say," Crow

mused. "I wonder how long it would've taken you to find this out if Thisbe had been around."

"I might never have," said Fifer. "I hope she can learn to like them. Especially since they're really well trained now. I'll teach them to not flutter up at her."

"She'll probably get used to them," Crow agreed. "I totally have, and I used to be terrified of Queen Eagala's threat of sending the birds after us Warblerans. When she actually did it, I thought that was the end for me. Then you broke the spell with your scream. It was amazing. I was there with you, hiding in the giant rock."

"I remember," said Fifer, though she meant she remembered the story as Lani had written it, not from her own memory.

"It seems odd that these falcons started turning up after that, doesn't it? I've been thinking about that. Ishibashi told Seth that they'd never seen them until about ten years ago. And the scientists have been there over sixty years now I think."

"That is odd," said Fifer. She looked down and could see a road leading from the castle to the west. It was the one she and Thisbe had traveled on in the back of a vehicle. "Maybe when

I broke the spell, the ravens turned into these magical falcons."

"And maybe that's why the birds obey you," said Crow. "Because you broke the spell."

"I'll bet the Revinir will be really mad if she finds that out," said Fifer. "I hope I get a chance to tell her."

Crow smiled. In general he could tell that Fifer was maturing, and she seemed to be putting a bit more thought into her actions. But she still had her moments of recklessness, and this was one of them. "Again, you might want to think that through before you do it."

"I know, I know," Fifer muttered. "Sometimes I just say things that are in my head to see how they sound out loud. Sometimes they sound good, other times not." She didn't say whether she agreed with Crow and instead sat up and looked out. The birds were taking them safely above the trees so there was little chance of anyone noticing them. She wondered how far Alex and the others had made it. Maybe they'd even rescued Thisbe already. While Fifer would hate to miss that action, it would be more than worth it to have her sister back safely.

After a while, in the distance they could see the big city of Grimere and the Dragonsmarche square in the middle of it.

LISA McMANN

Shimmer uttered a sharp call to the other birds. They changed course slightly and headed for the edge of the forest that lay closest to the city.

"I think the birds found our rescue team." Fifer shifted nervously, then peered out but couldn't see anything through the cover of trees. The birds carefully maneuvered their cargo to fly above the river, where they could descend below the branches and find a place to set everything down. Crow and Fifer shaded their eyes, trying to see any sign of Alex's team.

The birds clipped a huge treetop, which slowed them down sharply, throwing Fifer and Crow off balance. The two tried desperately to lean in the hammock this way and that to avoid branches, but the ground came up fast and the birds screeched and fluttered to a halt. A few of them were forced to drop their ends to avoid smacking into trunks. The hammock tipped and spilled its contents onto the forest floor. Fifer and Crow tumbled out and sprawled awkwardly on the ground, unhurt.

When they could pull themselves to their feet, they looked up and around. Twenty feet away stood Alex and the others, staring at them.

"Oh," said Fifer, pulling leaves from her hair. "Hello."

Finding Common Ground

Carina, Thatcher, and Kaylee stared. Seth's mouth fell open in shock. Simber, who'd been ready to pounce, stood down and nearly smiled, but quickly looked stern instead. Arabis appeared startled but pleased, and Talon seemed unsurprised, though if he'd expected anything, he'd kept it to himself.

Alex's face went from shock to fury in about half a second. "What the— How did you—" he sputtered, and then, "Fifer, honestly! I don't know what to do with you anymore."

Fifer smiled meekly and inched closer to Crow for protection. But Crow looked at Fifer expectantly—it was up to her to explain.

"Take it down a notch, Al," murmured Kaylee, putting her hand on her brother-in-law's shoulder, lest he go barreling at his sister. "Let her talk before you go shooting off your mouth again and wrecking everything. Remember what you said yesterday."

Alex clenched his teeth and muttered, "That was when I thought she was in Artimé."

"Are you really that surprised to see her, though?" Carina asked him. "She's got more tenacity than all of us put together. It's admirable."

"*I'm* not surprised," said Seth. He grinned and ran over to Fifer and embraced her. "How did you do that? You got them to fly you this whole way? That's incredible! They must be really tired."

"They took shifts," said Fifer, keeping one eye on Alex. "Some of them would rest on the edges of the hammock when it wasn't their turn."

"*Cooo-l.* Ha-ha. Get it? Bird joke." Seth chuckled to himself and bent down to look more closely at the magical falcons.

"Hi, Alex," Fifer said finally.

He nodded. "Fifer."

"Look," Fifer began, remembering Crow's advice, "I know you're mad. But I couldn't stand being so far away from Thisbe. She's . . . she's my other half, like you and Aaron. Plus, I can help you all. And I know you'll never believe me unless you see me do it. So I'm here. To . . . to show you."

"Hey!" cried Seth suddenly, standing up again. "You're wearing a component vest! Who'd you steal that from?"

Insulted, Fifer smoothed the wrinkles from her vest. "I didn't steal it. I would never do something like that."

"Someone lent it to you?" asked Alex.

Fifer blew out a frustrated breath. "No, Alex. I earned it the way everyone else earns it. From the Magical Warrior trainer."

"Florence gave it to you?"

Fifer pinched her lips together. She didn't want to name Florence outright, though everyone knew that's who she meant. She didn't deny it. "Every other person in Artimé has earned their vest on their own merit. Nobody goes around asking the parents or guardians if it's okay to give a kid a vest. It's up to the trainer to decide. And she did. So."

Alex scratched his stubbly chin, his eyes narrowed and still on Fifer. He sighed and shook his head slightly, and then he emitted what almost sounded like a reluctant laugh. "You drive me crazy, Fifer," he said. "You really do."

Fifer nearly spat out an angry retort about how he drove her even crazier, but Crow touched her shoulder. She glanced up at him, and he frowned.

"Look," Crow whispered. "He's smiling. Don't blow it."

Carina, Thatcher, and Kaylee all seemed to be saying the same thing with their strained expressions.

Fifer closed her lips and dropped her gaze. She took a couple breaths. "I know I drive you crazy," she admitted. "It's like I can't help it, you know? Because I'm so worried about Thisbe. I can't stand not knowing. Like, remember when you thought Aaron was dead that one time? You said you could feel that part of you was gone."

Alex's smile faded as he remembered. He could almost feel it again just thinking back to those days. "I remember," he said quietly. After a moment he came over to her and knelt, putting his hand out to pet one of Fifer's birds. "I've actually been thinking a lot on this journey. And I get it now."

"You do?"

"Yeah. I'm still mad you disobeyed me. But . . ." He glanced at Lani, who raised an eyebrow at him and nodded encouragingly. "I think maybe you and I should take a little walk. Okay?"

Fifer nodded. "Okay."

Alex stood, and he and Fifer set out through the forest away from the others. Fifer glanced over her shoulder, and Kaylee gave her two thumbs up in encouragement.

When they were out of earshot of the others, Alex glanced at Fifer. To his surprise, she was a few inches taller than his shoulder already. "When did you get so tall?" he asked sheepishly.

Fifer shrugged. "I don't know. I'm strong, too. Want to see?"

He nodded. Fifer lifted her arm and flexed her biceps. He reached out and tested it. "Wow," he said, impressed.

Fifer dropped her arm, then said, suddenly impassioned, "Alex, I want to tell you things. Secrets. Confessions."

Alex looked surprised. "Okay," he said. "You can talk to me about anything. You know that, right?"

"I've tried to tell you things before, but you haven't been hearing me."

Alex opened his mouth to retort, but then he closed it. "That's fair. Will you give me another chance?"

Fifer was surprised and encouraged by his question. She nodded and began. "First confession: I watched out the window when Florence was training you on the west lawn."

Alex cringed. "Oh. I see."

"I was so proud of you, Alex." Fifer's voice hitched. Suddenly tears were surfacing in both their eyes. "I was there," she went on, "and Florence knew about it. And I learned how to use the components that way, as Florence retaught you. But mostly that time by the window was so important for another reason. Because I saw bits and pieces of the Alex from Lani's books for the first time. And I feel like I know you better now."

Alex stopped walking and stared numbly at the ground cover. "I haven't read them," he confessed.

Fifer stopped too and faced him. "What? How could you not?"

"It was too hard."

"What was?"

He pursed his lips, a pained expression crossing his face. "Reliving all of those losses. The battles, and my friends. It was too hard to see myself as I was before . . . and realize I'm not that person anymore. And the person I am now is someone I don't . . . really . . . like as much." He let out a breath. "It was too hard to be painted as some sort of hero when I wasn't feeling like one. It was easier to shove all of those memories away where they couldn't gnaw at me every day. Easier to pretend that 'fearless leader Alex' was just a character in a storybook I hadn't read."

Fifer was quiet for a moment. "But here you are again."

"Yes," said Alex. "I suppose." He slipped his hand inside his robe, pulled out a handful of spell components, and looked at them. "Here I am again," he said softly.

"Do you feel good about it?" asked Fifer. "About deciding to retrain and go? And about fighting again after so long?"

Alex looked at her for a long moment, revealing vulnerability in his eyes. Then he nodded. "Yes, I do." He replaced the components, then asked, "Do you?"

Fifer looked puzzled. "Do I feel good about myself fighting? Or about you?"

Alex gave her a crooked half smile. "Both."

"Yes," she said. "To both."

"Good."

They continued walking a few steps, and then Fifer stopped. "So . . . do you maybe want to throw scatterclips at each other?"

Alex frowned and looked like he was about to say no, which he would have automatically done in the past. But then he tilted his head and eyed her mischievously, one brow raised. "Yes. I do. Fifteen paces. Avoid the trees. Go."

Fifer almost shouted in delight—she'd never expected him to say yes. They turned their backs on each other and counted their steps, then faced each other again. Fifer pulled out a handful of scatterclips from her vest, praying she'd get the spell right, because if she messed up now . . . Well, she didn't want to think about the consequences.

Alex slipped his hand into his robe and took out a full set of scatterclips. He tossed them confidently in his right hand. "You're sure you want to mess with me?" he said. "I'm the head mage of Artimé, you know. Somebody even wrote a book about me once."

"I'm sure," said Fifer, laughing nervously. Her stomach flipped. This was the first actual component spell she'd be doing. What if it didn't work? Would Alex forbid her from fighting? Would he send her home?

LISA McMANN

"Wait," said Alex, holding up his hand. "You don't know the deadly verbal component to scatterclips, do you? I only ask because . . . well, talk to Aaron about that sometime."

Fifer's eyes widened. "I don't know that verbal component," she said.

"Okay, good," said Alex. He dropped his hand. "Ready?" He took a quick glance at what was behind him and drew his arm back, poised to throw.

"Ready," called Fifer, doing the same.

"Go!"

Alex and Fifer flung their scatterclips at each other. The two sets of components soared straight and true and had to dodge out of each other's way in the center of the distance between them. Fifer closed her eyes and stood firm as Alex's clips soared into her, grabbing her clothing and yanking her backward through the air until she slammed into a tree with a *thump*. The scatterclips hooked into the trunk, leaving Fifer hanging. She peeked out of one eye, cringing at the same time, hoping she hadn't done anything wrong with her throw.

Alex was pinned as well and laughing. "You did it!" he

called out. Fifer had nailed it. Just like with other spells, she'd picked up how to do it with hardly any effort.

"Release," said Alex, and he and Fifer both fell to the ground. Alex got up and ran over to her. "That was really good," he said, helping her up.

"Thank you," said Fifer.

"I'm impressed. How many times have you done that?"

Fifer wanted to lie and tell him that she'd done it dozens of times so he'd have more confidence in her. But she told him the truth. "That was my first time."

Alex shook his head, awed. "How did you get the throw right?"

"I watched you," said Fifer. "And I practiced the movements a lot. I just haven't done it with the components before."

"Do you want to show me some more?" asked Alex.

"I do," said Fifer, "but I don't want to waste my components."

"I'll reimburse you from our stash," said Alex. "Show me what else you can do. I really want to see."

Fifer grinned. They spent the next little while going through Fifer's vest pockets and having her try out each new component she pulled out. Fifer knew Alex needed to see her do them—and she was okay with that. She needed to see what she could do too. And it was nice that they were actually having a conversation without either of them arguing.

After Fifer had tried out everything successfully, the two walked back to the group, talking about magical strategy as if they'd been fighting together for years.

Kaylee watched them return and smiled as she saw them in animated conversation. "Looks like you two are seeing eye to eye," she remarked.

Fifer grinned. "Alex let me try out my new components on him."

"And she didn't even kill me," Alex quipped.

Crow flashed a thumbs-up at Fifer. It was heartwarming for all of them to see the two Stowe siblings getting along for once. Things were looking up, and the team was growing anxious to move.

"When do you think Kitten will reach the exit?" Alex asked Arabis, who was holding her mouth open in the river and scooping up fish.

The dragon swallowed them down and lifted her head. "She

probably won't make it there until sometime after midnight. It's a lengthy journey on foot."

"I think we should be cautious and wait until morning to send the seek spell, then," said Alex. "So Kitten will certainly be in the right place."

"But if we're to be stealthy, we don't want a lot of people roaming about in the square," Thatcher pointed out.

"We'll go before dawn," said Alex. "Before the townspeople start their day. How does that sound?"

Everyone agreed it was the best option.

"Also, after dark this evening," said Lani, "I was thinking some of us could check out the area and maybe see if we can find the exact location of the cylinder. Perhaps there's an out-line visible in the stone."

"That's a great idea," said Seth.

"I agree," said Thatcher. "I'm not positive I can find the exact location, especially if the stage they put the girls on isn't a permanent fixture in the square. Everything is such a blur."

"I could find it," said Simber, "but I don't think I should rrrisk being seen."

LISA McMANN

"I can show you all exactly where it is," said Fifer. "I stood there long enough."

Kaylee smiled. "It's good we have you here, then, isn't it?"

Fifer grinned. She glanced at Alex, and he shrugged, then grinned back. It felt good not to be so frustrated and angry all the time for once. Now if they could just get Thisbe back without anybody getting hurt or captured, that would be truly amazing.

A Shocking Turn

The rescue team shared a late-afternoon lunch in the cover of the forest while a small group of them made plans to venture out, hoping to find the Revinir's cylinder entrance to the catacombs in the square.

In her packing and planning, Fifer had been thinking ahead, and she'd brought along clothing and accessories that would disguise her black eyes. She dug through her travel bag and pulled out a scarf and some stage glasses with tinted lenses that Thisbe had worn in a recent play. Samheed glanced twice at her when she put them on, then smiled when he realized what she was doing. "Incognito," he said. "Very nice."

LISA McMANN

"I don't want anybody to notice me. I was up for auction out there once—I don't want to be again!"

Before they left, Arabis bade them good-bye and good luck. As soon as darkness fell, she'd be on her way to warn the dragons in the land beyond the forest. "I'll be swift," she promised them.

Simber and Talon chose to stay in the forest so they wouldn't draw attention. "Maybe I should stay back too," said Lani, looking down at her contraption. "Does this look too magical? Will people suspect?"

"I've never seen any wheels that look that advanced in my world," said Kaylee, skeptical. "If this world isn't magical at all, you might want to wear a long jacket that will hide some of it."

"Stay toward the middle of our group," Fifer suggested. "We'll cover you."

Lani agreed. Soon the humans were heading toward the road that led into the square. They went up the road in two groups. Fifer, in disguise, led the way with Alex and Kaylee. Seth, Carina, Thatcher, Samheed, and Lani went behind them. It was a lengthy walk, but when they got close, Fifer filled in the others on some details.

"The soldiers in green are the king's soldiers. They're from the big castle. If you see any soldiers in blue uniforms, those are the Revinir's. They sort of seemed to work together when Thiz and I were on the auction stage—though I'm not positive if they are friendly or not. The green ones let the blue ones come in and surround the stage. So I think that means the Revinir and the king aren't enemies, but I don't think they're friends, either."

"Maybe they just warily tolerate each other," said Lani.

Alex nodded. "Arabis mentioned that the Revinir would be furious at the king for allowing the dragons to escape and she'd demand something in return. That could create a problem."

"So tomorrow," Thatcher clarified, "we're most likely going to end up fighting the blue-uniformed soldiers. Leave the green ones alone unless they attack."

Dragonsmarche, the weekly market in the center of Grimere, was teeming with shoppers. The Artiméans looked on curiously as people traded gold nuggets for other goods. Kaylee explained to those who were puzzled by the exchange that the gold nuggets were the currency and they were worth something—at some point someone had decided gold was

305 « Dragon Bones

valuable, and people began to seek it and collect it, and they could use it to get other things.

"Why doesn't everybody just share everything like we do?" asked Seth. "If they need something, get someone to make it for them, or do it themselves."

"It's easier to do that in magical worlds, I suppose," Alex mused. "We have everything we need. But when Artimé's magic was broken and we were starting to starve, people began fighting and stealing from each other. It was ugly."

"Dev stole our fruit on the mountainside," said Seth, remembering his severe hunger.

Fifer glanced back at him and nodded. They'd had their eyes opened to a different world with Dev. "I wonder how he's doing," she said. "Princess Shanti was so mean to him."

"Yeah," said Seth. "I hope he's . . . okay." They both had ambivalent feelings about Dev, but he'd helped them at least as much as he'd hurt them. He was intriguing, at a minimum.

As they neared the center of the square, an explosion in the distance rocked the ground. Most of the people of Grimere ignored it, but the Artiméans startled. Fifer and Seth remembered they'd heard it before, and they looked to the west. "Look that way," said Seth, "beyond that hill. There'll be smoke rising up." Sure enough a plume of gray smoke rose.

Alex narrowed his eyes, puzzling over it. "It sounded like . . . like . . ." He shook his head as if he couldn't quite figure it out.

They meandered and weaved through the crowds, trying not to look like foreigners, though their clothes were quite different from everyone else's. Fortunately it was crowded enough that not many seemed to take note. Fifer led the others toward the center of the square. The stage wasn't there now, so it was hard to figure out exactly where the girls had been. Fifer looked around, trying to remember if there were any other landmarks she could recall. Then she spied the huge aquarium in the far corner of the square. It looked like the glass had been broken and repaired, and there were fewer sea creatures inside than before. Once Fifer found that, she could remember how the stage had been set in relation to it and about how far away from it she'd been. She moved toward the area where she thought the stage had been.

"It was here," she said in a low voice. "We faced this way, right, Thatcher?"

"Yes, from what I can remember. Simber and I circled and

flew in from that direction." He pointed toward the aquarium.

Fifer envisioned the auction and the way the crowd had grown and spread out. "It's got to be somewhere nearby."

The group, attempting to not appear suspect, milled around the area looking at the ground and tried to detect any sign of cracks that would indicate a break in the mortar. But the uneven cobblestone was covered in cracks, and there was no apparent pattern.

As Fifer and Seth worked their way around a stand where someone was selling tiny bottles of liquid, a blue-uniformed soldier stepped out and nearly knocked Fifer over. She stumbled and caught her balance on the edge of the table. The bottles shook and threatened to spill off.

"Watch it!" snarled the boy behind the table.

"Sorry," said Fifer, pulling her hand back. She glanced at him and nearly gasped. "Dev?" she said before she remembered her disguise.

The boy behind the table looked startled but didn't seem to recognize her.

Seth came up behind Fifer. "Are you all right?"

Dev froze in fear. "Seth," he said, then glanced at the blue-uniformed soldiers behind him, who were talking quietly together. He leaned forward and squinted, taking in Fifer's scarf and glasses. "Fifer? Is that you? You're okay?"

A musical fanfare began at the mouth of Dragonsmarche, and the three moved closer so they could hear one another.

"What are you doing here?" Dev said sharply. "It's dangerous!"

"Have you seen Thisbe?"

"I—I—" Dev seemed frozen in his ability to tell them everything that had happened. "Yes!" he sputtered. "She's down there! In the catacombs. Same hallway as the elevator."

"She's alive?" Fifer exclaimed, and Dev nodded.

"Elevator?" asked Seth. "You mean that cylinder thing?"

"Yes," said Dev.

The blue-uniformed soldiers stepped toward the group, suspicious. "If you're not purchasing any dragon-bone broth, be on your way!" shouted one over the noise of the band. He moved closer, looking menacingly at them, and Fifer and Seth turned and rushed away.

Dev watched them stiffly as another soldier came and stood

behind him with a dagger pointed at his back. He was help-less to do anything. But he consoled himself with the news he could share with Thisbe later—that her people had finally come back for her. She'd be so happy.

It almost made Dev feel emptier inside. Part of him wanted Thisbe to be with her family, but that meant he'd have no one again. He closed his eyes as pain washed through him, and then took a deep breath and opened them, ready to sell the dragon-bone broth. The sooner he could move everything, the faster he could get back inside to tell Thisbe.

Seth and Fifer found Alex and the others again and hurried to tell them what they'd found out—Thisbe was alive! They exclaimed their relief at the news as the marching band got closer and louder. And then the crowd parted and the band pushed through. Behind the band was a small chariot that was drawn by two jewel-adorned tigers.

Sitting in the front, wearing a petite crown that sparkled in the waning light, was Princess Shanti. All around her chariot were soldiers with green uniforms who looked about uneasily, almost as if they were assessing the number of the Revinir's soldiers in the area.

Shanti was looking around too, but not at the soldiers. Finally she spied Dev and halted the tigers, then ordered the band to be quiet. When the band ceased playing, the townspeople looked over to see what was happening.

"There he is," Shanti announced loudly to her soldiers. She pointed at Dev. "I want him back. Now! Seize him!"

LISA McMANN

On the Run

Fifer and Seth hid behind the others so the princess wouldn't recognize them. But Shanti was focused on Dev. "Bring him to me now!" she ordered. The soldiers in green marched over to Dev, who was beginning to quake with the dagger point pressed in his back. He quickly grabbed something off the table and slipped it into the money belt around his waist, then put his hands in the air. "Shanti, no!" he said. "What are you doing?" One of the Revinir's soldiers whistled for help, and more in blue came running. They pushed Dev around the table and out into the open.

The princess's soldiers drew their swords, prompting the blue-uniformed soldiers to do the same. "Help!" cried Dev, caught between them. "Princess, please!" he pleaded. "Does the king know what you're doing? The Revinir will be furious. Don't make this mistake."

Shanti jumped out of the chariot and stormed toward Dev, unafraid. "Stop this nonsense," she said to him, then chided the soldiers on both sides. "Put these swords away. I want my servant back. I am the princess. Therefore, you must give him to me."

The soldiers in blue stood firm around Dev—they took their orders from the Revinir. "Stay back," one of them ordered her. "This slave was given as restitution and belongs to the Revinir."

"Perhaps we should take the princess as the final payment," jeered another of the Revinir's soldiers.

Shanti's eyes burned. She continued forward, acting like she couldn't imagine anything bad ever happening to her. Her soldiers followed her, staring down the ones in blue.

"Shanti, stop!" shouted Dev, his eyes wide and fearful. "I mean it! Just go back to the palace before you start a war!"

"Don't speak, Dev," said Shanti coldly. She stood between the two groups of soldiers and began telling them what to do like they were five-year-olds.

The Artiméans shifted uneasily. "What should we do?" asked Fifer, peering between Alex and Kaylee.

"I didn't bring my sword," Kaylee muttered.

"I've got components, but we can't do anything," said Alex. "It'll jeopardize our chances of rescuing Thisbe. Besides, I'm not sure whose side we're supposed to be on. Are you?"

Fifer and Seth looked at each other. "I guess Dev's," said Fifer, "but why is he being guarded by the Revinir's soldiers? It sounds like the Revinir took him after what happened with the dragons."

"That would explain how he knows where Thisbe is," said Seth.

Shanti reached out to grab Dev by the collar and pull him with her. A soldier in blue struck the princess's hand away, then pointed her sword at Shanti. It glinted in the sunlight.

"Don't touch her!" shouted the captain of the king's soldiers. They drove the Revinir's soldiers back, and Shanti grabbed at Dev again.

"Come on, Dev," she said angrily. "Soldiers!" she shouted. "Take care of this."

Swords clashed.

"Shanti, please," Dev begged. "Stop them." A few soldiers in blue shoved Shanti away from the booth.

The princess screamed, and the king's soldiers charged to protect her and fight back. Some of the Revinir's guards grabbed Dev, who struggled to get away, but all he could do was watch, terrified. From the chariot, the tigers growled.

The skirmish became a fight. The king's soldiers attacked full on and knocked over the table of dragon-bone broth, sending the glass vials smashing to the ground, the broth spilling everywhere. The Revinir's army charged.

"No!" shouted Dev, and with a huge effort managed to escape the soldiers' grasp. He shoved Shanti out of the line of fire. Losing his balance, he tried to roll out of the way, but the soldiers kicked and stepped on him, leaving him squirming and unable to get up. Shanti stumbled and fell against one of the Revinir's soldiers, who turned sharply and slammed the pommel of his sword into her stomach. She doubled over and yelled out for Dev to help her as another blue soldier swung wildly with his sword, swiping at her. His blade left a deep gash in her neck. Her eyes widened in fear, and then the blood started flowing. She dropped to the ground, her princess crown falling off her head and rolling over the uneven pavers. Another of the Revinir's soldiers slammed his sword down on the princess. She stopped moving.

The tigers growled and yanked at their tethers, and the crowd of townspeople pushed back, many of them running for their lives. One of the tigers bucked and broke free of the chariot, then began stalking random people around him. The blue soldiers fought the green, swords clashing, blood and bodies flying. Shanti lay still in the midst of it all, bloody and broken. Dev got up and fought his way to her, shoving people aside even as they trampled her limp body. He knelt next to her. Reaching for her shoulder, he shook her gently and called her name. But he could see the truth. Shanti was dead.

Dev clutched his head, beside himself, and yelled, "You killed the princess!" His face awash in terror, he got up and stumbled into the fighting, numb and disoriented and yelling in the Revinir's soldiers' faces. "You killed the princess!"

Running townspeople stopped and turned. "The princess

is dead," they murmured. "Killed by the Revinir's soldiers!"

"Surely the king will declare war."

The Artiméans watched in horror. "Run, Dev!" screamed Fifer before she could contain herself. "Get out of there!" Hearing her, Dev looked wildly around. He came to his senses, dashed through the remaining onlookers, and disappeared.

"Look out, friends," muttered Carina to the others. "One of the tigers is loose and it's coming this way. Time to get out of here!" She and Alex found everyone from the rescue team and sent them running toward the forest.

But Crow stayed back as the royal tiger continued attacking injured bystanders who couldn't get away. People screamed. Crow reached into his pocket and pulled out his slingshot and a handful of stones. With a troubled look on his face, he loaded a small stone and took aim, then fired. It got the tiger's attention.

Crow stepped toward it and reloaded, this time with a big rock. The tiger recognized its enemy and stalked him. Crow waited. The rest of the rescue team turned from a distance to see what was happening.

"Crow!" screamed Fifer. "No! Look out!"

Crow took careful aim and pulled the stone back as far as he could, his hand shaking. The tiger came at him. He let the stone fly.

It hit the creature between the eyes. The tiger roared angrily, then retreated to nurse his wounds. Crow turned and ran to join his team.

"At least he's distracted," said Crow when he reached them. "Enough to give the people a chance to get away."

"Wow," said Seth. "That was really brave."

Crow didn't answer. Instead he cringed as he watched the battle, his face drawn. He hated fighting. But he'd do anything to protect his friends, just like they'd done for him so many times in the past. Soon one of the king's uniformed soldiers was able to stun the loose tiger long enough to reattach him to the chariot.

The rescue team retreated farther to the edge of the square, where the buildings began. There they watched from behind an abandoned wagon as the king's soldiers fell at the hands of the Revinir's soldiers.

Eventually the Artiméans slipped away to the forest again, all together this time.

After the blue soldiers had fought off the last of the green and declared victory, they descended on the princess's chariot and looted the jewels that encrusted it. Leaving the dead scattered, one soldier lifted and turned a particular cobblestone in the square near where Dev's market booth had been. The Revinir's elevator rose. The victorious soldiers piled in, helping their wounded.

The last one in grabbed Princess Shanti's crown and held it high in triumph. They left her dead body on the ground in the middle of the square.

A Change in Plans

The end of the day drew near, but Thisbe's work wasn't done. She bottled the new liquid alone, lost in her thoughts. The images of her ancestors that had overwhelmed her after taking in the bone broth occasionally flitted through her mind, making little sense. Yet the Revinir hadn't experienced anything after drinking the ancestor broth. Why hadn't this same thing happened to her? Thisbe wondered if it was because the woman wasn't a descendant of the royal black-eyed people.

It made Thisbe thoughtful—was her lineage the real reason the Revinir wanted Thisbe to join her in taking over the land? To use her somehow because of who her powerful ancestors were, like she wanted to use the dragons' power?

It had to have something to do with her magical abilities, too, or the Revinir could have chosen any of the other slaves. The woman desperately wanted to be great at something, even if by association. Since she wasn't royalty, having Thisbe as an assistant—and more importantly, a *willing* assistant—was of the utmost importance to her. That much was clear. Perhaps she wanted validation. Perhaps Thisbe represented some sort of proof that she was powerful and respected because this black-eyed servant thought good of her. Knowing the incredible ego that the Revinir had, this made the most sense.

Thisbe wasn't having any of it. But she was extremely nervous. She'd nearly gasped when the woman had mentioned escaping, as if she knew full well about the plan. Was the dragon-bone marrow really that strong that the Revinir would have gained such strong intuition? Or was it just a random threat that happened to be accurate? She'd find out soon enough. She and Rohan were breaking out in a few hours. *No matter what.*

As she finished up for the day, she kept looking anxiously

for Dev. Maybe he wouldn't have to come back here after working in the market all day. She wished she'd said a more meaningful good-bye to him. And had somehow been able to hint to him that they'd be coming back for him and the others eventually. If they survived the escape.

Just then there was a ruckus among the soldiers at the door. A moment later Thisbe could hear faraway shouts from the main hallway. The soldiers ran out, and Thisbe went to the doorway. Rohan was nearing with his load of bones. He was clearly agitated.

"What's going on?" Thisbe whispered.

"Something terrible has happened," he said. "The princess came to the market and ordered the Revinir's soldiers to stand down," he said in a low voice. "She demanded to have Dev back. There was a fight, and the princess was killed."

"What? *Killed?*"

"Yes, and Dev ran off."

"He did?" She clutched her throat, feeling sick for him. "I hope he's okay."

"He ran toward the forest is what I've heard, not back to the castle. The Revinir is fuming. And I'm afraid my fears of

LISA McMANN

the past weeks will be realized. The king will surely declare war on the Revinir after this. I have no doubt. And after losing the dragons and now Dev, she will certainly welcome it. We're in for it, Thisbe. All of us."

"Oh no," Thisbe said under her breath. Stunned, she couldn't imagine what Grimere would be like in the middle of a war, or what it would mean for the black-eyed slaves.

"It's chaos in the square," said Rohan. "And it soon will be down here. It'll only get worse as time passes."

Thisbe searched his eyes. Then she peered down the hall-way. "We should leave now while everyone's distracted."

"You read my mind," said Rohan. "Is that the dragon ability?"

"No. I'm just smart. Let's get out of here."

Rohan flipped his load of bones onto the kitchen floor and rolled up his harness while Thisbe put her things away in the kitchen as usual, so nothing would seem suspicious. At the last second, Thisbe grabbed a few bottles of the ancestor broth and slipped them into her pocket. She wasn't sure why she'd taken them—perhaps they'd hold some value down the road. Then the two snuck out toward the main hallway. They could hear soldiers shouting. They reached the main passage and peered in all directions.

"We'll pretend like we're walking back to our crypts," whispered Thisbe. "It's the right time of day. We'll go one at a time so we're not seen together. And we'll just keep going."

"Maybe we should grab dragon bones to drag toward the extracting room so we look like we have a purpose for going that way," said Rohan.

"Perfect," said Thisbe. "Though it'll seem a little odd to go in that direction in the evening. But we could say the Revinir is punishing us for something. Maybe we can get by everybody without having to fight at all."

Rohan slipped his hand in hers and gave it a squeeze. "Whatever happens . . . ," he said, and trailed off.

Thisbe turned to look at him. She saw the worry in his expression. "We keep going," she said, finishing his thought.

He flashed a crooked smile. "That's not what I was intending to say, but all right."

"What were you going to say?"

"I'll tell you once we make it out of here."

With no time to waste on words, Thisbe nodded and stepped into the hallway, then moved toward her crypt like normal. Rohan waited a few minutes, then followed.

The trek back to their crypts went smoothly enough. Thisbe turned off to her hallway and Rohan to his. A few soldiers ran past Thisbe toward the elevator exit, and she could see a larger crowd of soldiers there. She slipped into her crypt and drained the last of her water from the pitcher. Then she climbed up her bone pile, sending a small dragon bone tumbling to the floor to use as an excuse. She slid down after it and reached for her harness.

As she did so, Mangrel appeared and pushed a food tray inside the room. He slammed the door shut, locking Thisbe in for the night. "Wait!" Thisbe stared at the door. "Buckets of crud!" she muttered, using one of Alex's common expressions. For a split second her heart fell, and she thought all was lost. But then she remembered.

"Rohan, wait!" she cried, turning toward the tunnel. She quickly attached the bone to her harness and started climbing again, but became hindered by it getting caught on the other bones. She had to stop to unhook it and carry it, and her panic increased. Had the crypt keeper been to Rohan's room already? Or was he gone? "Rohan!" she called again, growing frantic. She finally made it to the top. She reattached the bone to the harness and dove into the tunnel. "Rohan!" she called again, and crawled through.

Emerging into his crypt, Thisbe looked out. There at the door was Rohan . . . being held fast by the Revinir.

Breakaway

Thisbe stared at the woman.

The Revinir sneered when she saw her and realized what the tunnel meant. "Aren't you clever?"

"Leave him alone!"

The Revinir shook her head. "You've been very devious, teaching this good boy to do evil things."

"He hasn't done anything!" Thisbe said, feeling her scales rise and her body's fiery magic heat up. "Let him go."

"I will," said the Revinir. "But only if you stop your nonsensical escape and share just one of your secrets with me."

"What secrets? Which one?"

LISA McMANN

"I want to know what you learned from that broth. I know you were lying. Something happened to you. Tell me what it was!"

Rohan looked confused. Thisbe hadn't had a chance to tell him about *that* yet. She let out an exasperated noise. "It was nothing. Let go of Rohan. I'm warning you." Thisbe raised her arm and pointed at the woman. She could feel the electricity pulsing through her, ready to explode.

"Don't make me kill him," said the Revinir. "He's so good."

Rohan gulped and gave Thisbe a wild look. Thisbe realized that behind the folds of her robe, the Revinir was holding a knife to Rohan's chest. Didn't the Revinir have any dragon powers to threaten him with?

Thisbe felt her heart beating wildly. She didn't know what to do. Rohan was so close to the Revinir—what if she fired and hit him by mistake? "What do you want me to do?" she asked the crazed woman.

"I want you to join my effort to take over the entire land of the dragons. Then we'll fight against the people who betrayed you in the seven islands."

"I think you have a lot of other trouble you're going to have to deal with first, lady," Thisbe said.

The Revinir jabbed the knife against Rohan's chest, making him yelp. "Tell me what happened to you when you drank the ancestor-bone broth!"

Rohan gulped down a breath, and his eyes stretched open even wider. He gave Thisbe a hard look, and without him saying a single word, she knew he was telling her it was okay to say no.

Thisbe swallowed hard and tried to be brave. "And if I don't join you or tell you—what then?"

"I'll kill Rohan right here in front of you."

Thisbe's fingers wavered. "Okay, then," she said. Then she slowly dropped her arm, carefully watching every move the woman made. "I'll tell you."

The Revinir looked appeased. She relaxed her grip a little, and Rohan inched to one side. Quickly Thisbe threw her arm forward and pointed at the woman's neck, fingers dripping sparks. "Boom!" she cried.

A fireball burst forth and flew across the crypt. Rohan dove. The spell hit the Revinir in the chest. She flew back into the wall and dropped to the floor, but she didn't break into dozens of pieces like Thisbe had expected.

LISA McMANN

Thisbe stared for a moment, then started skidding and sliding down the dragon bones, her harness dragging the extra one along with her. Rohan scrambled to his feet and checked the woman's pulse. "She's not dead," he said wildly.

"It's her dragon scales," Thisbe muttered. "They protect her." She thought about trying to finish the woman off, but didn't want to waste an ounce of energy—she had a lot more fights to be ready for. If they started moving fast now, the Revinir might never catch up. "Let's go. We'll lock her in."

"Brilliant." Rohan grabbed his harness and slipped it on; then they went out his door as quickly as possible and closed it behind them, automatically locking the Revinir inside the crypt. Staying together now for safety, they moved as fast as they could with their cargo.

"That was quite a powerful spell," said Rohan, a bit breathless. "Thank you for saving me."

"I wasn't about to go along with her," said Thisbe. "Not for any reason. Even if nobody ever comes back for me—which is what she keeps reminding me about." She frowned, thinking about how the people of Artimé had left her here. It was deeply painful and probably always would be. But she didn't hate them for it. Not the kind of hatred the Revinir seemed to feed on and expected Thisbe to feel. Thisbe shook her head. "I don't care how evil I am. I'm not like her."

"Is she still selling you that bunk? You're nothing like her. Besides, I think she makes up half of her dragon abilities to scare us. She's got scales and a little smoke and that's all. That's my guess. Otherwise why would she need to hold a knife on me?"

"I wondered about that too." Thisbe thought the woman might have a bit more dragon power than what Rohan had suggested—some sort of mental advantage that Thisbe had felt the tiniest bit of herself ever since she'd drunk that cup of dragon-bone broth. There was no telling the quantity the Revinir had ingested to produce such a full blanket of scales on her body. But Thisbe was quite sure the ancestor-bone broth hadn't done anything for the woman like it had for her. It was intriguing that the Revinir wanted to know so badly what had happened after she'd forced it down Thisbe's throat, as if she expected it to be something very important. And perhaps it was. Thisbe hadn't had time to contemplate the images she'd seen, but they remained burned in her mind as solidly as her own memories. But she might never know their significance now.

They passed through an intersection with only a few suspicious glances and hurried on toward the river. When the soldiers were out of earshot, Thisbe looked at Rohan. "She made me drink the ancestor-bone broth."

"So I gathered," Rohan said gently, and studied her face. "How ghastly that must have been. Are you okay?"

"I'm—I'm not sure. The Revinir threw it in my face. I didn't swallow much, but enough, I guess. It felt . . ." She recalled the dizzy feeling and stumbled in the hallway. Rohan reached out and steadied her arm. "It felt weird," Thisbe said. "I saw some things. Like images of things I've never seen before, but now I feel eerily like I've experienced them. It's hard to explain."

"I'm really sorry."

"Thanks." Thisbe was quiet for a time as they moved along as quickly as they could. They were both hungry and weak, not having eaten since dinner the previous day. How Thisbe wished she'd grabbed some food off her tray after the door had closed. But she hadn't thought of it in her panic. She had the ancestor broth, but she'd rather trade it for food than drink it.

Her mind turned back to the day. "The Revinir told me there are other dragons somewhere."

"Yes, I believe that. When I was a child, my mother and father told me about the ghost dragons beyond the forest—they were something to be feared. Is that what your dragons were like? Wild and fierce?"

"Not to us, because we are at peace in the seven islands. For now, anyway. The Revinir wants to take over the rule there, too."

"She makes a lot of plans," said Rohan. "But she's barely conquered one city here, and now that's in jeopardy."

"I thought everyone was afraid of her."

"They are. It's because she's so secretive and sneaky. She managed to capture dragons and build an army right under their feet—the people up there fear the unknown. How big is her underground army? How strong is she? How rich? How many dragons are under her control? No one knows because they can't get in."

"How did you find that out? From the soldiers?"

Rohan nodded. "And other newer children when they come in—I try to find a way to question them."

"You are very popular. I wish I could learn the common

language so I can speak to the others. I've only picked up a few words so far."

"I can teach you once we're out of here."

Once we're out of here. Thisbe bit her lip anxiously. They both grew somber and hurried on, knowing they might not ever get out of here. And now that the Revinir knew of their secret tunnel, they'd most certainly be kept far apart if they got caught.

At the next intersection, two soldiers stopped them, a man and a woman. "Where are you going at this time of night?" the woman asked.

Rohan smiled to appear sheepish. "The Revinir is punishing us again. I'm too friendly—it's really becoming a hazard to my rest time." He laughed, and the male soldier gave a reluctant smile. The female soldier remained stern but didn't press him.

"Has anyone found the traitor who ran away?" Rohan asked them.

The woman remained suspicious. "Not yet. What do you know about him? Did he tell you of these plans?" She looked at Thisbe. "How about you? You worked with him."

"I had no idea. I despised him. We barely spoke."

The woman studied Thisbe, then stepped aside. "Go on, then. Don't let the Revinir catch you talking together or you'll have even more work to do."

"You make an excellent point," said Rohan. "Thank you for the advice." They continued on in silence, with Rohan dropping back from Thisbe for appearances until they made the next turn. All they had left now was the group of guards at the river exit, and there was no telling how many were there—with any luck at least some of them would've been called away to help with the wounded soldiers from the square and the search for Dev.

Thisbe was quiet, wondering if Dev had known about the princess coming for him. She doubted it greatly—his earlier heartbreak had been too real to fake. Thisbe could tell that much just from her time studying acting with Samheed. It took a lot of studying to appear that realistic when pretending to cry. She was sure Dev hadn't ever had the opportunity to act in his life. He was manipulative, sure. But he'd tried fighting off those tears with all his might, and he hadn't succeeded. She believed the princess must have surprised him by showing up at the market. The thought made her angry. Princess Shanti hadn't been nice to Dev. She'd used him as a whipping boy, making him take punishment for the wrongs she'd done. That wasn't a friendship. If Dev considered that to be what friends do to each other, he had no understanding of the meaning of the word.

In that moment, thinking on friendship, Thisbe's heart wrenched. She missed Fifer and Seth. She missed her writing class with Lani and her dance class with the lounge band and her fencing class with Kaylee, which she'd only just begun. She longed to see Aaron again—he'd always made her feel better when Alex had been angry with her and Fifer. And even as confused and upset as she was about no one coming to rescue her, she still missed Alex, and she felt terrible about leaving like they'd done. She knew he loved her and Fifer dearly. A little too dearly, but was that all bad? She bet Dev would give anything to have someone care so much for him. Something had to have happened for Alex and the others not to have come after her. "I hope you're okay out there," she said under her breath.

By now Rohan had caught up with her. "What's that?"

"Nothing." They continued on. When the sound of the

river became evident, Thisbe began flexing her fingers and trying to work up some anger to cover the melancholy feelings she had. It didn't take long—she just needed to think about that morning, when the Revinir had ambushed her with the broth.

Rohan glanced sideways at her and stayed quiet, seeing she was concentrating. Soon they came up to the narrow hallway where they'd need to turn. They stopped to look all around, and then Rohan, growing anxious, asked Thisbe what she thought the best plan was.

Thisbe had forgotten that she'd never told him. She'd thought of it two nights ago but hadn't seen him since then, and with the excitement about Dev and with the Revinir, she'd forgotten all about the fact that he was approaching this without insight or instructions.

"When we get within sight of the soldiers," Thisbe said, "unhook your dragon bone and leave it behind, but keep your harness on. We'll need it later."

"Okay," said Rohan. "To get across the river?"

"Possibly. If not that, we'll need them eventually for

something, I'm sure." She tapped her lips, then said, "We're going to have to fight them. I'm not sure how many good shots I have before I start shooting worthless sparks. I should have several, but I haven't eaten anything since yesterday, so I'm not feeling terribly strong. We'll just have to wait and see. I'll go for the biggest ones first. Stay out of my line of fire, but if you can do anything at all to help, that would be grand. I wish you had a weapon."

Rohan bent down and pulled up his pant leg. There was a dagger, tied to his leg. "Like this?"

"Where'd you get that?"

"I lifted it off a soldier yesterday. I figured we might need it."

"Well done," said Thisbe. A spark of hope grew inside her. Maybe they'd have a chance. "Stay back until they come at us. We may need to make a break for it past them. Then stick close to the left wall. If we're lucky, we won't get wet at all."

Rohan raised an eyebrow while Thisbe detailed the rest of her plan. When Rohan was clear on the procedure, they locked eyes for a moment, then moved forward and went around the corner.

There were five soldiers there, guarding the river exit. As Thisbe headed toward them, Rohan turned sharply. "Thisbe!" he whispered.

She looked back. The two guards from the last intersection were running toward them from behind, and the five in front of them had noticed them coming. They were surrounded.

The Plan Backfires

I t's now or never," Thisbe said quietly. "Let's go!" She
stayed far away from the soldiers, hoping the distance
would give her better aim, then shot a ball of fire at the
largest soldier by the river. It exploded on his chest and,
like the snake in the desert, he flew into dozens of pieces that
mostly landed in the river. "Whoa," said Thisbe. She let out a
breath. "Okay. That's one down."

The soldiers tried to figure out what had just happened, but
they were flabbergasted and couldn't make sense of it.

Thisbe felt terrible. But she had to continue. She used a little
less power on the next one, knocking him to the ground almost

as easily. Even if the remaining three didn't understand magic, they knew enough to rush at the source of it. The closer they got, the poorer Thisbe's aim was. She pointed again, her finger burning and throbbing, and shot off another fireball. It slammed into a soldier's legs and flipped her up into the air. She crashed to the floor, conscious and crying out, but unable to get up.

Meanwhile Rohan took on the two advancing from behind. He yelled out an apology, then punched the woman in the face, dropping her. He looked at the other guard, who was one of his friends, and just gave him a pleading look. "Please, Gustav," he said. "Just give us a chance."

The man looked uncertain for a long moment, then sighed heavily. "All right. Go, before I change my mind." He dropped to the ground, faking an injury.

"Thank you," said Rohan. He turned quickly to help Thisbe with the remaining two soldiers.

Thisbe's finger was black with soot and searing with pain. She tried her other hand and shot off another medium-size ball of fire. It missed wildly. She wished she'd practiced with that hand. She tried a second time and missed again as the two soldiers closed in.

Rohan came running, brandishing his dagger. The soldiers had swords and ran at them, leaving Rohan trying to dodge and weave without getting hit, and trying desperately to get close enough to get a jab in himself. He had no experience, though he was pretty good at avoiding the sword.

Thisbe slipped past them toward the river and turned around, shooting off sparks with her eyes when the guards spun around to go after her. A pair of sparks slammed into a soldier's eyes and he cried out, covering them and moving about in serious pain, unable to see. Thisbe quickly dispersed some more sparks at the remaining guard, aiming for and hitting her hand. She dropped the sword and Rohan moved in, slamming his knee into her stomach and grabbing her sword. But she dropped to the ground gasping for breath, and he held off hurting her further.

"Come on!" said Thisbe. "Quickly!"

They ran to the river and stood at the edge. Thisbe quickly cast invisible hooks, like the one outside her bedroom window in the mansion, just above the water line, putting them all the way across. Then she cast another line of them at shoulder height.

"One of the soldiers is getting up," said Rohan under his breath.

Thisbe glanced back. "You go across first. I can swim better than you in case they knock me in. Just feel around on the wall for the hooks, and trust me. They'll hold you fine. Step on the low ones and grab on to the high ones and walk across." Thisbe turned and shot sparks at the soldier coming at them. The woman cried out in pain but kept coming.

Rohan reached out, feeling for the first hook. When he found it, he grabbed on, then moved his foot above the water along the rock wall, trying to find the foothold.

"No hurry or anything," said Thisbe, seeing another soldier stirring.

"I'm trying to go as fast as I can," said Rohan.

Thisbe tried a wrong-handed throw and ended up accidentally shooting an invisible hook instead of a fireball at the woman. It apparently struck her, and she yelped and reached for her nose. Blood streamed down.

Thisbe was getting tired. She didn't have any sparks left. She glanced over her shoulder at Rohan, who was reaching for the next hooks. He needed to go faster. But if he faltered and slipped, he'd be dead. Thisbe didn't want to rush him.

A second soldier was getting up now. Thisbe ran at the man, who swung his sword at her. She jumped, but the blade caught her in the lower leg, slicing into her. "Ouch! Hurry, Rohan!"

"I'm trying!"

Thisbe summoned all her strength and sent a weak fireball from her burning finger. It hit its mark, dropping the man temporarily. But the woman soldier was moving more quickly again.

"Okay, Thisbe!" Rohan shouted at the last set of hooks. "Come on!" He jumped to safety.

Thisbe ran for the wall, then placed a glass spell in front of the woman who was chasing her. She banged into it and recoiled, giving Thisbe enough time to turn and reach for the first hook. Her fingers were growing numb from the burning pain, but she swiped them along the wall, desperate to find it. Finally she felt it and grabbed on. She put her foot out and slid it along the wall.

"Look out, Thisbe!" shouted Rohan.

Thisbe couldn't look. Her foot struck the first hook and

LISA McMANN

she pulled herself onto it, then, shaking, reached for the next ones. Stretching precariously, she turned her head to see the man maneuvering around the glass barricade and coming toward her.

"Thisbe!" screamed Rohan.

The soldier lifted his sword and batted the side of it against Thisbe's hand on the first hook. She shrieked in pain and let go, balanced for an instant on one foot. Then the soldier struck her again, and she plunged backward into the rushing river.

More Trouble

Thisbe hadn't had time to take a breath. She choked and sucked in a mouthful of water and flailed as the river's current whipped her upside down. She couldn't find her bearings. She couldn't tell where the surface was. All she knew was that she didn't have much time before she'd be swept under the wall.

Finally she righted herself and surfaced, the wall coming fast at her. Coughing and sputtering, she lifted her arms and turned her face, and slammed into it. Her fingers raked at the sheer stone as she tried to find something to hold on to. It was that or be forced under.

"Hook," she cried, but it didn't appear where she needed it. She was slipping, her legs and midsection already pulled beneath. The only thing holding her here was the pressure of water against her back, pressing her face and chest against the wall just above the surface. But the river's grasp on her legs was strong. She took a deep breath and continued to struggle as it pulled her down an inch at a time.

"Thisbe! I'm here!" Rohan yelled. "Reach for me! Grab my harness!" He was safely on the far bank, throwing the end of his harness to her, but it was too far away. Thisbe couldn't get there, and she couldn't let go of the wall to reach for it.

When her hands slipped, she submerged and was swept under the wall. She cast a glass spell in front of her and immediately slammed into it feetfirst, her knees buckling. It stopped her and kept her from being swept away, but she couldn't swim upstream against a current like this, and she wasn't sure how far under the wall she'd gone. Blindly she cast another glass spell in front of the one that was there, making the glass twice as thick and putting her a half inch closer to where she needed to be.

She could hold her breath for a long time, but was it long

LISA McMANN

enough to cast enough glass spells to inch her way back into the hallway?

She tried again to cast hooks, and this time she managed to place two of them on the rock above her. She reached for them and pulled herself against the current. Then two more. Once again she could hear Rohan shouting—he had no idea that Thisbe could survive underwater for so long, and she knew he must be beside himself. But she couldn't think about him right now. She hung on to the hooks and pulled her legs up to her chest, then cast another glass spell to push off against with her feet and to stop her from losing the ground she'd gained. Then she cast two more hooks and nearly reached the hallway wall. She gripped them and pulled with all her might, until finally her head was back in the hallway. She used her chin as leverage and her face broke the surface. She sucked in a big breath, then quickly cast more hooks on the wall. Reaching up, she found them and grabbed hold. She pulled her body along with her, casting another set of hooks just above the surface toward Rohan's side of the river. She moved sideways one hook at a time, fighting the current, her arms aching. She could hear his muffled shouts, and then she felt something hit her in the head.

It was his harness, in a loop. Thisbe grabbed on, trying to slide her arm through the loop, and managing to hook it around her elbow. "Got it!" she cried, her voice ragged. When it grew taut, she let go of the hooks.

Rohan pulled her to his side of the river. When she reached it, he got on his knees and yanked her up and onto the passageway floor. He rolled her over.

She looked up at him and coughed. "Thanks."

"How are you possibly alive?" he exclaimed. Then he glanced across the river at the soldiers, and his face changed. "Oh no," he muttered, getting up. The one who had batted Thisbe into the river was coming across on the original invisible hooks like Rohan had done. "Get up, Thisbe. Look!"

Thisbe lifted her upper body and turned to see what was happening. Then she held her hand up at the hooks. "Release!" she said weakly. The invisible hooks apparently disappeared, for the soldier plunged into the water and was swept away, never to be seen again.

LISA McMANN

"Gods of nature!" muttered Rohan as he watched the soldier disappear. "Who are you?" His face was stricken, and he looked to Thisbe to know what to do next.

Safe for the moment, Thisbe released the other spells so the soldiers couldn't use them, and slowly got to her feet, dripping wet. Together she and Rohan moved toward the fresh air. By now it was nearly dawn, and they'd made it across the river.

When they reached the exit, they peered out to see where their journey would take them next. The sheer wall of rock, almost perpendicular the ground, landed at the edge of the crater lake, hundreds of feet below them. Thisbe's stomach turned—her fear of heights hadn't magically gone away. She swallowed hard and stepped back. "Blurgh," she muttered, trying to calm her butterflies.

"Now what do we do?" asked Rohan, still rattled. He didn't look excited about the prospects either. It seemed impossible.

Thisbe took a few deep breaths and shook out her arms, which felt weak after performing so much magic and struggling in the river. How was she going to climb down from here? She glanced back at the soldiers, two of whom were helping the remaining injured ones now. The one that had let Rohan go was one of them, and he refused to look up at the escapees. It seemed strange that no new soldiers were coming to this area. Hadn't anyone gone to summon help? Or had they given up on the two and simply considered them a loss?

Perhaps there would be soldiers waiting for them by the time they reached the bottom. Then again, Thisbe imagined the soldiers would never expect them to make it down alive. So it seemed most likely that they'd ended pursuit to spare their own lives.

Thisbe took another deep breath and let it out, collecting her thoughts. "Okay, well. We have to climb down, that's what. And it would be best to make it down before it's bright enough out for anyone to see us. Hook your harness to mine."

While Rohan connected the harnesses, Thisbe got on her hands and knees at the edge of the opening. She assessed the situation, with only shadows to hint at the variations in the wall, then carefully placed four invisible hooks directly to one side of the opening, where she expected she'd need her hands and feet to go in order to swing out of the mouth of the cave.

Thisbe glanced at Rohan. "Are you ready?"

Rohan's gray face was tinged with green, but he nodded.

Thisbe reached out sideways for the first handhold. She found it and grabbed on. "Watch where I go so you have an idea of where the hooks are. Okay?"

Rohan nodded again and gulped hard.

"And we'll move one at a time. If one of us falls, the other has to be hanging on tightly if we're going to have a chance of surviving this."

"My God," whispered Rohan. "You don't seem scared. Why in the world aren't you petrified? I'm shaking."

"I'm terrified," Thisbe admitted. "But we don't have any choice. Unless you want to go back?"

"No. We need to continue."

"Okay. Here I go. Watch the harness ropes so we don't get tangled." Thisbe sat on the edge and let her feet dangle out. Hanging on to the first hook, she slowly slid out, reaching her foot to find the invisible hook that was there somewhere. She felt the blood drain from her face and tried not to think about the height. She'd done something far worse before with Hux and Fifer and Seth. Now at least she'd remembered this spell.

As she slipped farther and farther off the edge of her seat, she began waving her foot, trying to find the hook. Finally her toe struck it. She relocated the hook and rested her toe on it, then eased her upper body out and started to reach toward the other handhold. "This is the absolute worst thing I've ever willingly done in my life," she muttered, then gasped and swung out. Her foot stayed solid as she pivoted and reached wildly for the other hook, slamming her hand into it hard. Fingers stinging, she found it again and grabbed on, pulling her face and body close to the rock wall. "Phew," she breathed. Then she found the second foot hook. She rested for a moment, her cheek against the cool rock, then turned her head and looked at Rohan. She blew out a breath from deep in her chest and tried to smile.

He looked back at her, fearful.

With her body frozen in terror, she wasn't sure if her smile had translated. "Everything's great," she assured him. She made another set of hooks next to the first set, and began the process of moving sideways, lifting her line of harness over one of the hooks to help in case either of them fell. "Eventually we'll go down one below the other, like descending a ladder," she explained, "but let's just get you out here first."

Rohan nodded. He found the first handhold, then began sliding out and searching for the first foothold like Thisbe had done. "This is utterly grim and horrifying," he muttered. "I'm not sure why I've become your friend."

Thisbe laughed softly, glad he was trying to make a joke. "You've really gotten yourself into a mess with me," she said.

"I had no idea you could do all of this magic," said Rohan. "You are a goddess, and I am but a mortal boy of no significance who will surely die in moments." He connected with the foothold a little easier than Thisbe, as he was taller and it wasn't quite as far of a reach for him.

"You're fine." Thisbe watched him and realized the conversation seemed to be helping him cope. "Just wait until you see me make things come alive. I didn't try it with the bones for obvious reasons."

Rohan managed a smile before he swung out and dangled precipitously for an instant, then hit the rock wall chest-first. He made a noise and flailed, panicking a little.

"Your handhold is right next to mine," Thisbe said, trying

to stay calm. "You're doing great." If he fell, she wasn't at all certain she could support his weight. The points of the hooks dug into the soles of her shoes a bit, but it wasn't the most uncomfortable thing Thisbe had ever endured, though it might be by the time they neared the bottom. Rohan found the top hook and gripped it tightly. He was breathing hard. "Was it really necessary to make the hooks invisible? What was the thinking there?"

"Not my spell," said Thisbe, eyeing him. "Are you doing okay?"

"Yes, for now," said Rohan, panting. "Tell me more about something. Anything. Your world. I don't care what." He pushed his face into the wall and couldn't slow his breathing. "Help me," he said.

"Try taking one deep breath," Thisbe said. "That's what my friend Seth would suggest. He has trouble breathing sometimes when he panics. It just happens. It's real, though, and he says it feels awful, but it's going to be okay. One deep breath, if you can, and blow it out."

Rohan tried to do what she suggested.

Thisbe told him a little bit more about Seth while she

LISA McMANN

planted two more sets of hooks, one set directly below each of them, equidistant apart like a ladder so it would be easier to find them. "The hardest part is over," she told Rohan. "You made it out. Still okay?"

Rohan nodded. He took in a couple more breaths and blew them out as slowly as he could. "My arms . . . and legs . . . are rubber."

"That's just how they feel on the outside. Inside you have strong muscles from all the work you've done. They won't fail you now." She watched him for a moment as his breathing evened out. "Your next hooks are just a couple feet directly below the first set. Let's do this together. Which foot do you want to start with?"

"Left," said Rohan.

"Okay. Here I go. Did I ever tell you about the Island of Graves? It's covered in saber-toothed gorillas." Thisbe found her left foot hook and moved to the right foot.

"No," said Rohan, copying her when she was solidly in place. "I'm quite sure I'd remember that. Tell me."

As Thisbe talked about the Island of Graves and how

Kaylee had lived there in a tree for a year before Alex, Sky, and Aaron had rescued her, they moved down another set of hooks. Thisbe kept planting new ones directly below the existing ones as they went, and soon both of them became a bit more comfortable.

"How did you stop yourself from being swept down the river back there?" asked Rohan after a while. "I thought you were lost for good and I was stuck forever."

Thisbe told him about the glass spell and how she'd used it to make walls to push herself back against the current. Then she told him how most people in Artimé could hold their breath for several minutes.

The edge of the sky tinged orange, and while the two of them remained in the shadow of the wall, at least they could see the ground. But their limbs were growing weaker. It became harder for Thisbe to tell stories because it was wearing her out, so she stopped. Every step required concentration on their shaking legs.

By the time they were two-thirds of the way down, they were spent and beginning to really worry they wouldn't last.

LISA McMANN

Thisbe couldn't place her hooks properly anymore, and both of them slipped at least once. The bottoms of their feet became tender and painful.

But they couldn't stop. Eventually, because of how taxing the magic was becoming, Thisbe stopped making double ladders and moved over to Rohan's ladder. That helped her magic fatigue, but they were exhausted all around. They'd been up all night and hadn't eaten in ages. At one point, the volcano in the lake erupted with a huge blast of water, scaring them both—they'd never been so close to it when it had gone off before. After the water had slapped the lake, a fireball flew out. The spout spewed lava and a second fireball. Then after some time, the volcano plunged into the water and disappeared. "We have one of those in our world too," said Thisbe. "Pirates used to live under it in a big glassed-in world." The image of a pirate ship flitted into her mind—the same one from when she'd taken the ancestor broth—but it disappeared, and with her exhaustion, she soon forgot about it.

Rohan couldn't respond. They continued, fighting through pain and weakness.

Finally they made it to the ground. The sun was coming

up. They looked around for soldiers but saw no one. Then they crawled on shaky limbs to the edge of the lake to drink some water. Soon they took to the thick foliage beside it and collapsed under some bushes, unable to go any farther without rest.

Before they fell asleep, two giant shadows passed over them, heading straight for the opening to the catacombs. But the brush hid everything from view.

Mass Confusion

The Artiméans had spent a troubled night in the forest, with Talon and Simber keeping careful watch over the others while they slept. They'd all hoped Kitten was safe after the unexpected ruckus and would make it to the elevator sometime during the night. They were comforted by the fact that she was so tiny she wouldn't be noticed, and even if someone stepped on her, she had more lives left.

Before dawn the first wave of the rescue team set off toward the cave entrance: Talon flying with Alex, and Fifer and Crow in the hammock being carried by the falcons. They rose above the trees and swept over the quiet city and the empty square. Few signs of the previous evening's fight remained. Talon and Alex headed to the hill beyond the city square, in the direction of where they'd seen the smoke. Fifer commanded the falcons to follow Talon's lead. It took them quite some time to reach the far side of the hill where the cave entrance was, but Crow and Fifer didn't speak much. They were anxious and focused.

Fifer was a bit perturbed not to be going in the elevator entrance, which, according to what Dev had said, was much closer to where Thisbe's crypt was. But she and Seth had told the others where to look for her. Plus, Talon and Alex needed more help at this entrance, and Fifer was the only other flying option small enough to fit into the cave.

Simber would stay behind in the forest—feeling helpless, Fifer supposed. At least she didn't have to do that. Alex hadn't even suggested leaving her behind. It was a relief to really and truly be doing this without him always telling her no. She finally had a chance to show him what she could do. She hoped she wouldn't mess up.

When Talon and the birds rounded the hill, the quiet crater lake came into view. There was no volcano in sight, not that

LISA McMANN

this team was expecting to see one. They circled above the lake as they waited for sunrise, barely able to see anything but the outline of the shore and a stream that rushed to meet the lake. When the sky began to lighten, they finally spotted the cave-like entrance to the catacombs. They moved toward it, trying to get a look inside at what they faced, while also being careful to stay out of sight of anyone who might be looking out.

"Do you hear that?" asked Crow when they got close to the cliff side. "That river? It's coming from inside the hill."

"That's strange." Fifer strained to listen, and she could hear it faintly. "Maybe it runs through the hill and somehow becomes that stream we saw." When they pulled up alongside Talon, Fifer told him and Alex about it. They waited for the signal to go in, all the while fidgeting and worrying.

Alex looked back at Fifer. "Are you ready?"

Fifer nodded. "Are you?"

Alex gave her a broad smile. "I've never been readier."

Crow nodded at Alex and said with respect, "It's really good to have you here, Alex."

"Thanks," said Alex. "It's good to be back." He hesitated, then added, "Once we have Thisbe, we're going to find Sky. I know everyone thinks she dead, but I don't. If Queen Eagala could survive the plunging volcano, Sky certainly must be able to. I . . . I can feel her still. Somewhere."

His face was filled with such conviction, it made Fifer believe it too.

But Crow smiled sadly. "If you say so, I'll take heart in that. Though I fear I'll never see my sister again."

At last Seth's seek spell came flying toward Fifer. It stopped and exploded into a little dance diagram that Fifer had sketched and given to him.

"Okay," said Fifer, feeling her nervousness ramping up. But she sat up quickly to remind everyone of the plan. "That's it. Let's go in. Talon, you and Alex first. We'll be right behind you. Go as fast as you can so we can get to Thisbe."

"Yes, ma'am," said Talon very seriously, and Alex nodded.

Fifer smiled to see them treating her as a valuable team member, and the nervousness washed out of her. "Let's do it."

Talon, carrying Alex, flew toward the cave opening, hovered for a moment, and disappeared inside. Fifer waited a beat, then directed Shimmer and the other birds. "Forward!" she cried. "Into the cave!"

LISA McMANN

The falcons turned sharply. Crow and Fifer sat up so they could see over the edge of the hammock. Crow held his sling-shot ready, though he hoped he wouldn't have to use it. Fifer fingered the spell components in her vest pockets, knowing by heart where each kind was placed. She was ready to take down anybody in her way.

Back in the city square, Samheed, Lani, Kaylee, Carina, Seth, and Thatcher waited, trying to guess exactly where the elevator would come up based on where Seth's seek spell to Kitten had gone down. It seemed to be taking her some time to figure out how to make the elevator move, and for a little while Seth worried that he'd sent Talon, Alex, Crow, and Fifer into the cave prematurely. Then he worried that something had happened to Kitten, and he began imagining all the disasters that could occur if he and his part of the rescue team couldn't get in.

But his fears were assuaged when the cylinder began to rise. The team ran over to surround the spot, armed with components in case soldiers were coming up with it, but the contraption appeared empty.

"Inside! Quickly!" whispered Lani. They flooded over and squeezed inside.

"Mewmewmew!" came a muffled sound from the top of the lever on the control panel. Kitten jumped up and down on the lever until it switched and the elevator began making a whirring sound.

"Kitten!" Seth cried, reaching out to her. "You did it. Great job! Come here and have a rest."

Kitten climbed into Seth's hand as the elevator began dropping again. "Mewmewmew?"

No one knew what she was asking, and Simber, the only Kitten interpreter, was hiding back at the edge of the forest waiting for a sign from them. Now that they were descending, everyone focused on what they would face at the bottom.

As their eye level dropped below the ground, they were horrified to see dozens of soldiers watching the elevator and waiting for them—no doubt they'd noticed it going up a moment before.

The rescue team was poised to fire spells from their cramped positions through the opening. As soon as they could cast an accurate spell, Samheed and Lani fired clay shackle

LISA McMANN

components at the nearest two soldiers. The elevator stopped, and they shoved the shackled ones out of the way. Then they exited and, while each firing off a round of scatterclips, moved aside so their teammates could get out too. Some of the spells hit just right, sending multiple soldiers stacked and pinned to the wall. The soldiers, unaccustomed to fighting against magic, were so surprised they hardly tried to retaliate at first—they'd never seen nor expected anything like this before.

Behind the soldiers stretched a long hallway with several huge doors, and thanks to Dev, the Artiméans knew that Thisbe resided in one of these crypts. But was she in it now? She could be anywhere in the maze. And, unfortunately, more soldiers were arriving to keep them from finding out.

Kaylee swung out expertly with her sword, driving the soldiers back so her magical friends had room to take proper aim. She winced now and then as a spell whizzed by her ear, but she had faith that they wouldn't accidently hit her after all the training they'd done. Besides, she had other things to worry about. The soldiers had regained their senses and were fighting back hard.

The rescue team pressed forward a few steps, but another rank of soldiers came running from a side passage, pushing the Artiméans back against the elevator again. Despite making no forward progress, the mages leaned in and continued pelting the soldiers, setting off several dizzying backward bobbly heads just in time to stop from being skewered. At the moment, that was what counted the most. If they could stop the army from getting too close and capturing them, they might be able to knock some of them out of commission permanently. And hopefully Talon, Alex, Fifer, and Crow would be coming to help after a while. It was probably a good thing that they'd ended up having a head start.

As the first few soldiers' spells began to wear off and even more soldiers appeared, it became clear that the rescue team was far outnumbered, and their opponents were well trained. Samheed took a sharp hit to the side, knocking him down. Kaylee fought on, but the soldiers' swords connected with her and left her battered and bloodied.

While Seth and Thatcher covered the others, pelting the soldiers with spells, Carina dragged Samheed to safety and

LISA McMANN

called out to Kaylee, who was still struggling to fight. Kaylee gratefully dropped back behind the others and took Carina's medical kit so she could apply Henry's magical ointments to herself and to Samheed's wounds. Carina rejoined the fight.

Kitten was alarmed to see that two strong Artiméans had already fallen. Having overheard that somehow Crow and Fifer had arrived while she'd been gone and were now with Alex and Talon, she slipped out of Seth's pocket unnoticed to find them. She ran along the passageway, sniffing the air wildly in search of Crow, who, other than Fox, was her favorite. She could tell he was down here, but where? She paused at a hall-way, noticing the symbols on the wall that she'd been study-ing all along on her underground journey, and darted down it. She galloped at full Kitten speed, which was quite impressive, determined to find the others and lead them to help as quickly as possible.

Every now and then Kitten slowed and sniffed the air again, then charged up a different hallway, always seeming to follow the same red arrows. But would she find her beloved Crow before he was struck down too? She raced, veering close to the wall when more and more blue-uniformed soldiers ran past her. Sometimes she had to dart between their feet. Magically she avoided being crushed, but how long would that luck last? Despite knowing she had seven lives left, she didn't want to lose even one of them to these smelly keepers of the bones. She had to get to Crow, and fast—or there wouldn't be a rescue team left.

In Pursuit

Fifer and Crow soared into the mouth of the cave, blinking hard as their eyes began adjusting to the firelit passageway. The hammock skimmed the floor and dipped precariously into the rushing river as they crossed it. The birds rose to the ceiling to lift the cargo a little higher as they continued into the catacombs.

"Wooo!" cried Fifer, thrown backward in the hammock as the birds screamed forward. "We are cruising!"

She regained her balance and planted herself on her knees, holding on to the edge of the hammock. Crow did too, and they could finally see where they were going again. Talon and Alex were a short distance in front of them, Talon taking care not to scrape his big bronze wings or body in the narrow passageways. He held Alex around the chest, and the head mage's robe flapped in the breeze. There was no one around.

"This seems too easy," Alex called out warily to Fifer and Crow. "Something feels off. Don't let your guard down."

"Okay, Alex!" said Fifer. She grabbed a handful of scatterclips in one hand and a clay shackle component in the other. She glanced at Crow, whose jaw was set in a hard line. He held his slingshot and a sharp stone.

They flew through the hallways, Alex and Talon making split-second decisions as they tried to decipher the symbols on the walls, choosing the paths that went downhill. They saw no one for many minutes. And then they came to an intersection.

A group of soldiers heard and saw them coming, and they lined up across the hallway to stop them, swords raised. "Everyone hold on!" shouted Talon. He turned his body to shield Alex, made a fist with his free hand, and put his head down. Without slowing, Talon slammed head- and fist-first into the center of the lineup, sending several soldiers flying and skidding left and right. Alex fired off a series of backward

LISA McMANN

bobbly heads, blinding highlighters, and shackles, which cleared a wide enough path for the birds to advance without being struck down. Fifer cast her components at the remaining soldiers, hitting two and missing one, leaving him to help his fellow soldiers back to their feet.

They kept going. The soldiers charged after them but couldn't keep up.

When Talon and Alex reached another intersection, they did the same as before, and the results were just as predictable. Behind them Fifer nailed all three of her opponents this time. They pressed forward, seeing no one again for a long distance.

"I hope the others are all right," shouted Alex. He was deeply worried about them, imagining that the majority of the soldiers would be stationed near the elevator entrance since that one seemed the most vulnerable of the three.

When they neared a third intersection, spotting more soldiers on the run toward them, they heard a familiar cry. "Mewmewmew!"

"It's Kitten!" cried Fifer, looking around. "Where is she? Does anyone see her?"

Talon reversed his wings and stopped suddenly, forgetting to warn the birds. The falcons screeched and veered around him, trying and failing to stop in time. Some of them hit Alex and others crashed into the wall, causing chaos in the narrow hallway. Crow and Fifer were thrown from the hammock and found themselves rolling and scrambling among the birds to get to their feet.

Alex leaped out of Talon's grasp and ran to help them. But just as Alex, Crow, and Fifer were upright and reaching for their weapons, the soldiers from the intersection reached them and began swinging their swords, knocking them down again. More birds squawked, others lost hold of their ropes, and several scattered to save their own lives. Feathers flew everywhere. From the ground, Alex began pelting spells expertly at the enemy like he was a teenager again. Fifer grabbed a handful of components as she rolled and dodged the swords and cast freeze spells and scatterclips, trying to protect Crow, who was scrambling to get away.

Alex got up, sending a steady stream of spells at the soldiers as Talon plowed into a line of them. Then Talon chased after a few who were trying to make a run for it. With him far down the passageway, one sneaky soldier who'd been faking injury jumped to his feet. He slid behind Alex and grabbed him, holding his arms down and pressing a dagger into his back.

Alex struggled but couldn't free himself from the soldier's grasp. "Fifer!" he yelled, trying again to get loose.

The soldier jabbed the dagger harder into Alex's back, making him yelp.

Fifer turned to see what had happened. Her eyes widened. "Alex!" She took a step toward him, but the soldier jabbed him again.

"Argh!" Alex cried, then tried to wrestle free. "Stay back!"

"Fifer," said Crow urgently. "Here!"

Fifer stopped and turned to Crow.

Crow, who'd been fumbling in his pockets, pulled out the heart attack components that Scarlet had given him. He shoved them at Fifer. "Take these!" he cried. "I don't trust myself to do it right. Just say 'heart attack' when you throw one."

Fifer took them as Alex called out for help again. He had a wild, frightened look on his face that Fifer had never seen before. It scared her. But she didn't dare get closer, worried that the soldier would stab Alex again. She looked at the heart attack components, then up at her brother. The soldier was using him as a shield. Could she risk trying to hit the soldier without hitting Alex by mistake?

Alex had seen the exchange and heard what Crow had said. He stared at what Fifer held in her hand. Then he flinched and cried out in pain again as the soldier brought the dagger to his throat. "If the girl makes a move, you die," snarled the soldier in Alex's ear.

But Alex had been threatened before, many times. And he wasn't about to let this soldier kill any of them. "Fifer!" he yelled. "Do it! Use three!"

Fifer froze. She'd never even used one of these before, much less the lethal dose of three. But the soldier was threatening her brother's life. Cringing, she picked three of the heart attack components and shoved the rest in her pocket. Taking aim and praying to miss her brother, she wound up and, focusing on the soldier, let them fly. "Heart attack!"

The components sailed through the air. Alex closed his eyes and swallowed hard, holding himself deathly still. All three of the little red hearts missed Alex. But they didn't miss the soldier. They struck him right where Fifer had aimed.

The soldier's face paled, and an instant later his dagger slipped from his grasp and clattered to the ground. His body dropped next.

Alex blew out a breath and stepped away from the soldier. A moment later Talon came flying back. Fifer ran to her brother.

Shaking, Alex grabbed Fifer and hugged her hard, not letting go. She could feel his heart pounding. "That," Alex said quietly near her ear, "was brilliant work. Brave and precise and true, just as I knew you would do it. Thank you, Fifer. You've saved me."

Fifer's eyes shone. She'd saved Alex's life. And he'd trusted her to do it. He'd instructed her to use a lethal dose of a spell, knowing he was putting his own life in danger but not hesitating, believing in her to get it right. She didn't have any words to say back, but her heart soared. They released their embrace, and smiled, and Fifer nodded. "You're welcome," she managed to whisper. Alex rested his hand on her shoulder and gave it an extra-brotherly squeeze. And then they turned to see some of the other soldiers getting up to fight, and the moment was over. But Fifer knew she would never forget it.

Kitten mewed again, and Talon located her and swept her

out of the fray. Then he plowed into the soldiers who were getting up.

"Let's keep moving!" Alex shouted, running over to Talon.

Fifer signaled to the birds to regroup.

In the larger space of the intersection, Shimmer and the birds flocked together again and straightened out the hammock, then took their ropes in beak and waited. Fifer laid down one last struggling soldier with a backward bobbly head, then grabbed Crow's sleeve, and the two ran and dove into the hammock before the soldiers could revive and come after them again.

Talon swung around with Alex and tossed Kitten to Crow, who caught her and set her on his shoulder. Then Talon and Alex continued forward. The birds took off right behind.

Seeing that the hallway before them was clear, Alex turned his head to look back at Fifer. "Are you okay, Fig? That was a big spell you did."

Fifer smiled. She'd known it was a major one, and she'd thought briefly before about what it would be like to use a lethal spell like that. But in the moment she hadn't really had time to dwell on it. She knew she could do it, and she needed to

LISA McMANN

do it, so she did. But it dawned on her as they traveled through the passageway that over her lifetime, being as powerful as she was, and reading about the adventures in Artimé and knowing the stakes her brother and the others had faced in the past, this hadn't been a difficult decision at all. She hadn't hesitated, and she didn't have any regrets. She would do anything to save and protect her friends and family. And she wouldn't blink before using another lethal spell on the next enemy who threatened her brother. "I'm okay. Are you?"

"I've never felt better in my life," said Alex. "You're an excellent partner, and I'm so glad to be fighting alongside you."

"I think the same about you, Alex," said Fifer, imagining them fighting many battles together and wondering with pride what Lani would write about *her* in future books.

They exchanged a look of mutual respect and admiration. Fifer could tell by the expression on Alex's face that this adventure, plus the near-death experience, had truly made him come alive again in every way. Here was Alex the hero from Lani's books, right in front of her. Fifer's heart soared—seeing him in battle for the first time that she could remember, his spirits so high. She loved every part of this.

And he'd trusted her with his life. She was feeling just as euphoric as he most certainly was.

"Mewmewmew!" cried Kitten from Crow's shoulder, pointing. "Mewmewmew!"

"That way?" guessed Crow. "She's leading us to the others!"

"Mewmewmew!"

"Are we nearly there?" asked Fifer.

Kitten nodded.

"We're nearly there!" Fifer called to Alex. She looked down at Kitten. "Are there any more intersections with soldiers first?"

Kitten nodded wildly. She held up her paw and extended a single tiny claw.

"One more intersection?" Crow asked.

Kitten smiled and nodded again. Then, her duties complete, she yawned and curled up in the folds of Crow's shirt.

"One more intersection, and then we'll be there," Fifer called to Alex and Talon.

Crow set down his slingshot, took Kitten off his shoulder and slid her into his pocket so she could sleep. "Well done, Kitten," he said, and she began to purr.

As they neared the next intersection, they couldn't see any soldiers.

"Perhaps they've gone to the elevator area to fight," Talon said, sounding worried. He went forward into the large space, and suddenly a group of men and women jumped into view. Swords slammed into the bronze man, clanging like a thousand ancient bells, sending him hurtling off course. Startled and spinning, Talon shielded Alex the best he could and tried to take the brunt of the swings.

Behind them the falcons put on their air brakes, but they didn't have enough time. The hammock swung wildly, which messed up Fifer's aim, and she accidentally sent a clay shackles component into Alex. It pinned his arms to Talon so he couldn't throw.

"Whoops, sorry!" said Fifer, starting to panic. "Release!" she called out, freeing him. Then she pelted the soldiers with scatterclips and blinding highlighters. She was starting to run out of components. As she fumbled with the bag to reload her pockets, a sword went flying through the air straight at them, knocking two falcons to the ground and continuing toward the hammock. Crow, who'd turned to fire off his slingshot at a soldier, didn't see it coming. The sword hilt barely missed Fifer and smashed into Crow's head. He slumped against Fifer, unconscious.

Fifer shrieked his name, then kept flinging components until they were out of immediate danger. When she had a moment, she looked at Crow again and gasped. He had a lump on his head the size of a platyprot egg. "Oh no!" She checked him over and was relieved to see he was breathing, just knocked out.

"Let's push through this mess!" Talon called out.

"Right behind you!" Fifer said, signaling to Shimmer. The birds regrouped, leaving their two fallen ones behind, and diligently followed Talon.

When they finally neared the elevator passageway, they were relieved to hear sounds of battle—which meant the Artiméans were still alive and fighting. But then they saw that their team members were either wounded or doggedly fighting the mass of soldiers, looking like they were about to collapse.

Talon landed and set Alex on the ground. Fifer jumped out of the hammock, leaving Crow, still unconscious, for the birds to protect. Talon began punching soldiers left and right, and Alex and Fifer worked as partners, flinging spells at the rest of them, giving the others a chance to recover and take a breath.

They fell into a routine, as if knowing instinctively what the other was about to cast and working to enhance the effects.

With Talon's great help, finally all the soldiers in the elevator area were down and unmoving, and the Artiméans had a chance to fix up their wounds.

Alex and Fifer exchanged a satisfied look. "Good work," Alex said, giving her a quick side hug.

"You too," said Fifer, squeezing him around the waist and peering at the thin cut on his neck where the threatening soldier's dagger had left its mark. The blood had dried by now, and the wound looked like it would heal fine on its own.

"Let's go help the others," said Alex. "And check on Crow. He's going to have quite a headache when he wakes up."

Fifer nodded. The faster the others were back on their feet, the sooner they could start their search for Thisbe. They tracked down Carina's medical bag and helped to administer the healing salves to whoever still needed them.

After a while Crow regained consciousness and left the hammock to help Fifer and Alex. Fifer gave him some medicine for the huge lump on his forehead, and soon everyone had recovered enough to continue with the quest.

"Let's find Thisbe," said Alex. He quickly assigned duties pertaining to the new job of breaking down crypt doors. Talon led the way with Alex and Fifer right behind. Lani and Samheed followed.

"We'll take care of these goons in the hallway so they don't wake up," said Carina. She and Thatcher showed Seth how to do a permanent freeze spell, and the three began to freeze the many soldiers in place.

Talon went to the first crypt and knocked tentatively on the door to see what it was made of. "Clear the area!" he called, in case there was a person behind the door. Then he smashed his shoulder into it, breaking the lock and ripping the door off its hinges. He stumbled inside the crypt. A frightened girl with black eyes screamed and cowered behind some bones, but it wasn't Thisbe.

"Come out, come out," Fifer said, running inside and waving the girl toward the door. "It's okay. Do you know where Thisbe is?"

The girl looked puzzled and shook her head, then said something in another language.

Fifer shrugged helplessly. "Sorry," she said. "I don't

LISA McMANN

understand. *Thiz-bee*," Fifer repeated, slower this time, in case the girl would at least recognize her sister's name. But the girl shook her head again.

"Let's keep going," said Alex, glancing around uneasily. "I don't want to spend any more time down here than we have to. There may be more soldiers. And I'd like to get out before the Revinir learns we're here."

Talon led them to the next crypt. He smashed in the door like he'd done before, and this time Samheed ushered out a bewildered black-eyed boy. He and the girl they'd freed began talking fearfully together when they saw each other. They pointed to Talon, who was clearly unlike anything they'd ever seen before, and then at the soldiers being frozen on the floor. They started sneaking away.

Lani stopped the black-eyed children and tried to convince them that they were safe as Talon freed another boy and two more girls. But with the frightening happenings and scary bronze-winged man breaking down doors, combined with not being able to speak their language, it was impossible. The five of them pushed past the Artiméans and ran through the catacombs, out of sight. Lani and Samheed gave up trying and let them go.

LISA McMANN

Talon continued to the last crypt in the hallway.

"This has got to be hers," said Fifer, "unless Dev lied. I wouldn't put it past him." She stood on one side of the door, watching anxiously as Talon stepped back and prepared to break in. From the other side Alex strained to see. With extra exuberance, Talon smashed against the door and pushed it aside, then got out of the way so Alex and Fifer could be the first to enter.

"Thisbe!" Alex called out, going a few steps inside the dark room. "Are you in here?"

Fifer moved in behind him, trying to look around him and over his shoulder. "Thisbe!" she said. There was no reply.

At first Alex didn't see anyone at all—there was only a stub of a lighted candle near the door, its fire being drowned by wax. Imagining how scared Thisbe must be, he called out again. "Thisbe, it's me, Alex. We've come to take you home."

He thought he saw movement off to one side, and he stepped toward it. "Thisbe?" he said softly.

From out of the shadows came a horribly familiar face— it was the face that had plagued his nightmares for a decade. "Thisbe isn't here anymore," said a familiar voice. "But I'm glad we finally meet again."

Alex sucked in a sharp breath. He fumbled for a spell component.

From behind him Fifer had heard the woman's voice, and then, looking around him to see who it was, she witnessed the Revinir's scales beginning to glow. She screamed, "Alex, look out!" and reached for her vest pockets.

But they had no time to react. A long, thin spear of dragon fire shot out of the Revinir's mouth, striking Alex in the center of his chest. It threw him violently backward, limbs flying, knocking Fifer into the hallway. Then he hit the floor with a crack and skidded to the doorway, the lightning-like spear sticking with him. Skewering his chest.

Alex's body came to a stop. The dragon-fire bolt faded, and the Revinir stared as if she couldn't believe what she'd done.

From the hallway Fifer shot off her last two heart attack components into the dark crypt, but forget to yell the verbal component. She couldn't tell if they hit their mark. "Help!" she called out. Blind with fear for her brother, she abandoned further attack and scrambled to her hands and knees over to him.

"Alex!" Fifer shouted as Talon leaped over them, charging

into the crypt. The Revinir slammed a dragon-fire bolt at him, too, sending him back out the doorway and crashing against the wall of the passageway, stunned.

Several of the others had all grabbed spell components by now and took cover, peering into the crypt.

Still stunned by what she'd done, the Revinir's eyes widened to see so many of her former enemies. She took another dragon-fire shot, narrowly missing Lani's forehead.

"Fire!" Lani cried, retaliating with a spell Fifer had never seen before. But Lani's wheels seemed to catch and she lost her balance and missed.

The Revinir ducked and took a few steps back, like she was worried she couldn't take all of them on.

"Heart attack!" cried Carina, and she and several others sent a round of heart attack spells at the woman.

The Revinir turned and tried to dodge the components by scrambling up the bone mountain. But there were too many to avoid. The components slammed into her, and she cringed. But then they bounced off her, causing no harm. They hit the ground and rolled around.

"Carina, help!" Fifer called out. "Alex isn't breathing!"

The Revinir looked surprised to be still standing, and took the distraction as her cue to get away. As the Artiméans let go another round of heart attack spells, the Revinir turned and deftly climbed the pile of bones, again unaffected by the components. She slipped into the tunnel and disappeared.

Lani struggled with her wheeled vehicle to get back up, but it wasn't working right. Carina and the others rushed over to Fifer and the head mage. His face was ashen. His robe had a burned spot the size of a fist on his chest. Carina tried to revive him. Samheed ran for the medical kit and brought it back.

"Alex," Fifer pleaded. "Please wake up."

"Everyone stay back," said Carina, sounding frantic. Finally Lani was able to pull herself upright, and she gently pulled Fifer next to her in the hallway so Carina and Samheed could work. And that's when Lani saw what else was happening. The permanently frozen soldiers who lined the area were beginning to move.

"Oh my," Lani whispered. She quickly looked down at her wheels and noticed her contraption no longer had the magical shine it normally had. "No. This can't be."

"What's happening?" cried Fifer, straining to see Alex's face.

Lani let go of her and pulled a heart attack spell out of her pocket. She aimed it at one of the soldiers and flung it. "Heart attack!" she cried. The component bounced off him, and he kept moving. Lani gasped. "Oh no!" One hand rose to her throat, and the other rested on the belt around her hips. She turned sharply and nearly fell again. "Alex! No!"

The others of the rescue team looked up. Kaylee rushed over when she heard Lani gasp. Talon, who'd regained his senses after being speared with dragon fire, slowly got up.

"What is it?" Samheed asked, eyes wild and fearful.

"My wheels won't move magically anymore." Then Lani pointed at the soldiers. "And look."

"What's happening?" Fifer asked again, her voice breaking. Seth came to stand by her, trying to figure out what was going on too.

"Why didn't the spells work?" demanded Talon.

There was a noise at the crypt door as Carina stopped working on Alex. Her face was drawn.

"There can only be one reason," Lani told them, voice

LISA McMANN

trembling. She started to cry. Seeing Carina's face, she pulled herself over to Fifer and took the girl's hand. "And it's only happened once before."

"No," said Samheed, as the truth came to him. "No! That's not what this is. It can't be."

But Lani continued, trying to steady her voice. "When the head mage of Artimé dies, the magical world disappears. All the magic in it, too."

"What are you saying?" cried Kaylee. "Quick, Carina—give him some more medicine! Why are you stopping?"

"It's too late," said Lani, tears streaming. "It's too late. Don't you see? The soldiers are moving. The heart attack spells don't work. My wheels won't move according to my thoughts anymore. The magic—it's already gone! See?" Blindly she took out an origami dragon. "To the elevator!" she commanded it, and sent it flying. It dropped to the floor.

Carina nodded. "Lani's right. I can't do anything for him. It's too late. He's . . . he's gone."

Thatcher stared. He tried a spell too, which failed.

Fifer was numb. Her head spun as she tried to comprehend

Dragon Bones » 390

what had happened. All she could do was stand and watch. Lani and Carina were telling the truth. It was too late.

Fifer's brother was gone. Alex Stowe, head mage of Artimé, was dead.

"We have to go immediately," said Carina in a low voice. "Before they realize we're weaponless. Talon? Will you . . . ?" She pointed at Alex's body inside the room, closed her eyes, and lowered her head. She couldn't finish.

"Yes, of course." Talon went in and picked up the mage as gently as he could.

The soldiers soon began to stagger to their feet. Kaylee kept them back with her sword so that they couldn't regroup. The people of Artimé slipped down the passageway, Samheed helping Lani move quickly. The first group of mages got into the elevator and rose out of the catacombs. They spilled into the square, where a few surprised townspeople traveled on foot. There was no market today. In the next elevator ride, Kaylee followed with Talon, who carried Alex's body.

With Fifer too distraught to instruct the birds, Shimmer ordered them to retrace their flight path to the cave exit,

LISA McMANN

carrying the empty hammock. Even with Artimé's magic gone, Fifer's birds seemed to be unaffected.

In the square, Talon ignored the townspeople who gaped at his strange bronze presence and the lifeless body in his arms, and he and Kaylee hurried off after the others to their meeting spot in the forest. There they found Simber's body frozen in place where they'd left him, all the magic gone from him, too. Crow reached into his pocket and pulled Kitten out, placing her on Simber's back. She didn't move either.

"Oh, Simber," said Lani, shaking her head. "How will we ever tell you this dreadful news?" Silently she imagined Artimé in chaos, but they were helpless to do anything without a ride across the gorge.

"Arabis's wings won't work," Samheed said, beginning to calculate all the devastation and complications that Alex's death had brought. "We're stuck here."

"There are other head mage robes," Lani said quietly. "And instructions. Alex made sure of it years ago. Claire Morning has one somewhere."

"And Aaron," said Carina. "Though he might not realize right away what happened."

"Oh, dear Aaron," muttered Kaylee, shaking her head. "He'll be devastated. But he'll do anything he can—"

"He'll be stuck on the Island of Shipwrecks," Samheed pointed out grimly. "The tube won't work. So it'll have to be Claire who restores Artimé."

Fifer and Seth stared wide-eyed, trying to follow the strange conversation, unable to understand the depth of what had just happened. All Fifer knew was that her brother Alex, whom she was just coming to understand and really enjoy, was dead. Dead! How could it be? She'd saved his life once that day, but he had died anyway. It felt so wrong. It was completely bewildering. The word "dead" echoed in her mind. She was too stunned to cry, or maybe just too numb to feel the tears.

Crow blew out a breath, recollecting what the world had been like when the last head mage had died. It was just a short time after he and Sky had arrived in Artimé. He exchanged a devastated glance with Carina, who was the only other one of them who'd been present in Artimé when it had happened. "It can't possibly be as bad this time as it was back then," he said, wanting desperately to believe it. "Can it?"

Carina pursed her lips, not knowing the answer.

LISA McMANN

"How long do you think it'll take to get the magic back?" Seth asked nervously. "Days?"

"Not that long," said Samheed firmly, but his face was troubled. "A few hours, don't you think, Lani?"

"If all goes perfectly," said Lani. "If Claire has the robe."

"And the spell," added Crow.

"Yes. The spell," said Samheed.

"We will make it through this," said Carina firmly. "We always have."

"Let's hope for that," said Kaylee through silent tears. She rested her hand on Simber's frozen neck and stroked it. Then she petted Kitten's cold porcelain back with her fingertip. "Hope is all we have."

After a silent moment, a faint sound of trumpets came from far off.

Talon lay the head mage's body on the forest floor. Crow stood beside him, all of the memories of those early days in Artimé hitting him hard. He looked down at Alex's body and the burn hole in his robe, centered on his chest. In tribute Crow raised his fist to his own chest and tapped it, a symbol of solidarity that Alex had begun using in the darkest days. Then

LISA McMANN

Crow opened his lips to speak the line that went with it but couldn't get the words out. So he said them in his heart. *I am with you.*

Carina covered Alex's body with a blanket. And they all gathered around to mourn their beloved leader. Their friend and brother.

There was nothing else they could do.

What Hope Sounds Like

When Thisbe woke up to the distant bleat of trumpets, it was dark—she and Rohan had slept the day away. Her body ached, and her stomach twisted in pain. She'd dreamed she was back home eating something delicious that the chefs had prepared. It was such a real dream that she could almost smell the food. She poked Rohan awake.

He groaned and lay there a moment. Then he eased up to sitting. "Everything hurts."

"Yes. But we made it."

Rohan nodded. "We really did." The horns sounded again

from a long way away. His eyes widened, and he sat up. "Do you hear that?"

"Yes. What is it?"

"It's . . . it's the king's call to arms. Or at least that's how I've always imagined it would sound. If it continues all evening, we'll know for sure it is."

Thisbe gave him a solemn look. "What does it mean?"

"It means the king is calling the people of Grimere to join his army and fight for the kingdom. I knew it was inevitable, especially after the Revinir's soldiers killed the princess. She was his only heir, and he's got to be sick over her death. But even sicker worrying about the kingdom falling into the wrong hands once he's gone, now that there's no offspring to take the throne."

"So . . . this is the war?" said Thisbe, alarmed. "It's happening? Like, now?"

"Not yet. He's sounding the trumpets to see how many will come to his side to fight against the Revinir. He'll want to train them and organize first."

"Oh." Thisbe relaxed a little. The thought of being stuck in the middle of a war the day after their escape was not at all appealing. She looked at her fingertips, which were still red and blistered from yesterday's battle. She pointed her forefinger at a dead leaf and let out a spark, setting it on fire. She grimaced in pain. The magic made her finger hurt more. She'd want to wait a few days at least to heal before doing that again. Thisbe put out the tiny fire, then went to get some water from the lake.

Rohan wrapped his arms around his knees and remained in his spot, deep in thought and brooding with the trumpets. Eventually the call to arms ceased, and the silence was overtaken by crickets chirping.

Thisbe returned with a fresh green palm leaf that she'd rolled into a cone and scooped water into. She offered it to Rohan.

"Thanks." He took it gratefully and drank. "What's that smell?" he asked. He sniffed the air.

"Something cooking? I thought I was imagining it. Maybe it's coming from the catacombs." Thisbe pushed the brush aside and peered out. She could see a faint glow of candle-light coming from the circular opening to the catacombs high above them.

"We've never consumed anything in the crypts that smells this delicious," said Rohan. He slapped at a bug, then peered at it curiously, like he might be tempted to eat it. He sniffed again and looked around. "There's smoke over there along the shore. A fire. Someone's camping out."

Normally Thisbe wouldn't consider approaching anyone when trying to hide from everyone. But she was growing delirious with hunger. They had no fishing equipment, and she didn't trust the unfamiliar plants enough to try eating them—the grandfathers had taught her they could be poisonous. "Let's see if we can beg for some food."

Rohan looked skeptical, but he was starving too. "Do you think people are looking for us? What if this master chef vagabond notices our eyes? We're nowhere near safe, you know."

"You're right." Thisbe hadn't really thought much farther than escaping the catacombs and getting to the ground. Now they were faced with a whole new set of problems. "I'll pretend to be a beggar and see if I can get at least a little food until we can figure something out. Give me your shirt—I'll wear it like a scarf and cover my eyes and face a little."

LISA McMANN

Rohan was hungry enough to agree. He took off his shirt, and Thisbe folded it and wrapped it around her head. "Shall I come with you?" he asked.

"Are you an actor?" asked Thisbe.

"Me? No. Why?"

"I'm an actor," Thisbe said. "I know what I'm doing. I've had a lot of training. I can play the part of a beggar and nobody will ever recognize me again. Plus, in case people were alerted to the two of us having escaped, they won't suspect as much if it's just me."

Rohan thought about it and agreed. "Just hurry before they eat all the food without us." He grinned weakly. "Be careful. Sneak up and make sure it's not a bunch of soldiers first."

"I will." The call to arms sounded again, as Rohan had predicted, and Thisbe and Rohan looked at each other uneasily. Then Thisbe slipped as quietly as possible out of the brush and went toward the smoke and the smell.

She stayed along the lake near the steep rocky hillside, and eventually she saw where the smoke was coming from. There was a fire burning in a small cave. Over the fire was a makeshift spit made from sticks and thin, scorched vines, and on the spit was a big open-mouthed fish speared from throat to tail. Thisbe didn't see anyone there tending it. She crept closer. Maybe she could steal it without having to beg.

Staying in the shadows of the rock wall, Thisbe drew near to the opening, the delicious smell making her mouth water. Slowly she peered inside the cave. No one was there. Crazy with hunger, Thisbe crept forward. She glanced over her shoulder into the dark evening. Seeing no one, she went up to the fire and touch-tested the stick that speared the fish, trying to figure out how to pick it up without burning her already scorched fingers. Remembering Rohan's shirt, she quickly unwrapped it from her head and used it like a hot pad, lifting the stick from one end. It was heavy. She hoisted it up and turned carefully, feeling a huge rush of adrenaline. She had to get out of there.

She heard a crackle of footsteps, and her heart stopped. She moved away from the light, stumbling in her haste. Before she could disappear into the darkness, a woman's angry voice called out. "Stop! You thief! Bring that back here right now!"

Thisbe froze when she heard the footsteps coming swiftly toward her. Weak and carrying a huge fish, there was no way Thisbe could outrun anybody. She turned sharply to see someone coming at her, looking fierce. Thisbe didn't know what to do—if she tried to run, the woman could follow her, and she didn't want that. She and Rohan needed to stay hidden. And she didn't want to drop the precious food. Maybe if she begged, the woman would feel sorry for her.

The woman stopped in the shadows at the edge of the fire. "Come here this instant with my fish!"

Thisbe took a few steps toward her and hung her head to keep her eyes hidden. "I'm sorry," she whispered. "I'm—I'm just very hungry." She held out the stick with the fish and stepped to the fire to put it back in place. "I don't suppose you can spare a few bites for me and my . . . uh . . . ." She thought quickly, trying to sound more pitiable. "My sick mother?"

Thisbe could feel the woman's stare nearly boring a hole through her head, but she didn't dare look up and risk capture. Finally the woman took a step closer.

Thisbe took a step backward and contemplated running for it.

"Wait," said the woman, less angry now. "Don't run." For an instant, Thisbe thought the voice sounded familiar. Was it one of the soldiers out of uniform? Someone else from the market or the prison? Or was Thisbe just out of her mind with hunger?

The woman knelt, trying to get a better look at the skinny, ragged thief in front of her, and then she sucked in a breath. "Thisbe?" she whispered. "Can it be?"

Thisbe's heart throttled. Despite her vow to keep her eyes hidden, she looked up. Her lips parted in shock, and her breath caught in her throat. She blinked and looked again, fearing a mistake due to her altered state of mind. But no—her eyes weren't playing tricks on her. A rush of hope surged inside her chest for the first time since her capture, and a gasp escaped. Someone from Artimé had come to rescue her after all.

"Sky," she whispered on a breath. "Oh, Sky. It's really you."

Fifer's and Thisbe's stories continue in

THE UNWANTEDS QUESTS

BOOK THREE
Dragon Ghosts

Turn the page for a peek. . . .

The Gray Shack

When the world of Artimé turned gray, Henry Haluki knew that Alex was dead.

The medicinal herbs he'd been picking turned to weeds in his hands, and the ground beneath his knees became hard and cracked. The enormous mansion swirled and disappeared, leaving a small shack in its place. Hundreds of Artiméans who'd been inside the mansion spilled out of the shack's doorway and burst through its windows, trying to keep from being crushed. The walls strained and bulged as if they were about to explode.

Henry stared for an instant, trying to comprehend what

was happening, and then he dropped the weeds and ran toward the chaos to help. As he went, he realized that his hospital ward and everything in it would have disappeared along with the mansion. He reached into his healer's coat pockets to see what medicines he carried with him, but those magical products had vanished too. His heart sank.

Cries and shouts rose from all over the property. It was impossible to know where to start helping. Henry looked around frantically as it dawned on him that his and Thatcher's adopted young Unwanteds were probably somewhere in the disaster. His breath caught as he thought about how scared everyone must be. With Alex gone, he had to step up.

With Alex gone. Not just away. Gone. For good.

A sharp pain speared through Henry. He slowed and stumbled forward, crumpling into the agony of the realization. A horrendous sob exploded from him, the sound of it lost in the chaotic din. *Alexander Stowe, head mage of Artimé, is dead.* Henry clutched his chest and tried to breathe, blinking the tears away. Then he got up and pushed through the growing crowd around the shack. He had to keep going.

"Henry! Over here!" Sean Ranger was inside, holding his

young son through the broken window and looking frantic. "Can you take Lukas? I can't find Ava!"

Henry rushed up and took the boy. Sean used his sleeve to clear out the rest of the glass, then helped a few others get through the window. He disappeared into the shack to look for his daughter.

"Go on," a man by the window said to Henry. "Move out of the way so we can get more people out."

Overwhelmed, Henry hurried away from the disaster with Lukas. The five-year-old was crying. He was missing a shoe, and he had a bruise turning purple on his arm and one on his cheek. A thin trickle of blood ran down his leg. Henry set the boy down and examined him. Finding his injuries to be minor, he tried soothing him. "There," said Henry, distracted and looking anxiously for his teens to surface from the stampede. "It's going to be okay." With relief, Henry spotted one of his and Thatcher's recently adopted girls, Clementi Okafor, at another window helping others out. Her natural spiral curls had a layer of gray dust on them, and her black skin shone with sweat. Henry caught sight of Clementi's brother Ibrahim, from the same purge group of Unwanteds, assisting her from the inside. "Thank goodness," Henry murmured. Hopefully the rest were close by.

Lukas sniffled, drawing Henry's attention back. "Where's Ava?" asked the boy. "I want my dad."

"She's . . . She'll be coming any minute. Your dad is going after her. It's just a little shack, so it shouldn't be too hard. They'll find us out here."

"Everybody fell on each other," said Lukas tearfully. "I got hit in the face."

Henry sucked in a breath, imagining what it must have been like to have the entire population of Artimé, on multiple floors and in a variety of additional magical rooms that took up no space, suddenly and entirely converge in the single gray shack when the mansion disappeared. He kept seeing more and more people struggling to get out. With other Artiméans rushing forward to help at the exits, there wasn't much Henry could do at the moment but stare and feel the horror he'd felt when he was ten years old—the first time Artimé had disappeared and Alex had taken him under his wing.

Alex is dead.

The reminder hit him like a sucker punch to the gut. It

repeated over and over in his thoughts. He tried to rationalize—
tried to come up with reasons why it couldn't be so. Maybe
Alex had just gotten too far away from home and had moved
outside of his magely range, assuming there was one. Silently
Henry counted the days since Alex and Thatcher and the rest
of the rescue team had left, and he knew Alex would have
been in the land of the dragons for a while. So it didn't seem
likely that he'd somehow be out of range now if he hadn't
been yesterday.

Alex. Is dead.

Sean came running over to them, bloodied and battered,
with six-year-old Ava in his arms. She seemed to be okay, with
just a few cuts and scratches on her arms and one of her legs.
Henry checked her injuries and made sure she was all right.
Then he looked up at Sean with dread, not sure what to say in
front of the children.

Sean held Henry's gaze for a moment, then shook his head
sorrowfully. "He's . . . gone. He's got to be."

Henry swallowed hard. Hearing Sean say it made it seem
real. Permanent. Sorrow enveloped him. But fear did too.
If Alex was dead . . . what about Thatcher? And Lani? And

Carina and the others on the rescue team? Were they dead too? He pushed the horror of that thought aside and nodded. "We need to get to Aaron—bring him over here right away. He knows the spell. He has an extra robe."

"Henry," said Sean, "we *can't* get to him. The tubes are gone. We'd have to take a ship. It'll take days."

"Can't we send a seek spell—" Henry cut himself off, annoyed and disheartened. "Sorry. Of course not." He thought for a moment as his anxiety built. "Who else knows what to do?"

Sean looked up. "Claire Morning does. She has a robe. She's familiar with the spell, too."

"Is she in Artimé?" Henry's eyes swept the area.

"I don't think she came today."

"Let's go to Quill and find her, then." Henry glanced back at the chaos surrounding the shack, confirming that, like Sean's and his kids', most people's wounds were superficial. His adopted Unwanteds would be all right—they'd been through worse. And there were people helping at all the exits. He spotted a few of the nurses assisting the injured, but without medicine or the hospital ward, they couldn't do much.

Neither could Henry. "Hang on a minute," he told Sean. He ran over to one of the nurses to explain where he was going and put her in charge while he was gone. "Keep an eye out for the rest of my kids, will you?" he asked. "Clementi and Ibrahim are there by the east window, but they're the only ones I've seen emerge so far."

"Of course," said the nurse, knowing it was more important for Henry to go after Claire so they could get the magic back as quickly as possible. Before chaos turned to disaster.

Sean and Henry each took a child on their backs and turned toward Quill, where Claire Morning now lived. At the sight of the larger part of the island, they both gasped, because they'd forgotten something else.

Quill was gone too. Everything there looked even worse than in Artimé. It was nothing but old burned land and sooty rubble. And angry, nonmagical Quillens were coming toward them in droves.

The Time Before

It had happened once before, when Henry was ten. Hours after Mr. Marcus Today, the first head mage and creator of the magical world, had been killed and Artimé had vanished, Henry's mother had died of injuries sustained in a skirmish with the Restorers of Quill. Henry's sister, Lani, had been taken captive on Warbler Island, leaving Henry with his grieving father, Gunnar, who was also trying to regain control of Quill.

The mess of problems that had surrounded Henry in those awful days had left a permanent, invisible bruise on his soul. He'd clung to Alex as a shadowy helper. Fetching him cups of water or a bit of broth if he could get some. Trying to come to grips with his losses when everyone else was feeling losses too. Comfort had been scarce. Artimé had seen its worst in the way people treated one another.

It had taken weeks for Alex to decipher the strange spell that Mr. Today had magically sent to the boy's pocket in the moment before he'd died. Sky had helped Alex—the world might still be gone if it hadn't been for her. People had turned desperate. Water and food had been nearly nonexistent. But they had survived . . . most of them anyway.

With Ava and Lukas on their backs, Henry and Sean forged a path through the increasing crowd of upset Quillens. The people of Quill were not magical, but the world they lived in was. When Quill had been destroyed by fire, Alex had come to the aid of the contentious neighbors, pushing the boundaries of Artimé's magical world to cover the soot and burned-out buildings and whatever else had been left. He'd created magical houses and workplaces and fields and even a lighthouse for them, and the people of Quill had accepted these things begrudgingly, having no other choice. They'd been tiresome and grumpy neighbors, but peaceful since then. Most of the Artiméans had at least a few family members there. But Quill's focus on what was important strayed far from Artimé's, and the two places, despite sharing an island, were still quite opposite.

As they traveled, Sean and Henry scanned the crowds for signs of Claire, hoping she was already on her way to Artimé. The shock they both felt was numbing. Henry could hardly fathom what had happened. All he wanted was for the magic to be restored as quickly as possible so he could send a seek spell to Thatcher. If he got one in return . . . well, it would mean at least they weren't *all* dead. Henry's throat caught. The desperate need to know if Thatcher and the others were alive was all consuming. He had to shove it down and get through this.

Sean felt the same way about Carina and Seth. "At least we were more prepared this time," he said. "I just can't believe . . ." He choked on the words, then kept going. "I can't believe Alex is . . . gone." He glanced up at Ava on Henry's back, not wanting to say anything to scare the young ones even more than they already were, especially since no one was 100 percent certain that Alex was dead. But Ava wasn't paying attention.

Rather, she was looking around in wonder and fear at the desolate burned-out mess of land that used to be Quill. She'd never seen it like this before.

It was slow going, pushing upstream the whole way. After an hour or more they came to a huge gathering of angry Quillens blocking the path, demanding to have their houses back. At the center of the gathering, hundreds of feet away, was Gunnar Haluki, Henry's father, looking frazzled. Beside him was Claire Morning, the musical instructor, raising her voice in a way she'd told many singers to avoid doing in order to protect their vocal folds. But now she was forced to do whatever it took to be heard.

"You must let me through!" Claire insisted. "I can't help you unless you let me get to Artimé! I need to talk to the people there. Please make way!"

The crowd around her grumbled louder.

Henry touched Sean's shoulder. "I'll go help them." He carefully lifted Ava off his shoulders and handed her to Sean so she wouldn't get stepped on. Then he shouted with authority, "Coming through! Move it! Look out!" which was so uncharacteristic of him, but as it was a new distraction, it worked. He pushed people aside, row after row all the way to the center, and caught his father's eye. Gunnar looked relieved to see him.

Henry reached Claire first and took her hand, then beckoned for his father to come and grabbed his hand as well so they wouldn't get separated. They weaved through the crowd until they found Sean. Sean quickly herded them out ahead of the mob toward Artimé. Henry took Ava back onto his shoulders as they went.

"Thank you," Gunnar said, glancing behind him. They began to pick up speed to stay ahead of the others. "They weren't quite grasping the fact that things can't be restored without Claire going into Artimé." Then he looked at Henry. "What news do you have?"

"None," said Henry. "We can only assume Alex is dead."

Gunnar Haluki looked pained, and he closed his eyes momentarily, then shook his head. "Of course, we thought as much. But it's . . . it's hard to hear that."

"It's terrible," Claire said. Her face was smudged with soot, and her cheeks had tear tracks running down them. "No word from anyone?"

Henry shook his head.

"Do you have the robe?" asked Sean, looking anxious. Claire wasn't carrying it.

"Not yet. I don't keep it in our house in Quill, since it would disappear with the world the moment I'd need it."

"Well, that's brilliant of you," said Sean. "Where is it?"

"It's inside the gray shack along with the clue and the miniature model of the mansion. Those were the three items that Alex used to bring the world back the first time. If all goes as I planned, I'll find the things in the little cupboard in the kitchen." She hesitated. "I hope everything's still in place after all these years. I've been meaning to go to the gray shack in the Museum of Large to check on the items once Alex left, but I'm afraid I haven't done it."

"Hopefully everyone will have emptied out of there by the time we return," said Henry. "There were hundreds of people inside the mansion when it happened. It was a disaster, all of them falling on top of one another from all locations—the living spaces, theater, lounge, dining room. The upstairs on top of down, I imagine—all squished into that tiny space. They were breaking windows to get out."

"Oh dear," said Claire. "That's horrible."

"It was frightening," Sean said. He glanced at his daughter and son, but they appeared to be handling their fear. They rode quietly on his and Henry's shoulders, sometimes pointing and talking with each other about the strange sights they were seeing.

Their little group went faster, but the way became more difficult the closer they got. People began chanting "Bring back Quill!" as they converged into the area that, with magic, would expand into beautiful Artimé. Without magic, it was a small plot of land, and there was little room to move.

"Let us through!" Henry called out. "We can fix this, but we need to get to the shack!"

Sean began hollering too, though it was hard for anyone to be heard. They lost Gunnar Haluki somewhere along the way, but Claire pushed on with Henry and Sean. They had to squeeze and weave through the people who were packed all the way to the seashore.

Then Henry stopped and grabbed Sean's arm. He beckoned to Claire and then pointed to the gray shack . . . or what was left of it. Only one wall remained standing. The roof had collapsed. The rest of the little house had apparently exploded due to all the people inside.

"Oh no," Henry muttered, looking at the others in alarm. "It's in shambles. Now what'll we do?"

"Come on," said Sean. "Link arms so we don't get separated. Children, hold on tight!"

Sean led the way with one elbow, shoving roughly to clear a path to the shack. The others plowed after him, fearing the worst. Would people be crushed under the debris? When they finally reached the area, they could see that the exterior walls of the shack had collapsed outward and lay flat, so if anyone had been in the way, they would have been pulled to safety by now.

Henry spotted the nurse he'd spoken to earlier and saw Clementi and Ibrahim and the other four of his wards present with them. He breathed a sigh of relief, then turned to look at the mess before them.

The interior of the shack was almost completely torn apart. Shredded.

"This is not good," Claire muttered. She pushed her way over to where the kitchen cupboards should have been, but there was nothing left except piles of splintered wood, broken shelves, and shattered glass.

"The robe has got to be here somewhere," she said as Henry and Sean caught up to her. She looked frantically around people's feet. "Maybe it's buried under the collapsed walls." Exasperated, she put her fingers in her mouth and emitted a sharp whistle, startling those nearby into silence. Then she put her hands in the air and shouted, "Attention everyone! We need to clear this area. Now!"